Never
Quite
Dead

# Never Quite Dead

## SEYMOUR SHUBIN

St. Martin's Press
New York

This novel is a work of fiction. Names, characters, incidents, and places are fictitious or are used fictitiously. The characters are products of the author's imagination and do not represent any actual persons.

*Design by Claudia Carlson*

Library of Congress Cataloging-in-Publication Data

Shubin, Seymour.
  Never quite dead / Seymour Shubin.
    p. cm.
  ISBN 0–312–02187–9
  I. Title.
PS3569.H754N48 1988                          88–11588
813'.54—dc 19

FIRST EDITION

10 9 8 7 6 5 4 3 2 1

For
my sisters Eleanor and Ruth
and
my brother Aaron

I want to publicly thank my son Neil for inspiring this novel and helping to point the way.

Never
Quite
Dead

He opened the door from the kitchen to the basement and looked down at the darkness before turning on the light. Walking down, he had the feeling of uneasiness he'd had as a kid when he used to come down here, sometimes with his friends, to take the dead little boy's pictures out of his father's files and stare at them, one by one, with a mixture of fascination and horror. The poor little boy, as he used to think of him. The boy of three or four with the bruises on his head someone had dumped on a vacant lot, and no one had ever come forward to identify—no mother or father, no aunt or uncle or cousin or neighbor or someone who might have just gotten a quick glimpse of him, like a door-to-door salesman or a repairman: *someone.*

Twenty-one years ago. Or was it twenty-two now?

Twenty-two. He'd been eleven then. Or eleven and a half, as he'd still been young enough to say.

Upstairs his uncle, his father's younger brother, was still saying good-bye at the front door, the last of the friends and relatives who'd come back after the funeral. All afternoon, over and over, he'd been at it—"Never made sense . . . Could see your father giving it one year, *two* . . . His *life*? It wasn't like he was a cop . . ." Twice David had said, "Please." And then, though Marie tried to stop him with her eyes, he'd had to say, "That's enough, you've said it enough." But it hadn't stopped his uncle from coming back to it every so often. "I used to say, 'Joe, you're driving yourself crazy, going to kill yourself, you're not a kid.' But you couldn't talk to him, never could."

With all his uncle's money, his real estate, there wouldn't be a clergyman—*anyone*—who could say in all honesty at his grave, "How fortunate he was to have a mission. How blessed . . ."

And he'd been right, the minister, even though all he'd known about his father was what they, he and his sister, had told him the day before; that, and the nice long story on the obituary page. It had been a mission, all right.

Christ, what a mission.

He took a deep breath.

In a way he felt sadder here than at the graveside, with all the slush and people huddled together for warmth. Here was the guy's life.

The poor guy, the poor bastard, here was his life.

He went over to his father's desk and stood with his hands on the back of the old typewriter chair, the seat and back patched in a few places with masking tape. He'd never wanted a new chair, and never a new typewriter—it was an ancient portable Corona. The desk was in a corner of the finished basement, on the far end from where the gas heater was housed, rumbling now behind the door. The walls at the front and side of his desk were hung with framed, black-and-white photos, most of them from his years on the *Boston Star-Post*, the little tabloid that died a few years after he retired.

He'd started off in sports, a copy boy, then covered City

[ 2 ]

Hall, then wrote a gossip column—dot dot dot "guess who we saw" dot dot dot—called DOWNTOWN WITH KYLE. And the photos mirrored those years, showed him, short, stocky, and his red hair gradually graying, with politicians, prizefighters, entertainers.

Except for two photos, dead center in front of his desk.

One, his hair pure white now, was of him looking down at the boy's grave, in an overcoat that seemed too long today and holding a wide-brimmed felt hat.

The other wasn't really a photo—it was a framed, yellowed news story, probably the first one about him getting involved with the boy.

"Anyone down there?" his sister called.

"Me." He didn't look up; was looking at some of the things on the desk.

"Oh, I thought one of the kids left the light on."

There were scraps of papers with scribbled notes, some old newspaper clippings, a letter from an out-of-state police department notifying him that they didn't have something-or-other he'd requested, some other letters—he frequently got letters from people who read about what he was doing—and a folder on which he'd printed CRNT, which probably meant "current." David opened it, fingered through some papers, closed it; it gave him a particularly strange feeling, knowing that this was what his father had been working on last. He touched some of the other things on the desk, straightening them a little—a digital clock, a Lincoln bust paperweight—when Marie's voice said behind him, "Where do we begin?"

He hadn't heard his sister come down. Looking at her, he wanted to say, "Hey, try to take it easy," because of the permanent little pinch of a frown he'd noticed for the first time when he came home, the tiredness in her eyes. But he didn't say it because he already had, three times, and she'd acted annoyed the last time, as if she didn't want to hear it—or, more likely, as if there was nothing she could do about it. It wasn't, he knew, just Pop's death. She and Bob and the kids had moved in with Pop three years ago, when Mom died—the same old frame house in North Cambridge Marie had thought she'd left forever. And it hadn't been easy—Pop could be murder to live with.

"Go through everything and take what you want," she said.

"Not today. I just felt like coming down."

But he did go over to the green, metal file cabinet. Three of the drawers were labeled BOY and were packed, he knew, with files crowded between alphabetical dividers, and piles of loose papers and envelopes that even spilled over to another drawer. He knew what he was looking for, and wondered if it was in the same place.

He felt surprisingly tense as he opened the drawer where he'd seen it last, years ago. He ran his fingers along the files quickly, then came to it—an old, nine-by-twelve manila envelope, with BOY handprinted on it in ink. He drew out five black-and-white glossies. One was of the body lying on the lot, near some newly constructed houses. The others were taken at the morgue. They'd touched out the wounds and dressed the body in a shirt, sweater, trousers, socks and shoes, and sat it on a hardback chair. Blond, one eye slightly open, lips with a trace of a smile, he might have been watching TV.

Or, as David often thought, he might have been sneaking a peak when he'd been told not to.

They'd sent his pictures to police departments across the country and abroad. And a lot of papers apparently ran them; some of the supermarket scandal sheets still did every few years. But though they'd gotten a million leads, checked everyone from known child batterers to carnival workers to foster parents, tried matching his footprints with hospital prints of newborns, they still didn't even know his name.

All anyone knew was that on the night of April 19, 1966,

[ 4 ]

two Boston officers took after a car that ran a stop sign, but it disappeared before they got the license number. The only thing they knew was that it was a four-door sedan, maybe maroon. The next day the body was found a couple of miles away. The police didn't know, of course, if it was connected with the car, but suspected it was, that the body had been dumped there in panic.

The boy had been skinny but well nourished, his clothes old but fairly neat. The medical examiner reported that at least one of the wounds, the fatal one, had been caused by some kind of weapon, probably a pipe; the others, when the boy fell or perhaps was flung against something.

David kept looking at them, going from one to another.

How many nights he'd spent in cold terror of the boy, never quite dead in the basement.

And how many nights he'd cried for him.

Looking up at Marie, he said quietly, "Did these ever bother you?"

"Are you kidding? Of course. But just at first, really."

"Did you ever used to sneak them out to look at them?"

"God, no. The only times I saw them they were on his desk." But she hadn't been a kid, she'd been what?—twenty-one then. A second mother. In fact, he remembered someone saying it to her once—"Is that your son?" They did look fairly alike—brown hair, though hers was graying now, slender, tall.

"They used to scare the hell out of me," he said, putting them away.

She looked at the desk. "I don't know what to keep, what to throw out."

"I'll go over it tomorrow. I'm not in the mood now."

"I'll get some cartons tomorrow." She kept looking at the desk, opened a couple of drawers and closed them. "I can't begin to tell you how tense he was these past couple weeks. Especially when he got back. Jittery. Couldn't sit still. Like he was almost frantic. I used to ask him, he'd get mad. I look back on it, I think it's like he knew his time was running out."

"Did he ever tell you why he went?" He'd flown to Philadelphia for a couple of days, a few weeks before he died.

"You know, I hate to say it, but those things have been going in one ear and out the other for so long."

"Don't. I know what you mean."

"And I was so angry. I begged him not to go. I mean—seventy. It was enough."

It was even hard to remember exactly how it all started. They'd sat around last night, trying to. Bob said it was two years after the boy was found, but Marie and he agreed it was only about a year later. Someone had given him some kind of tip for his column—about a baby-sitter who'd disappeared, as they recalled—and he'd passed it on to the police. But then when he felt they'd given up on it too quickly, he began looking into it. After a while, word spread of what he was doing—word spread, hell, he had it in his column—and even before that tip fell through, there were others. Then one of the scandal sheets came out with a story pretty much featuring him, and the tips really poured in. And what started as a kind of hobby worked itself into an obsession.

He'd taken early retirement, then spent a fortune traveling to follow up leads; had even, they'd found out just yesterday, remortgaged the house.

"You know," Marie said, "they say when your time's up, it's up. Well, I look on it as bullshit. That man killed himself. He came back a wreck, worn out. The thing I thank God about, he didn't suffer." He'd died in his sleep; she'd found him in bed, eyes closed peacefully, on his side and an arm flung over his right shoulder, as he always slept. "They say that only happens to good people. Do you believe that?"

"I believe it happened to that good guy."

She took his hand and squeezed it. "I'm still mad at you, you know." He was staying at a hotel, not here.

"That's all you needed." He hadn't wanted the kids to double up. And he preferred this, anyway.

They started to walk to the stairs. Then she stopped. "David? Can I tell you a thought I've had?"

He looked at her.

"It's corny, but it made me cry. Do you think Pop knows who the boy is now?"

• • •

In his hotel room, he took off his jacket and sat back against the headboard of the bed. He felt drained.

"There's no easy way to tell you," she'd said. "Pop died." Then the flight from L.A., and thinking, looking down, how this is the way he'd always known it would happen: getting a call somewhere, L.A., New York, Europe, and the flight home and the long remembering, looking down.

Pop would have climbed out of the box if he'd known there was going to be a service. He used to say no; in the clipped way he had of speaking, he used to say just throw in the dirt. They're all bullshitters, he used to say, meaning the priests and nuns of his childhood, and the ministers Mom, a Protestant, could never get him to hear more than once. But Marie wanted her minister. And if it made her feel better . . .

Actually, it did him too, in a way. Though the guy hadn't known his father, it was nice to hear him express their feelings. And nice to see a few of the old-timers from the paper, and a few people, strangers, whom the obit and the stories over the years had brought out in the gray slush and cold. There would have been a lot more, he guessed, if it hadn't been for the weather.

He looked at his wristwatch. Almost nine-thirty, which made it almost six-thirty in L.A. He wondered were they eating, but he didn't feel like waiting—he might want to go down to the bar. He wanted to let Gina know he'd be back in time to take Sara for the weekend; he hadn't known how long he would have to stay here. But it shouldn't take more than a day or two to sort out his father's things and some legal matters. Then maybe he'd go to New York for a couple of days to see his agent, perhaps an editor or two.

Gina's husband's teenage daughter answered the phone, and she called to Gina, whose first question to him was how was Marie, how was she taking it? She'd always liked Marie.

"Pretty well. She's doing okay. Look, I want you to know I'll be in Friday night, I'll pick Sara up in the morning."

"Good. I'd put her on the phone, but she's next door. You know Amy, don't you? She's staying over Amy's."

"Well, tell her I'll see her Saturday morning."

All very civilized, he thought later.

Occasionally it still surprised him, after four years.

They'd been married five years, and had gone together three: had done lots of wonderful things together—backpacked through Europe, worked at odd jobs—at restaurants, mostly—until he got his first newspaper job. And she was behind him when, after a few small freelance sales and then the three straight articles to *Esquire*, he'd mentioned wanting to quit. Had encouraged him, really, and they'd done fine for about a year. But finances got shaky, and now there was Sara, and there were arguments probably both of them took turns starting. And it was like something, once started, you couldn't stop, even though he began doing pretty well again, mostly with freelance PR and annual reports and speeches, and then there were some more articles, and then the first of his paperbacks sold.

• • •

"I think I'm getting close."

That, or something like that; there had always been

variations. And so many times. But the time David was thinking of now, a magazine on his lap, unable to concentrate and unable to fall asleep, was that evening of the basketball semifinals in junior high and only his mother showing up. "I think I'm getting close," his father said the next day, though not to him; to his mother. And it had been wrong to be angry at him, because of the poor boy, the boy he often pictured coming up from the basement, or staring, dead and lonely and frightened, into his bedroom window; whom he saw so often, standing in the night near his grave, the only little boy among all those big people.

Standing near the grave and gravestone that public contributions bought.

DEAR LORD HOLD TO THEE THIS UNKNOWN BOY

How could you be angry at your father when you had it so good, and no one would ever even admit knowing the poor little boy?

"David, I'm really close this time, I'm really onto something."

This time, the last time, about two months ago, in a call to L.A. And after they talked awhile of other things, the reason Pop had called came out.

"Any chance you coming home soon?"

It had been Pop's way of saying he needed him, maybe to drive, because he had said earlier his legs "feel a little weak," and that Marie and Bob didn't want to hear any more about the case, were always angry at him.

He would never come out and ask a direct favor. And so he'd moved on to talk of other things when David told him of his deadline.

David closed the magazine. He sat staring at the blank TV.

He'd turned it on and off at least three times, trying to fall asleep.

[ 9 ]

He could feel his heart thumping. He knew why, but didn't want to let it come full-blown into his mind: the thought he'd had a hundred times before.

But he had hated it coming from his uncle.

His uncle was right.

Still, he couldn't stop the twisting of guilt that he hadn't come home.

2

As soon as he opened the front door to the house he could almost feel the silence. Marie and Bob were at work, and the kids, two teenagers, were at school. It called back the days when he would come home from grammar school and no one was there. It was a silence that used to change with certain seasons: in winter, heavy; in spring, thin, almost transparent in the sunlight. But he always felt a little uneasy in it for some reason. And he felt it now, though much more so in the emptiness filled with his father.

He closed the door against the February bite and picked up the mail under the door slot. He put it on a table while he took off his thin raincoat—he'd had to buy one here; he hated coats and ties—then sorted through the mail. Most were condolence cards, some to the "Family of Joseph Kyle," some to Marie and Bob, one to him. He opened his. It was from an old friend, Judy Sears. He read it several times. She'd written just a few lines, and they were just right: what proud memories he would have.

He opened the ones to the family. Each that he read and set down was from a stranger: we just had to say; we felt we knew him; he will be blessed for all eternity . . . And this one, like some of the others—who knew?—was possibly from one of the many people who'd given him tips over the years, a Sam Goldberg: "I want you to know I had the pleasure of meeting your father and what a wonderful man he was. He didn't care if you bothered him, he was grateful. God bless him. He will bless him." And this one—

Oh, you bastard!

You bastard.

A Halloween card. Unsigned, of course.

HEADLINE GRABBER! MAYBE HE'LL DO SKYWRITING NOW!!!

David quickly ripped it up and stuffed the pieces in his pocket. He didn't even want to put them in the trash.

He'd gotten plenty of crank mail, Pop. And calls. And the cops, they could have lived without him, had even threatened him with "charges" at least once, if he ever kept evidence from them.

"I turn over just about everything. But do they want it?—they don't want it, just want to file it away. It's *old*. But they don't want anyone else doing anything either."

Bad enough murdered, he used to say. But for no one to want the child, to care. "Not a parent, not a relative, not a neighbor! Someone had to of seen him. Once. For a second. *Something*. Isn't there someone, somewhere, who *misses* him?"

Headlines . . .

A lie. He wouldn't have devoted so much of his life just for that.

Would he?

• • •

He looked at the few jackets and pants hanging in his father's closet, touched something in one of the pockets as he moved them along the rack, and instantly knew what it was: the remains of a cylinder of Lifesavers—his father used to like to suck on Lifesavers. David held a couple of ties against his palm, tried to remember his father wearing them, then let them slide off and went to the drawers.

Open, close. Open, close. More of a man's life. Underwear, shirts. He'd drop all of it off at a Goodwill dump. This drawer held things like tie clips, two watches that were going to the boys, a couple of ballpoint pens, cufflinks—he moved all of it around with his fingers, taking nothing. Except, he decided, this old press card from the fifties. He didn't know why he wanted this in particular; just did.

The pictures, he had some pictures back home, so Marie could keep the one of Pop in uniform—he'd been in the landing on Anzio—and their wedding picture, smiling, Pop's cheek almost on hers.

He felt he should take something more, and would. But suddenly he felt tired, wanted to hold off; would come back up after he did the basement.

He started for the steps, then stopped at the banister.

He remembered standing here one night, he must have been seven, and hearing them fight for the first time. His job, she was saying, everything his job, out every night, never home.

"But that's my job, damn it! I write a column! A stinking column, but a column. You want to eat? You like to eat?"

"But every night?"

"It's not every night! You know it's not every night!" And the next he remembered hearing was "Cow! A goddam cow!"

"Irish should never get married!"

And he remembered the feeling, could almost feel it now, of heat rising up from his chest, and wanting to go down there and beat at him, hurt him, all the while crying don't talk like that to my mother. And after that, maybe the next day, his wonder at how they were speaking to each other again. Actually, they probably didn't fight more than most couples, but whenever they did it was like they were doing it all the time. But then there were silences, often, that were just as threatening. And sometimes—though he'd never heard them fight about the boy—she'd complain to Marie and him about how lonely it was, and once about how she was afraid he was going to lose his job, and a couple times pretty much what his uncle had said—how this was none of his business, he wasn't the police.

David used to feel terribly sorry for her. And sometimes, without really knowing why, for him.

As he started down the stairs he wished he was leaving tonight. It was something like the feeling he'd had in high school. He had been happy here as a kid, at least thought so; but by high school he not only wanted to get away, but get away far. So he'd applied only to colleges in California, as far as you could go. So, Berkeley, and even geology, thinking it would take him even farther, though he lost interest after the first year and dropped out after the second.

• • •

Marie had gotten five cartons and left them piled near the file cabinet. Where the hell to begin? He opened one of the BOY drawers, then stood there looking at it. What he should do is just reach in, grab a handful of things, and dump them. Instead he lifted out a bunch of clippings his father had filed under "Miscellaneous," and sifted through them and put them back. He ran his hand along some of the files. A few of the headings still meant something to him. Here was a woman who'd run a camp where some children were abused; here, an illegal immigrant a neighbor said had had a child who disappeared . . .

He had no idea how many of these his father had actually looked into. And as he'd said in an interview once, "No, I don't expect anyone to go confessing to me. No one's even obligated to talk to me. What I hope is to give the cops something they can use."

Had squirreled away so many things.

Look at all this.

Copies of old police reports—he'd had a million friends in the department once. Letters back and forth to out-of-town reporters. Even clippings from foreign papers. Names of all kinds, addresses, scribbled comments. Correspondence with people who sent him leads, clergymen who apparently knew someone he was trying to locate, doctors, lawyers, DAs, police departments, wardens, mothers who'd given babies up for adoption, the French consul . . .

How do you just throw all of this away?

He pushed the door closed and began looking through the regular *A* to *Z* drawers. Bills, all sorts of letters, of course, old driver's licenses, a letter from a men's club back in the fifties—

Hey. They'd selected him for their humanitarian award for a series of articles he'd written, apparently about some destitute families.

David put aside the letter. Never knew that.

And these here? He drew out some manila envelopes that were old to the touch. They were addressed to his father, from magazines—the *Saturday Evening Post*, *New Yorker*, *Esquire*, another from the *Post*, *Atlantic*, several he'd never heard of.

Rejected short stories—they still had the printed slips attached.

This was staggering.

He'd never known his father had tried publishing fiction, had ever tried writing anything for magazines.

The earliest postal date was fifty-one, the most recent seventy-nine.

Never knew. Jesus.

He sat down with them at the desk. Just sat there, the little pile in front of him . . .

After a while he drew over the CRNT folder, began flipping through it randomly. A few ripped-out looseleaf pages with names on it; scraps of paper with scribblings; another looseleaf page, this one listing flights to Philly; a snapshot, a—

He brought the snapshot closer.

And his heart released flame.

It was a picture of a middle-aged woman holding a little boy in one arm and trying to control a little dog with the other. A boy of about three, with an amazing resemblance to the boy.

Quickly he looked at the back. Printed in his father's hand was: SAM GOLDBERG.

**3**

His sister and brother-in-law walked him to the door. Bob, a thin, balding man, said, "I want you to know we really appreciate it."

"There's nothing to appreciate, it's yours, it's your house, he wanted you to have it. I'm just sorry he complicated it."

Marie said, "Well, we mean it. We do."

"Come on, we've already been through it. I'll see you tomorrow."

"Good night." She kissed his cheek.

"I'll see you."

Thrusting his arms through his coat but leaving it unbuttoned, he walked to his car, a Mercury he picked up at the airport. It started instantly, but there was glaze on the windows, and he waited, headlights on, as they gradually defrosted.

He'd tried not to show how frustrated he felt. And how annoyed at the Old Man for screwing up. Ever since Marie and her family had moved in with him, his father had said he wanted them to have the house. Well, they should have it. They not only lived there, but they were just about making it as it was—Bob was a foreman in a warehouse, Marie a secretary, and their oldest boy would be going to college next year. But the Old Man had never gotten around to making out a will. And what could have been straight and simple had to involve a lawyer now.

So he couldn't leave tomorrow. Not until about six anyway, after the lawyer. Which would give him only a day in New York instead of two.

At the hotel he gave the car to the doorman, who was waiting on the other side of the revolving door. In his room he tossed the CRNT folder on the bed and hung up his coat and went to the bathroom. Afterward he sat on the bed and opened the folder to the snapshot.

Yes, Marie had said, Pop had showed it to her.

No, she didn't know who they were. If Pop ever said, she didn't remember. "You know how he was. Excited over everything. And you know how many pictures he got."

You know how he was, Bob had said.

David looked at the picture, then flipped through the loose papers, looking for some kind of notation that might indicate who the woman and boy were. But just all those names, addresses, phone numbers, scribblings, many of them crossed out, some impossible to read.

"Why?" Marie had asked.

Which, from her tone and look, meant not only why are you interested, but you too?

No, he assured himself, not him too.

It was just . . . sort of interesting. A piece of the Old Man. A part of Pop.

He closed the folder and set it on the dresser and went over and looked out the window. Then he looked at his watch. It was early, just a few minutes after seven. He'd been anxious to get out of there, but things to talk about had run into dinner. He felt restless now, was thinking of Judy Sears. He'd debated with himself at the house whether to call her, had decided no, but could feel himself getting closer to going over to the phone.

They were good friends, weren't they? Just friends. And she knew it, he knew it. Nothing more.

He started to look up her number in the directory, but some of the pages were crumpled and he lost patience and got it from information.

• • •

David watched from the sofa as Judy walked to the foot of the stairs in her home in Newton. "Okay, kids," she warned, "can it." She had two children—a boy seven, a girl Sara's age, six—and they were jumping up and down in bed. "You hear me? Okay? Or it's no food tomorrow."

They roared at that, and she grew instantly serious. "Come on, I mean it . . . That's better. Come on. Okay. Good night."

"Good night, you and you," the girl called, giggling.

"Good night, honey," David said.

Judy came back, with a slight roll of her eyes. She stood waiting for the jumping and yelling to break out again, but it didn't, and she gave him a little look of amazement. Sitting in the wing chair next to the sofa, she tucked her bare feet under her, as he remembered her always doing, and gave a quick touch of her hand to her black bangs. She'd worn bangs since he'd first dated her, in high school; had the same slightly round impish face. It seemed untouched by the sadness she'd known: her husband had died lingeringly of cancer when her daughter was two.

She said, "Sure I can't get you anything to drink?"

"No, I'm fine."

"But you wanted to go out."

"Not particularly. I wanted to see you."

"It's too cold. And I'd have to get a sitter."

"And I gave you all of two minutes' notice."

"Ah," she said, smiling, "but I didn't say yes right away. The trick is not to seem anxious."

He laughed.

"Oh, God," she said, still smiling and tugging her feet in tighter, "you know what I happened to remember just before?"

"My first name."

"Liss-en. I'm being very serious." Did he remember that time when they were driving his father's car to Chuck's party and something happened to an axle or wheel so that the only turns he could make were left turns? And they got there by making a series of left turns?

He grinned. "I don't know why you kept complaining. We saw parts of the city we never saw before."

"I wasn't complaining. God, you have no memory. All I wanted was to have a turn driving."

"My—father's—car," he said solemnly. "With only a hundred and twenty-five thousand miles on it. I should let someone else drive it?"

She laughed. "Hey, you never said—what did your father say?"

"Oh, he became very strict. I wasn't allowed to take out the garbage for a month." He shrugged, smiled. "He didn't take things like that to heart."

He leaned forward, elbows on his knees. "Speaking of my father."

He told her about finding the short stories. No, his father had never said anything about them to Marie either, obviously because he didn't want anyone to know he'd been rejected.

"You know," he said, "it made me think of something that makes more sense now—he couldn't understand why I didn't use my real name."

David had published eight paperbacks, the first a science fiction, then a series of seven novels featuring Cade, an emergency room physician and Nam veteran who had ingredients quite a few million readers seemed to like, took no nonsense from administrators, other doctors, anyone; was bright enough to come up with clues in the emergency room that uncovered crimes and sent him after criminals throughout the world. An amalgam of superheroes, but he'd clicked. The first of the series was being filmed now; the others were under option to the same producer.

"I used to tell him I was just learning my trade, I didn't want to be categorized yet," he said. "But he just couldn't understand."

"Look, he'd have given anything."

"I'm sure."

"Did he ever tell you what he thought of them?"

"Liked them. Said he did. But he was a stickler for grammar. Did I tell you? Nothing got him more upset. He said it was the only thing he liked about parochial school, they taught him grammar. So he'd always let me know. But you know what it was mostly. Don't start with 'and,' don't end with a preposition."

"I meant to tell you about them prepositions," Judy said, nodding.

He looked at her and smiled. "Look, they're addictive. Then once you get hooked, you're on dangling participles."

They laughed. "Hey," she said, "I feel terrible not giving you anything. You sure? How about at least a cup of coffee?"

"If you're going to have it."

He watched her walk into the kitchen. He could see her across the room divider.

Could remember that first date so clearly, both of them seniors, and how he'd kissed her and his hand soon slipped without resistance through her blouse and under the cup of her bra. He could relive the feeling of it now, the texture of the skin, the surprising plumpness; even how flat the nipples stayed, though her lips opened against his and her tongue kept darting out.

They hadn't done it then, maybe only because he hadn't tried; but after that it had been in her home—almost a mansion, her father was a neurosurgeon—and several times in his, in his car, and then miles away in motels. Then when they came back from college that first year, she from Sarah Lawrence, they dated just once; and though it happened in the car, sloppily happened, he found himself separating from her. He had too long a way to go, and he didn't know where; and though she was fun and brainy, she was more than a little spoiled, and one day there'd be a rich guy.

Then a year ago, after all these years, a letter from her, care of his publisher, saying she'd heard about what he was doing from a mutual friend and that she'd seen a few of his books at an airport and loved them. He'd answered her, and when he came home for a few days six months ago, they'd seen each other, but nothing happened. Just two old friends . . .

"You like cream?" she called.

"No. And no sugar."

She brought it out. He said, "Tell me, how's the business going?" She owned a little boutique on Newbury Street with another woman.

"It's doing pretty well," she said. "My problem's leaving the children. But I've got a good woman who comes in. And whenever I can I'm only at the place half a day."

"I don't know if I told you, they're great kids."

"Oh, they can be other than great. But they're good kids. I had a rough time for a while with Donny. Meg never really knew her father, but Donny, he's only a year older, but it was hard for him. He went to a marvelous psychiatrist. He's fine now, they're both fine. I can honestly say it."

He looked at her. She'd been through a hell of a lot. Not only the long dying, but it turned out that her husband, a corporate lawyer, had put them in debt through investments she'd known nothing about. It was amazing how she didn't look as if she'd been through anything.

She saw him looking and smiled. He said, "I'm just sitting here thinking. You look—well, not sixteen. But not much over. Twenty-one."

"Twenty-one? David, are you selling something?"

He laughed. "All right, twenty-five. I lied. But that's the truth."

"Talking about looks, how do you keep so thin? You've got that dark, gaunt look I'd give anything for."

"Dark, live near the beach. Gaunt, worry about plots and whether you're ever going to think of another one . . . But I'm not complaining." He smiled.

"Yes, you are. Hey," she said after a moment, "I got the most delicious coffee cake. I forgot."

"No. Really."

"You'll love it. Let me play mother. Let me bring it out."

"Only if you stop playing mother."

"Okay." And both of them laughed.

He followed her into the kitchen, watched as she lifted it off a pan, then as she looked through a drawer for a certain knife; watched, suddenly thinking of some of those times . . . then of that one time in particular, in a motel called the Blue Moon; thought of it simply because she'd gotten such hell when they came home late.

He wondered did she ever come to enjoy sex. Strange, how it never dawned on him that she really hadn't, nowhere near fully anyway, until he thought about it years later.

She cut two slices and put them on plates.

Why, she was saying, was she was suddenly thinking of this? Remember when Bill Henlin—was it Bill Henlin?— when he was dancing so hard his shoe flew off and knocked the assistant principal's, whatever his name was, when it knocked his toupee down on his face?

He laughed. "That was Bill."

"What happened to him? I forget."

"He just straightened his toupee, that's all."

"I don't mean *him*—very funny—I mean Bill. Wasn't he suspended?"

"No, he was just kicked out of the dance. And he danced all the way out."

"Now I remember. That was funny."

She started to extend a plate to him, then stopped and looked up at him. His own look, he knew, stopped her. They kept looking at each other. Then she set it down and came against him as his arms closed around her. He kissed her lightly on the lips, then harder, his lips opening. He could feel her hands clenching at his back, trying to draw him even closer. He touched her left breast, just touched it, and her shoulders seemed to go in spasm; he couldn't recall it ever happening. He held onto her, his cheek against hers. Then, as if on signal, they released each other.

She let out a little breath, looking at him. She touched his hair, where it fell over his forehead.

Although he didn't say it, he was sure she was thinking the same thing: not with the kids, not like this, not this way after all these years.

•  •  •

And later, in his room, lying in the dark, he was glad. And it had nothing to do with kids, or that they would have had to do it standing up, or on the basement floor or in a closet. The whole thing just made no sense. He couldn't see himself getting hooked up again for years. And she deserved, and with two kids needed, a solid citizen . . .

He reached over and turned on the lamp.

Funny. Pop thought she was the one who headed him

into geology and then was the reason he'd dropped out. She'd had nothing to do with either.

"Why don't you go into journalism?" his father had said. "You're a good writer."

Maybe one of the reasons he hadn't, David thought, was because his father had suggested it. There was a time, in his teens, no one could tell him anything. Or maybe he'd simply had to find out on his own that that's what he wanted.

He looked over at the bureau, at the CRNT folder. But his mind went back again to those stories in the basement. Pretty good stories. No reason why one or two, at least, couldn't have been published.

A terribly frustrated man, he thought. The boy. The stories. Everything, maybe; who knew? And, toward the end, frantic.

"I'm really close this time, I'm really onto something."

David kept looking over at the folder.

It would be nuts. And he wasn't going to do it. But even if he did, which he wouldn't, but even if he did call Sam Goldberg, he was sure the real reason would be to prove that even if he'd come in from L.A., it wouldn't have meant anything.

4

He woke the next morning with the feeling that there was something he had to do but couldn't think of. Then he remembered: the damn lawyer. Had to be at his office on Boylston at four with Marie and Bob. He reached for his wristwatch on the night table, saw with a rush of annoyance that it was almost quarter after ten. He never slept this late, then realized he had nothing to do until the lawyer, anyway.

Except, he remembered, to call Loni. His agent.

He called her after he showered; was still drying himself as he walked from the bathroom to the phone.

"I'm sorry, Mr. Kyle," the receptionist said, "she isn't in. Could you call her, say, four-thirty? Is there some place she can reach you?"

"I'll call her around then. But take this number."

As soon as he hung up, however, he remembered he wouldn't be able to call, he'd be at the lawyer's. Well, maybe.

He wasn't even sure what he wanted to see her about, except it was a good chance to. He was under contract for two more Cades and was about three weeks away from finishing the first one—they rarely took him more than four months—and he had a vague idea of what the new one would be about. They all started pretty much the same way—an emergency brought in, and Cade would detect something suspicious but no one would believe him, and the hospital was always threatening to fire him for taking time off (but he never took more than a week or so to solve a crime), then being forced to kill one or two villains, much to the consternation of the American Medical Association. It was pretty much just a question of who the villains should be—Russians, U.S. super-agencies, evil corporations, religious fanatics, radical left, radical right . . .

He'd even thought a few times about doing a takeoff on the boy, making him the son of spies in this country who couldn't reveal themselves, or a young human guinea pig in a secret medical experiment, or the son of a couple in the Witness Protection Program who'd killed him and whom the government was forced to shield.

But of course he would never have done that to his father; and now it would be wrong to his memory.

He wondered what the hell he was going to do today. He looked over the few clothes he'd brought: "California" things—a thin suede jacket, light sweaters, linen slacks; he'd had to go out and buy a suit and shoes for the funeral. He slipped into chinos, a linen open-throat shirt, loafers. He'd probably look like a nut in the dining room.

As he started to go downstairs for breakfast, he stopped and looked at the CRNT folder.

"It's something very ordinary," his father used to say. "That's why no one's been able to solve it."

Like a boy in a snapshot with a gentle-looking middle-aged woman and a little dog?

David kept standing there. Then he opened the folder and took out Sam Goldberg's condolence card.

He'd gotten his phone number and jotted it across the top, thinking maybe.

But it was crazy, it really was. He sat down at the desk.

But let's say he did call, what would he say? Thanks for the card, for the thought? Thanks for trying to help my father? And by the way, who's the little boy?

That's all, just that. Then cross it off and go. Go to New York and see Loni and talk over some floating ideas for a hardcover, and be open—that you're getting tired of Cade, and it's time for hardcover, but you're worried about giving him up. It was comfortable not having to think up a new character each time, and of course there was the money, the waiting readers. Not that he needed her okay, or didn't know what she'd say—what do you want to write about? And he'd say suspense and whatever I feel like. And she'd say write what you want to. What else could she say?

He reached for the phone, held his hand on it. Then he lifted it and dialed quickly.

"Hello?" A woman's voice.

"Hello, is Mr. Goldberg there?"

"Just a minute."

When he came on, Mr. Goldberg's voice sounded aged and hostile. "Yes? Who are you?"

"Mr. Goldberg, my name's David Kyle, I'm—"

"Who?"

"Kyle? David Kyle? My father was Joseph Kyle—Joe Kyle? You were kind enough to send us a card?"

"You're his son?"

"Yes."

"Oh," he said. "A real fine gentleman."

"I want to thank you for your card, your very kind note. My sister and I deeply appreciate it."

"Who?"

"The card you sent, the note. My sister and I deeply appreciate it."

"Oh, he was a fine gentleman."

"Mr. Goldberg, can I ask you something? Did you give my father a picture of a little boy with a woman? And there was a little dog?"

"Who?"

"Didn't you give my father a picture of a woman with a little boy?"

"Yes."

"I'm very curious. I wonder if you'd tell me. Who are they? Who's the boy?"

Oh, he said, it's very complicated. And he didn't hear so good on the phone. "You want to come over? You can come over. You're welcome."

"I don't know if I can . . ." Christ, no. He wanted bing bang, be able to forget about it.

"You're welcome to come over," Mr. Goldberg said.

"Hold on a second." He had to think. It would be absolutely crazy. "I'm sorry, I'm afraid I can't."

"Tomorrow, it doesn't have to be today. Look, whatever you say."

"I—" Had to think. Oh, Christ . . . Then, "Are you free now?"

Afterward, he sat staring at the picture.

He was angry at himself. Furious. For letting his father grab him by the conscience.

And the boy.

It had come back all at once, how many times—his father off somewhere, or just down in the basement—how many times he had hated the boy.

•  •  •

"I could tell the first two minutes I met him he was a wonderful man," Sam Goldberg said. "To do what he was doing. My, my. But you know? He worried me. His face

[ 29 ]

was so red. I said, how old a man are you? He said, I think, seventy. I said seventy?—look, I'm seventy-six, by seventy it's time to slow up. His face was so red I was afraid for him. And when I read he died, my God. What did I say, Doris?" he called to a woman—his second wife, as he'd introduced her—who was watching TV in the next room. "Didn't I say what a wonderful man? And I told him to slow up?"

Doris, as heavyset as he was thin, may or may not have nodded. Sam Goldberg settled back in his rattan chair. They were sitting in the sun-filled porch of his home in the suburb of Wellesley. It was warm enough without the small electric heater. And he wore a heavy sweater, a button-down. Bald, his scalp was splattered with the same kind of brown marks that were on the back of his hands.

"You know," he said, "there comes a time a man works enough. Enough is enough. I worked hard in my day, and let me tell you something, I enjoyed it."

I look back, he said, believe me—those were good days, those old days. He and Hilda—that was his first wife—he and Hilda and the two boys lived on top of their store in the city. You know what kind of store? No, you were too young. It was a candy store, for five cents—it used to be three cents one time—you got a cone this big, and there was a time, you can believe this or not, he used to give six cents worth of penny candy for a nickel.

Some store—he had magazines, newspapers, he even sold them model airplane kits, had all kinds of medicines, cigars, people were nice. You know what?—he used to keep pictures of the neighborhood boys on the wall they went off to war; some never came back, some became lawyers, he knew one an engineer. Today, he had a store, he wouldn't sell them magazines they got girls all naked. His store, those kids they said one dirty word in his store, he wouldn't put up with it; they knew. And they could hang outside all they wanted, just be nice, play. Why, his best friend was the priest, Father Kelly, a real real gentleman.

"So I was friendly with everyone, you know? Mrs. Dougherty—she used to be there every day. She bought ice cream every day, and then she didn't have a phone, she'd use our phone. I'd send a kid to call her to the phone. We did that for a lot of people."

"Who's Mrs. Dougherty?" David asked.

Sam Goldberg looked surprised. Then his face became anguished and he clapped the side of his head. "I'm getting all mixed up. It scares me sometimes, I get mixed up. It's like I've told you already. I told your father and it's like I told you."

She was the one in the picture. "The Doughertys—a real nice couple. Like gold. The two of them, always worked hard. And never had any children. I used to wonder why, you see a nice couple you wonder. Anyway, she comes in one day with a girl who got a stomach out to here. If she's fifteen she's a lot. I'm telling you. And no ring. So she introduces me—I couldn't think of the name for your daddy for a long time, but it was Sandy. In the middle of the night, I remember. Her sister."

Sam Goldberg suddenly seemed out of breath. After a brief wait, he said, "Your father didn't tell you none of this? I'm not repeating?"

"No."

"Well, what could I say? It was very sad, she had the face of an angel. Now the Doughertys and us, we were very friendly—I remember I once got him a job, they couldn't be more appreciative. He was always fixing things for me. But about this, this I never asked, I never questioned. It's none of my business, and I see they don't want to say, so why should I ask? But there are some things you don't have to tell me. Either she ran away from home or her parents, you know, sent her to her sister's or kicked her out."

Sam Goldberg leaned forward a little, head tilted toward the living room. "Doris, darling, would you lower just a little?"

He waited. David wasn't sure if there was any change, but Sam Goldberg went on. "I was where?"

"You felt she ran away or her parents sent her or kicked her out."

"Well, whatever. But she was there I'd say a month, two. Then I don't see her anymore. All I know is Mrs. Dougherty says one day 'everything's fine, she went home, everything's fine,' and she's even smiling. But I can tell something's still wrong, she's not telling something, that it's still trouble. I got eyes. But again I don't ask and she doesn't say."

Then maybe a year later, maybe two, the Doughertys moved away. "But we would always hear from them Christmas. They'd send a card, sometimes they'd send a picture of themselves, and we stayed in touch. And she kept it up after he passed away—a heart attack, a young fellow. Anyway, she sent the picture. It's hard to remember what she wrote—it's been a long, long time ago—but I remember she said it was Sandy's son, he was living with her. Then a couple years later, I don't know what happened, we stopped hearing from her."

He forgot all about the picture until sometime last year, when he was rummaging through boxes of old pictures. Then about five months ago he saw the picture of the dead boy in one of those terrible papers Doris was always bringing home, and he began thinking how close, and he went and got the picture and, you know, it was close. "But I thought I was imagining, you hate to get involved, and Mrs. Dougherty's sister, I mean what are the chances? So I didn't do anything," he said, shrugging. "But I saved the paper, off and on I would look at it. It mentioned your father, it mentioned the police. But I didn't want to get involved with police. And your father had such a kind

[ 32 ]

face, I figured let me get in touch with him. The worst he'll say is I'm wrong. And I don't have to think about it anymore."

David wondered what else to ask. Then it became obvious. "Do you have any idea when Sandy came to stay with her sister?"

"I know because your father asked me, he kept calling and asking me, I had to think. And I remembered it was a few months after my Bernie had his bar mitzvah. So it had to be sixty-three."

Which, David realized, would have made Sandy's child the right age—three in 1966. He said, "You say you kept hearing from her every Christmas. Do you remember when she sent the picture?"

"I don't know the year exact, but it had to be six, seven years. At least."

David frowned. "And she said it was Sandy's child? And he was living with her?"

"Like I said."

But the child Sandy had been pregnant with, David calculated, would have been at least seven or eight at that time. The boy in the picture was no more than three or four. "Do you remember if she said it was an old picture?"

"That's what your father asked. Like I told him, why would she send an old picture for Christmas? Anyway, it couldn't have been an old picture. You could tell—she'd aged like fifteen years since I saw her."

So, that was it. The child in the snapshot had to have been alive after the dead boy was found.

"And my father knew this?"

"Sure. But it didn't stop him," Sam Goldberg said. "I know he went back to the old neighborhood, kept going around looking for people who might have known them. Asked me for names. Asked did I know where Mrs. Dougherty lived—all I remember it was somewhere Chicago."

But for Christ's sake, why?

"Like I said," Sam Goldberg was saying, "he worked so hard, a man his age."

But why this?

And then a thought suddenly broke in him.

"Mr. Goldberg, the baby Sandy was pregnant with just can't be the child in this picture. She had this one later on. Do you have any idea what happened to the baby she was carrying when you saw her?"

"No." There was a touch of amazement on his face. "And I'm gonna tell you something, you got a head like your father's. And I think I know what you're gonna ask, he asked. And I'm gonna tell you what I told him. They were Catholics, I would swear no abortion. And they'd have to be crazy, she was too far gone."

David stared at him.

Pop—he was sure of it—had been trying to learn what became of her first child.

•   •   •

He got back from the lawyer's office a little after five. He was still annoyed—it had been a bunch of crap, they could handle his end by mail. He stopped at the desk and picked up a message. From his agent; just that she'd returned his call. In his room he called her, but an answering machine said they'd all gone for the day.

His mind went back to Sam Goldberg. It had been on him off and on most of the afternoon.

He tossed his jacket on the bed and sat at the desk with the open folder. So, she'd sent her second child to live with her sister. But that didn't mean she wasn't raising the first one. Or hadn't decided to give it up for adoption.

This whole thing was so way-out.

Still, look how the Old Man had worked.

David was looking at a few pages in particular. They were folded length-wise, sort of crumpled as if they'd been in and out of his father's pocket, and had some forty names on them. What made them stand out was that he recognized some of the addresses as being in the area of the store.

He could see him going from door to door. Saw him with that ancient wide-brimmed hat of his, the long coat.

This is where he must have wanted the help.

Christ, this was it.

He felt a kind of emptiness around his heart as he looked at the names.

Some had arrows going to other names, possibly meaning that one had referred him to the other. Most of the names on the papers were crossed out. Of those that weren't, four, no five, had a little star or check next to them.

Like this one, Madeline something-or-other—for a few seconds he couldn't make out his father's handwriting. Two last names, one probably a maiden name—(Magglio) Schwartz.

Or this one. Or this one.

He looked at them, just curious, then all at once his eyes darted back to the second name.

It was a man's name, with an address that said "Phila" after it.

The person his father had gone to Philly to see?

•  •  •

He gave in just after he'd convinced himself he shouldn't, that there was no point to it.

After all, just to ask had his father been there? Just that and . . . see where it went?

He looked at the phone. Then after a long moment picked it up. Philadelphia information gave him the number.

After several rings a woman answered. He said, "May I speak to Mr. Tucker, please?"

There was silence, then the sound of quiet gasping. Another woman came on, demanded, "Who is this?" He was too startled to answer. Only wanted to hang up.

"You another one? Animals! Hasn't she been through enough? Can't you animals leave people alone?"

Then the phone went dead.

# 5

What was that about?

He sat there for a long while, knowing only that that was the last of the calls.

That was it. No more.

He went over to the window and stared out briefly. Harvard was just across the Cambridge Common. He thought of getting something to eat in the Square, picking up an L.A. paper; but his thoughts kept going back to the phone.

He could feel his heart racing, but wasn't sure why. Then after a while he knew.

Though he might fight against it, might not do it right now, sooner or later he would call the four other people.

•  •  •

At a quarter after eight that night, about fifteen miles from Boston, Madeline Schwartz and ten other teachers were leaving a split-level home and walking to their cars. She walked quickly, a hand clutching the collar of her coat; it must have been fifty in that house, felt as cold as out here. In the car she let go a shiver and turned on the ignition; the motor strained, hesitated, then caught.

It would be a damn shame, she thought, idling it, if they went out on strike because of some hotheads. She was all for unions, for strikes, God knows—but a teachers' strike, a strike against *kids*, you should use every option you could, and then some.

She was a little surprised at Fran and Max in particular, getting up and saying they were all for a strike, it was time we thought of ourselves. And yet Fran and Max were always complaining about everyone else's strike.

She pulled away from the curb, honked good-bye at Rose and Sharon who were talking on the sidewalk.

Well, maybe there wouldn't be. Even if the committee voted yes—and they hadn't yet—the committees at the other schools might not, and it also had to go to the membership.

Driving, she started to think of other things. Her weight—she was thirty-two pounds over, this morning. She'd made a good start this evening, with just a salad, but that could have been because Herm hadn't been home, he was staying late at the hospital. She found she couldn't really diet unless they did it together, but they were rarely in synch.

Turning into her driveway, she saw that Herman's car wasn't there—they'd converted the attached garage of their rancher into a den. As soon as she came into the house, Cindy called from upstairs, "Mom?"

"Me." She was taking off her coat.

"Did they decide anything?"

"Not yet. Did Daddy call?"

"No."

Cindy came partway down the stairs as she was hanging up her coat. Except for Herman's coloring—she herself was dark-complexioned—she could have been

Madeline's twin at sixteen. Glossy brown hair, big eyes, nice figure.

Well, once she took off thirty pounds—even twenty—she'd have her figure back.

"Mrs. Weiss called, she asked you to call her."

"When did she call?" Not that it made any difference.

"Half hour ago, hour."

"You finish your homework?"

"Still got some French."

As Cindy headed back upstairs Madeline went to the kitchen. Cindy had left a few of her dishes in the sink. Could you believe she wouldn't take the two steps to put them in the washer? After putting them away, she wondered should she call Rose Weiss tonight. She'd made up her mind she wasn't going to take over for Rose as head of the sisterhood at the Temple, but somehow couldn't get around to just saying it. Maybe because a part of her felt flattered that Madeline Magglio, who'd become more "Jewish" than her husband, had really made it there.

She would do it from her room. She also had a pile of papers waiting up there to be graded. But even though she was a little tired she was looking forward to it, to see if they were still doing so well. Her kids this year—sixth graders—every one of them was bright, nice.

She was walking upstairs when the phone rang. Cindy took it.

"Mom, for you. A Mr. Kyle."

She stopped, reached out for the banister.

He was dead! Wasn't he dead?

"Mom?"

He was dead! She'd read it, knew it! Then who?

She wanted to say get a number, she'd call back. And then never call back. But whoever it was he'd only call again. And what did he want? She couldn't live through the night without knowing.

"I'll take it downstairs." But in the kitchen, not the den; there was no door to close off the den.

In the kitchen she fought for calm. Then lifted the phone from the wall.

"I have it, Cindy." And waited for the change of sound that indicated Cindy was off. Then, "Yes."

Mrs. Schwartz, he said, he was sorry to bother her, but his name was David Kyle. "I really hate to bother you, and I hope you don't mind, but I'm just calling to find out if you ever talked to my father. Joseph Kyle?"

"Who?" Stalling. Trying to think.

"Joseph Kyle."

She wanted to say no, but he might be testing her. "Yes."

Had his father asked if she'd known a girl named Sandy, this would be back around 1963, the sister of a Mrs. Dougherty? And again she wanted to say no, but maybe he knew that Mrs. Danzig in the old neighborhood had told his father about them. "Yes. Why?"

"I was wondering if you knew what happened to her after she left her sister's."

And this time she didn't care what he knew. It just came out. "No."

And no, she didn't know her last name. And no, she didn't know where Mrs. Dougherty lived, which was the truth.

"Can I ask you one more thing? Did you know a Roger Tucker?"

Oh, God! "He— Just, you know, he was one of the kids in the neighborhood."

"Would you happen to know if he knew Sandy?"

"I really don't." She wanted to say she was busy and hang up, but was afraid to, but then she didn't have to because once again he said he was sorry to bother her, and thanked her and said good-bye.

She sat at the kitchen table, hands clenched near her

face, trying to control her trembling. It would come in spasms.

When would it end? Never?

"Mom?" From upstairs. "You off the phone?"

She couldn't stop the trembling. Must.

"Mom?"

"Yes, sweetheart?"

"Could you help me?"

"I'll be up. I'll be up in a few minutes."

Would do anything, *anything*, to protect all of this. And she thought, as she often did, of that time out in the field when Nick, his dark eyes narrowed, had first handed her a revolver to shoot at cans. And how, though she'd never touched a gun, was even repelled by it, she was sure she'd use it if she had to.

● ● ●

Herman folded the newspaper, set it aside on the sofa, yawned, then said, "I think I've had it. Coming up?"

"Soon."

He lifted himself off the sofa, hands on his thighs. He yawned again. "If I don't see you in five minutes, good night."

"Good night."

She watched him walk up the stairs, a heavy man with such skilled hands, one of the top general surgeons in Boston. Now that he was up there, out of sight, she clasped her hands on her lap, kept tightening them.

What should she do? Try to contact him? No?

She looked at the French provincial commode across the living room. She kept looking at it. Then she went over to it and took out a *Time* from a stack of magazines in the bottom drawer. It was the oldest by far; over a year old.

Strange how she knew which page it was on but kept forgetting the name of the foundation. She opened it to the page, to a long story on a French film director. But she was interested in just one paragraph, which told of his receiving a large grant from the McInstery Foundation, in Washington, D.C. And there was a quote from its president, Nicholas Ellis.

Should she? Had he heard from Kyle too? And if he hadn't, shouldn't he know?

But she was afraid. Afraid of the son out there, and afraid of . . . him; afraid of letting him back in her life.

**6**

For the past half hour, from the time he woke up, he'd been trying to think of it.

What the hell was the guy's name? Derry? Derrick? . . . Did it even begin with a D?

David, elbows on the desk, pressed his fingertips against his forehead, as if that would loosen the name—the guy in Homicide his father had mentioned talking to a few months ago.

Or was it a P? It was a P . . . Petty? Perry? Perry.

That seemed sort of right. Perry.

He called police headquarters, asked for Homicide. When he was connected he said, "Is there a Detective Perry there?"

"Sure is. But he's in with the boss. Any message?"

"Yes, please have him call me."

After leaving his name and number, he finished the last of the cup of coffee on the desk and began to get dressed. He felt uneasy about the call, had thought it back and forth before making it: if Perry was like most of the others there, he'd probably had enough of Joe Kyle. But all he wanted to know was if they were interested in him dropping off this folder, in having the names, hearing the little he had to say. If they were, fine; if not, fine. Do what they want. He was going.

Perry called back within fifteen minutes. And as soon as David told him why he'd called he knew in the pause that followed that he was right to feel uneasy. He could picture him raising his eyes to the ceiling.

"And you say you're his son," he finally said.

"That's right. And I'm going to be leaving. I just want to know if you want this, that's all."

"I see." And there was a trace of a sigh in his voice. "Well, look, bring over what you want to bring over, but I'm checking out in a few minutes. So talk to whoever's here. But let me ask you one question, okay? Is whatever you have something that looks real hot? Because if it's something that's going to take us from here to there and up the hill and back again and all around, we"—and he enunciated the next few words carefully—"just ain't got the time. That case is a hunnerd years old and more guys have broken their balls on it. Not that we're not interested anymore, sure we're interested, but we can't go up and down and around anymore.

"So unless you have something real hot, something that looks like it's got a real chance of breaking it, that case is still for the history books. Now you sound like an intelligent guy, so I'm going to leave it up to you. If it's something hot, okay something *warm*, come in, you can talk to anyone he'll take it down. Okay?"

"I understand."

"Not that I'm trying to discourage you," Perry said. "I mean, sure, bring in anything. You know, leave it, we'll look at it. But I'm just telling you. If it's got no heat to it, you know, how much can we give it? So I'm leaving it up to you. We're right here, okay?"

[ 44 ]

"I understand."

"Look," he said, after a pause, "let me say just one more thing. I'm sorry about your father. I was sorry to hear it. He was a good guy."

"Thank you very much."

"Take it easy."

The phone cradled, he sat back in the chair, tilting it. His face was tight with anger. How many times his father must have been humiliated, made fun of, talked down to. And had to take it, because there was only one thing that mattered.

He could just see himself going over there, telling someone I'm Joe Kyle's son, and my father was looking for someone named Sandy because one of her children looked remarkably like the dead boy, and the other one would have been the dead boy's age. And here were all these names, three of which he'd called last night before giving up, learning nothing except that someone in Philly was terribly anguished.

He kept sitting there, thinking, trying to calm down.

There was just one more thing he had thought to do, but had decided on the call to Perry instead. He told himself now not to bother with that either.

He just wanted out of here.

Had enough of the boy, didn't want it anymore. And didn't want to think anymore of his father's hurts.

He rested his mouth against his tented fingers.

But this one last thing would only stick with him, something left unfinished . . .

Maybe, maybe just do it—fast and out.

•  •  •

Madeline Schwartz took a quick glance at her wristwatch against her lap. It was twenty to one. She had to make up her mind fast; had to be back in class by one.

Dorothy Taylor, one of the group of teachers at her table in the cafeteria, said to Stanley Miller, "So you're very lucky. All you have to do is hold out two more years. I'd give anything to be on pension in two years."

"Three-quarters pension," he said.

"Three-quarters pension. I'd give anything for that. It doesn't pay to wait for full pension, what's going on. Three-quarters pension, you can still work, you can live in Florida, California, anywhere you want. And you'll do better than you are."

"Oh, I'm looking forward," he said. "I never thought I'd look forward."

"Well, there's just no satisfaction anymore," Dorothy said. "The administration—should we even have to be *thinking* strike? How much money are we talking about? And the kids, I try to tell friends the kids are different than when we went to school, they think I'm talking about the blacks, the Hispanics. I tell them no, it's the kids. And they think, they say, aah, look who's bitchin', you're home three-thirty, you're off the whole summer."

"No, they're definitely different," Madeline Schwartz heard Oscar Simpson say, and she gave her wrist a little turn to see how much time had gone by. She drew in a deep, quivering breath.

She stood up, managed a slight smile. "Will you excuse me?"

"You may leave the room," Oscar Simpson said with a smile.

She walked to one of the doors leading outside, putting her arms through the sleeves of the thin sweater she'd been wearing over her shoulders. She should go to her locker and get her coat, but that would be five more minutes at the least. She walked quickly to the sidewalk, then to a partially sheltered pay phone at the corner.

She'd already gotten the McInstery phone number, and now had the operator put through the call on her credit card.

"McInstery Foundation."

"May I speak to Mr. Ellis?"

"One moment, please." Then, his secretary: "Mr. Ellis's office."

"May I speak to him, please."

"He's not in right now, he'll be back in about an hour. Who's calling?"

"I'll call back." She hung up quickly, then felt herself go limp. She was aware all at once that she was sweating in this cold; that she was chilled and shaking.

Thank God he wasn't in. It had to be a sign that she mustn't call.

• • •

He sat at a table in the library with the last three weeks' issues of one of the Philadelphia papers. Whatever had happened to the Tuckers surely had happened recently.

He worked his way back, scanning everything for the name—not just the news sections, but sports, business, society, editorials, letters to the editor. After a while he found himself going too fast, skipping stories, and had to go back.

But again he had to fight against turning pages too quickly, just skimming them. Wanted the end, out of here. But he kept going slowly, now and then going back to a previous page.

Suddenly he stopped. Halfway down the front page:

PROMINENT CLERGYMAN FALLS TO DEATH

The Rev. Roger Tucker, 42, the well-known social and political activist . . .

He'd either jumped or fallen from the balcony of his twelfth-floor apartment, where he'd lived with his wife. Former pastor of a church, he'd spent the past eight years in charity work, was in the forefront of antiwar activities, in the fight against abortion, and was the founder of a shelter for runaways and a suicide hotline.

[ 47 ]

A passerby had seen the body strike the sidewalk but had not seen Tucker on the balcony. According to a "police source," the railing around the balcony was four feet high, thus intimating that the clergyman who'd started a suicide hotline had ended up committing suicide.

Which could explain, David thought, the crank calls.

He looked at the date of the paper. January 29. Tucker had died the night before.

He wondered if he'd overlooked a follow-up story on it—certainly, the funeral—but then saw that some of the issues weren't in order. He searched and then pulled out the January 30 issue. And again on the front page:

TUCKER'S WIFE SAYS NO TO SUICIDE

Anne Tucker, 41, widow of the Rev. Roger Tucker, who fell to his death Thursday night beneath their twelfth-floor apartment, says it's "inconceivable" that he committed suicide.

"I'm not just speaking from emotions, but from what I know of my husband," she said.

Not only was he opposed to suicide on religious and philosophical grounds, she said, but there was nothing to indicate that he was contemplating it. He showed no signs of depression, had even made plans for a trip, and had left no note.

Mrs. Tucker, who had been attending an evening adult class at the time of her husband's death, said he had told her he was expecting a visitor.

"He didn't say who it was, just that someone had called to ask to see him," she said. "But he did refer to the person as 'he.' It wasn't unusual for him to have visitors—he was active in so many things, and so many people came to him with their problems . . ."

David kept staring at the story, his heartbeat gradually building, then going in tumult. For he was thinking of how Marie had described the Old Man when he'd returned—agitated, almost frantic.

## 7

There was another story, the following day, on the second page.

### SECURITY QUESTIONED AT TUCKER APARTMENT

Several tenants were quoted as saying they'd been complaining about lax security for months, and two people said they hadn't seen the guard at his station in the lobby for at least an hour around the time of Tucker's death, which could account for there being no record of a visitor. There were also quotes from several people who'd known Tucker, saying they couldn't believe he would have committed suicide. And the last couple of lines mentioned that the funeral would be private.

Sitting back, David could feel himself breathing heavily.

Had to be out of his mind to give this even a second's thought. His father kill someone? *Him? Pop?*

Yet whom had Tucker been expecting? And why hadn't that person come forward?

Almost against his will, David began thinking of things that could have happened. Like, his father could have accused Tucker of something—the murder, maybe knowing something about it, and there'd been a fight. Or he could have just snapped out after all these years.

He couldn't believe this, no way, and yet things—things just began finding their way into his mind. Like how strong his father was. He really was. He had complained for the last year or so how his legs weren't the same, and maybe so, but he always did exercises in the morning, by his bed, would pump those arms, do crackly knee bends; and he still had those big biceps and powerful chest, though the skin was so white and wrinkled in places.

And his temper came to mind.

Sometimes you'd forget he had one, because it could be months between times you saw it, when suddenly he'd begin yelling over nothing, like where were those newspapers he'd been saving, and his mother would go tearing through the trash to find them. And then there'd be an argument why she was always throwing things out she knew he wanted, and afterward when she was alone with Marie and him she would bite her lips and say something like "You just don't know," so that the sorrow filled up in him for her, and the fury against him. And then that time his father came into his room, he was maybe thirteen, and said, "Did a Mr. Ruan call me yesterday?"

And suddenly he'd known what was going to happen, so he'd started to lie, but then couldn't and said yes.

"Why didn't you tell me?" And his voice kept rising. "He told you to tell me, didn't he?"

He nodded quickly, wanting to tell him the truth, that he'd been afraid it would keep him from going to the Sox game with him, but instead he said, "I forgot."

And that's when his father slapped him. It was only, he

was sure, the second time he'd ever hit him, and Pop was so sorry maybe a half hour later, but he could never forget that one.

And he knew that ever since, though it never happened again, though they'd laughed about a thousand things, he'd feared his father.

And was afraid now of what he might have done.

Could even see him doing.

•  •  •

When he got back to the hotel he called Marie at work.

"I hate to call you here, but I didn't know if I'd have a chance to later. Can I ask you a fast question? Did you ever hear Dad mention anyone by the name of Tucker? Roger Tucker?"

"Tucker." She thought. "No. I don't remember. Why?"

"I'm just trying to check on something."

"David, is something the matter?"

"Nothing." He was sorry he'd called. "I said I'm just trying to check on something. I just wanted to know if he knew him."

"You sure now? There's no problem?"

"There's no problem. Nothing. I was just curious. It's a long story. And not very interesting . . . So, look, I'm still leaving this evening."

"What time did you say your plane left?"

"Quarter after six."

"Well look. Davey, you take care of yourself."

"You too, sweetheart."

"Take care."

He lowered the phone slowly. What he should do was just get the hell out of here, forget it . . . But why the hell did his father go all the way to Philly to see him? Did the guy actually even know Sandy?

But even if he could find out now, what then?

Somehow it was just important to know.

He opened a drawer and glanced at the phone book, then pushed it shut again. One of the stories had listed a couple of Tucker's relatives—a mother, a brother—but he couldn't remember their first names. And he'd never call them anyway. As he started to get up from the desk his eyes went to the crumpled sheets of paper with the names.

Of course. Why hadn't he thought of this right away? He found Tucker's name, saw that a penciled arrow pointed to it, and that the line curved back to an Alice Ozek. She'd also given him other names, but they were crossed out. Apparently Tucker was the only one his father hadn't spoken to at the time.

There was a scribbled address and phone number next to Ozek, but they were hard to make out. The phone number, it seemed, could be either of two combinations.

He looked at the phone. Then after several moments he dialed one, just to find out. It kept ringing. He tried the second one. This time a girl, a child, answered.

"Is Alice Ozek there?"

"My grandmom's not here."

"Do you know when she'll be home?"

"No. She went to the store."

"I'll call her back."

He hung up quickly, before anyone else came on. He realized then how hard he'd been clenching the phone. He hadn't been prepared to talk to the grandmother, wasn't sure he even wanted to. All he might end up doing was implicating his father.

He looked at his watch. Twenty to twelve.

He and Judy had left it that if they were free they might meet for lunch.

He wondered what she'd say if he asked her to come up. He wanted to slide in bed naked with her, and lose every trace of thought, all of this heaviness, in her arms. He let himself fantasy it a little, but decided against it; maybe if he wasn't going home today. Instead, calling her at her shop, he asked her out for lunch. Though she wasn't able to go out—her partner was off, and the saleswoman was new—would he like to have a bite there?

•  •  •

She lifted her face for a quick kiss on the lips—she seemed shorter than five four against his six two; barely came to his chin in high heels. He said, looking around, this is very nice, very very nice. A small, elegantly decorated shop, it seemed to have a smattering of everything for the high-fashion woman—smart expensive dresses, handbags, belts, costume jewelry. Her own dress, a beige suit, might have been lifted from one of the hangers.

She'd ordered turkey clubs and coffee for both of them, and set them out on her desk in the office. She sat half turned from the desk, looking at him, her legs crossed, and smiled as she said she'd forgotten how he hated coats—how could he just carry one in this weather? And she asked about the legal business with the house, was it settled?—good. And he wanted to know did Donny come down with a cold as she'd feared, and she said no, thank goodness; and he asked had she decided about the guy she'd told him about who had been calling for a blind date, and she said yes, she'd decided against it, she'd had enough of blind dates. And once in a while she'd look out at the shop, thinking she had heard someone come in, and then look back with a slight head flick of her bangs, a habit he'd forgotten, and with her almost perpetual little smile. Her saleswoman was with a customer, and would occasionally go over to speak to another who was looking around.

She deserved so much credit, he thought. For someone who'd majored in English and whose only job had been a brief one as a teacher in a private school, she'd become quite a businesswoman in the past few years.

He said, "Maybe you ought to go out. Don't let me hold you."

"Are you kidding? And let you eat all my lunch?"

He smiled, and she said, after a long moment, "David, can I say something?" She kept looking at him. "That's the first real smile since you've come in."

"No."

"No yes. It's none of my business, I know, but I'd say you have something on your mind."

"Well—Dad won't give me the car."

"Aah." Even her eyes seemed to smile. "How will we go out?"

"We can't. We have to stay at your house."

"The folks are home."

"Hey, I just remembered. I can get the car."

She laughed, then began gathering up the bags and papers and coffee containers. He watched as she stuffed them in the wastepaper basket. She'd always been someone he could really talk to . . .

"Look," he said, "there really is."

"Really is what?"

"Something on my mind. But it's a little nuts-o. A lot nuts-o."

She looked at him with an edge of concern.

"Would you believe," he said, "I've got this thing in my head that my dad might have killed someone?"

She winced. "No. Come on."

"I said it's nuts. And the odds are it is. But it's in my head . . . Well, it's not only in my head, there's a damn good reason."

Judy, he said, I've gotten involved in something I had no business to. And now he told her about his guilt over his father's call to him in L.A., and about Sam Goldberg and Sandy and Tucker's suicide and being afraid to call Alice Ozek back, because though he was curious—more than curious—to find out what she'd told him about

Tucker, it might only implicate his father in a—in a murder.

"Jesus," she said.

"Jesus is right."

"Look, he didn't do it. It's been years—but I sort of knew your father. No way."

"Marie said he was like off the wall when he came back."

"That could have been anything."

"I know."

"Can I ask you something? What will you accomplish if you talk to this woman? Let's say she tells you yes, Tucker knew Sandy. So?"

"She might say something more. I'm sounding like a broken record, but I'd like to know what made Dad go to Philly."

"David, it's not the first trip he made."

"Yeah, but it's a little different. He was complaining about his legs, that he was old. I think it would have had to be something special."

"Didn't you say he was always getting excited about things?"

"I know."

She looked at him, frowning. "You know what concerns me? That you're going to get so involved it's only going to tear you up."

"Well, I'm sort of torn up already. But it's like the only way to put all these crazy thoughts away is to take just one more step."

She kept looking at him. "You won't rest easy, will you?"

"No."

She reached over and squeezed his knee. "Then you do it." She stood up and touched his face. "Hey. You didn't do anything wrong." Then she turned and went out of the office.

He looked at the phone on the desk. He knew the number, would know it backwards and sideways. He picked it up and punched at the digits quickly.

Again, the child answered.

"Is your grandmother there?"

"Grandmom," she yelled. "Grandmom."

Alice Ozek came on forcefully. "Mr. Angelo?"

"I'm sorry, this isn't Mr. Angelo."

"Oh. I'm sorry, I was expecting a call. What can I do for you?"

And now he was going into it again—who he was, and had his father Joe Kyle been to see her about someone named Sandy who'd once lived in her neighborhood.

"Oh, yes. That's the gentleman who died. I was very sorry to read that."

He'd been going through his father's files, he said, and was curious about something. "Did you tell him that Roger Tucker knew Sandy?"

"Oh, yes. Like I told your father, I know because it almost killed his mother. He brought this girl home and his mother was sure he was going to marry her."

"Did he?"

"No. But by the way, I'm sorry to say this, but did you know Roger died?"

"No." He felt a harder thrust of his heart.

Well, he did; someone had told her just yesterday he'd committed suicide. Imagine that. "He was a very unusual boy. Very wild, unkempt. And he disappeared from home for quite a few years. Then the next I heard he was a minister."

Did she happen to remember Sandy's last name? No. And she didn't know where her sister was either. "But I did find out something that interested your dad. I called Roger's brother—I hear his mother's in a nursing home—I called his brother to find out where he was living, and that's how I heard he was in Philadelphia. And I asked him about Sandy. He told me Roger spoke about her once, that she'd worked for him."

"In Philadelphia?"

"That's what he said. I asked him was Sandy still working for him, and he was sure not, that it was a few years back."

No, the brother didn't know where Sandy was.

He was sitting there now, the phone down, wondering what to do.

She'd given him Tucker's brother's name, but that would really be pushing it to call.

And yet it was so hard to let it go at this.

Should he?

Go to Philly? Maybe just a day or two? See who might have known her?

•  •  •

"Mrs. Schwartz?"

Startled, Madeline Schwartz looked up from her desk; her mind had been so far away.

It was one of her pupils; the others were filing out of the classroom.

"I just want to know when you think we might be getting our test back."

"Can't you see I'm busy?"

The girl, one of her favorites, went red. She mumbled, "I—I'm sorry," and walked off.

Madeline watched her, wanting to call her back. But her thoughts drifted back again. Yes, no—whether to call him.

•  •  •

He made up his mind on the ride back to the hotel. The first thing he did was call his daughter. Gina answered.

She said, "Are you home?"

"No, I'm still in Cambridge. Look, I'm afraid I can't make it Saturday. Is Sara there?"

"Yes. Hold on. She's going to be very disappointed."

Sara came on. "Daddy?"

"Hi, sweetheart, how are you?"

"Fine," she said in a singsong way.

"Honey, I'm afraid I have bad news. I won't be able to see you Saturday."

"Oh." It sounded anguished.

"I'm disappointed too, you don't know how disappointed, but I can't help it. I miss you."

"I miss you too."

"I'm really sorry, sweetheart, but I'll make it up. I love you. You know that?"

"Yes."

"I'm really sorry, sweetheart."

"That's okay."

But she said it flatly. And it was the flatness that stayed with him after he hung up.

Oh, Christ.

It sounded like his own voice, so many times, to his father.

8

He lifted his bag to his bed and started putting in his things, then stopped all at once as though thinking about this for the first time. He really had no idea what he was going to do there; just that he was driven to go. That it was as if Pop were still alive and had done some crazy thing and had to be pulled out of it. And that learning a little more about Tucker and Sandy might somehow help, or give some insight into whatever happened in that apartment. Odds are he wouldn't learn a thing. But the only chance was there, not in L.A.

And the big thing, probably, was that he'd feel better knowing that at least he'd tried something, even if he was there only a day, did nothing but go through old newspapers to learn more about Tucker. Then get the hell back to L.A, to his work, friends, Sara—then maybe go back to Greece for a while, get a place on Hydra.

He went over to the CRNT folder to pack it, but then, standing at the desk, remembered something and called Marie.

"Will you be home in about a half hour?"

"Bob and I won't. But one of the kids."

"Tell them to wait till I get there. I'd like to pick something up."

"Isn't your plane taking off at quarter after six? You're cutting it mighty thin."

"It'll be all right, I'll make it."

"Oh, Davey, you haven't changed. If you can't run for a plane you're not happy."

Larry, their youngest, was home.

"How you doing, kiddo?"

"Okay." But Larry couldn't wait to go upstairs to the computer Marie and Bob had bought for the boys.

David walked down to the basement. Although all the furniture was still in his father's corner, there was a feeling of emptiness his mother would have loved.

"I'm only trying to keep the place neat," she'd retort when the Old Man couldn't find something or found stacks of his strewn papers put into neat piles.

"I don't want it neat! I want it the way I want it!"

"I'm only doing it for you, you'll be able to find things."

"I don't want to find anything. I want to spend all day looking. I told you to stay away from it, leave everything alone. How many times I got to tell you!"

"You're a crazy man, you know that?"

"Just stay away from it! Stay the hell out of here!" And once David remembered his father saying stay the fuck out, which was like a punch to her face, and they didn't talk for maybe two weeks. He'd never heard her use any stronger word than hell.

He opened one of the cabinet drawers. He'd thrown out most of the things; the dividers and the few remaining folders and envelopes sagged against each other. He took out the manila envelope he knew so well, opened it and pulled out some of the pictures of the boy, just to make sure they were still there, then pushed them back in.

He walked upstairs with them. And with the eerie feeling that he was taking along the boy himself.

● ● ●

As the plane began its slow descent to the lights of the city, the seat belt and no-smoking sign going on and the plane rocking slightly in some sudden turbulence, he found himself thinking of the last time he'd come here. It was the first year he and Gina were married, and they had this old, old Chevy they'd bought for three hundred and thirty dollars. Hey, he'd said, we've done the Europe thing, hitched, biked, walked, so let's see our own country.

"Why not?"

That was one of her favorite expressions. That, and "No problem." In fact, it had been a kind of "Why not?" when he'd seen her waiting for a bus near one of the freeways, when it was threatening to rain, and he looked over at her, tall and very thin, with long auburn hair, and gunned his Honda bike so it almost lifted under him, and smiled and touched the back part of the seat. She'd looked him over for a while, then smiled—it was the smile that might have said "Why not?"—and walked over and climbed on back. She had the high boots for it, and a miniskirt that she'd had to hoist a little higher.

"I never did this before," she called into his ear as they took off.

"You mean hitch a ride or on a bike?"

"No, on a Honda."

And he'd laughed and looked back, and she was laughing. And in just a few miles he learned that she worked as a secretary at a small, barely making it animation studio, and before that as a photographer's assistant at weddings and bar mitzvahs; and she, that he'd said good-bye to Berkeley only a few days ago and was down here in L.A. looking for a job, but mostly looking around. And again it was a kind of "Why not?" this time in her eyes, when he pulled over to the curb near a phone and asked could she take the day off, and they just looked at each other before she eased herself off and walked over to it.

"This is crazy," she'd said, but by then they were heading up the coast, the sky suddenly clear, a part of him thinking they might go all the way up to Big Sur, but they stopped in Santa Barbara and had lunch and sat around on the beach, and on the way back stopped long enough in a field to make love. And that night he'd met her mother, the Greek part of her—her father, an Italian, was the second of her mother's four husbands—and the first thing she'd said to him was, "There's something I don't like about you." But he never held that against her, for he couldn't blame her: she wanted her daughter married, and he knew he wasn't going to be the one.

But then the deep fondness came, then the love, for she was quite a person, and they did all those things together, single and married, like that trip across the country— where they'd bussed and waited tables, and once he painted a garage—that brought them here to Philly and then finally up to Maine and back to L.A. And when she became pregnant, it seemed just as much of a surprise to her as to him, but then one day he came across her cylinder of pills, which had only one missing, as it did three months before. But he'd never said anything to her, and Sara turned out to be the love of his life, and Gina the best of mothers . . .

As the plane pulled up to the terminal he waited until most people got out before he stood up. Walking along the corridors to the baggage department, he glanced at some hotel posters along the way, trying to memorize them, not sure where he'd stay: maybe one of those, or maybe the Blaine, where his father might have stayed. Marie had recalled overhearing him make a call to what had sounded like the Blaine.

He carried his cordovan leather bag, raincoat over his shoulder, out to the cab stand, where several people stood hunched in the black cold. It suddenly made him feel cold, and he slipped on his coat.

When he got in the cab he said, "What kind of place is the Blaine?"

"So-so," looking back at him. "Not bad. Not the fanciest. I never stayed there, but I hear not bad."

"Is it downtown?"

"Yeah."

"Okay."

As they drove, the driver said, "You been under a sun lamp?"

"No."

"That was the Boston flight just come in, wasn't it? I don't mean to get personal but you don't get a tan in Boston in the winter."

"No, I'm from L.A."

"You a Lakers' fan?"

"I go to about three–four games a year."

"I see the Sixers every chance I get. How about hockey? You got lousy hockey out there."

"I've seen a few games. But I'm no big fan."

"We got the Flyers, you know. If you asked me which I like best, Flyers, Sixers, Eagles, I'd have a hard time. I'm really a Phillies' fan. That's my game."

The Blaine was a small, residential-looking hotel. If it had a doorman, he wasn't out under the marquee. David said to the driver, "Let me see if they have a room."

They did, and after paying off the driver he brought in his bag. A bellman approached him quickly and took it.

The desk clerk said, "How long will you be staying, Mr. Kyle?"

"I'm not sure. Two nights maybe, I'm not really sure."

"If it's credit card I'll need it now."

David watched as he ran it through. He didn't know

why, but suddenly it became important that this be the place where his father stayed. He said hesitantly, "Can I ask you a favor? My father was in town a few weeks ago. I'm curious to know if it's the same hotel. I think it is."

"I don't think I'm supposed to give that. I don't know, I've never been asked."

"That's okay, it doesn't matter. He died a few days ago and I'm . . . I guess just being sentimental."

The clerk looked at him. "Same last name, huh?"

"Same last name. Kyle. Joseph Kyle."

"And you say a few weeks ago?" But he didn't wait for an answer. He went over to a computer. He tapped a few keys, looked at the screen. "Yep. Checked in January twenty-seventh, out the twenty-ninth."

"Thanks very much. I deeply appreciate that."

But he could feel a tightening in his chest as he followed the bellman to the elevators. Checkout was eleven. This was the first he knew for sure that his father had checked out the very morning after Tucker's death.

In the elevator he wanted to ask the bellman, "Do you remember my father, seventy, about five eight, white hair. . . ? And did he seem nervous? And what did he do and how did he act?" And he wanted to ask the day people, cabbies parked outside, things like did he ever ask directions anywhere, do you know any of the places he went to? . . . But he quietly followed the bellman down the hall and watched as he showed him the closet, the bath, clicked the TV on and off, and then he overtipped as he usually did.

A nice enough room, though his mind was hardly on it.

That had been stupid, he thought. Asking the desk clerk. Who the hell knew what the police were doing? All he might have done was bring attention to his father.

He looked around the room again.

So. Here he was in Philly. Now what?

Tonight, probably the bar for just a little while. He

snapped open his bag, but only to take out his shaving things, mostly, then sat down at the kidney-shaped walnut table by the bed. He owed two calls—one to Judy, whom he hadn't been able to reach after deciding to go to Philly, the other to Diane, whom he'd been seeing off and on for about five months and whom he hadn't called since he left L.A. He called Judy first but got a baby-sitter.

"Tell her it's David, I'm in Philly. I'll call her soon—if not from here, from L.A. . . . . You've got that? Oh, and tell her I'm at the Blaine." He repeated it for her, spelling it. "But I'll probably only be here a couple days."

He immediately called Diane, but got her answering machine. He left pretty much the same message. He'd forgotten that today was the day they taped the show—she showed gifts on a daytime game show.

She was the closest to the original Gina he'd met, except she'd gone on for a couple of years to college and was ambitious—actually to be a screenwriter, and had sold two TV scripts—but not for another marriage, which was just fine.

A deeper silence closed in the instant he hung up. He was anxious to get started on something, wished the night were over. He sat looking at the phone, then opened a few drawers until he found the phone book. He paged through it quickly.

Tucker, Roger, Rev.

Two listings. One was the apartment house. The other just gave an address. He dialed the second number.

It rang for a while, then a man said, "Homeward House."

The youth shelter, surely. He said, "Could you tell me if a woman named Sandy or Sandra works there? Or used to work there?"

"Sandy?"

"Yes. Or Sandra."

Silence. Then, "No, I don't know anyone. Might try tomorrow. But I never hearda no one."

It was only after he hung up that he could feel the pistons going in him. He tried to relax, to let go; had a sense of being out of control.

•  •  •

Detective Ed Perry blew on his hands before taking off his overcoat and hanging it up. He was crazy staying up north; each winter he swore was the last. But next year for sure, though Mary said oh, yeah. And she was right, not that he wasn't finally retiring, but she'd been hearing it for so long.

He nodded hello to Harry, the only one in the office at the time, and settled his big body at his desk. Harry, yawning, was just getting around to nodding back. Ed Perry took a batch of papers from his IN file and was sifting through them when he remembered.

"You know if a guy Kyle was in?"

Harry made an act of looking shocked. "You mean Joe Kyle? If he comes in I'm gettin' the fuck out."

"Cut the shit. But it's his son. I think David. He said he might leave some stuff."

"I don't know."

Perry went to the clerk. No. He came back to his desk, frowning slightly.

He'd started thinking about the guy this morning. Though he knew he'd just about talked him out of it, still he found himself wondering. Why he hadn't brought in whatever it was, anyway. And whether it had been a mistake cooling him.

Perry had been maybe the fifth man to reach the scene. He'd been twenty-six then, the youngest detective on the force; hadn't been in Homicide yet, but the kid had been found in his area. A sad thing, but no sadder than a million other things they saw, and a lot less gruesome than a million others. But a kid—a kid always gets you.

It had been one of those cases you're sure will be solved quickly; certainly there'd be no problem about identity. So there's where it started getting real real sad. And he'd been one of the guys who every year went to the grave; every year, up until about five years ago.

Trying to shift his thoughts, Perry looked at a medical examiner's report on one of his cases. Now, this was a gruesome one. An old fairy, sliced from the chin down almost to his prick.

But his mind kept going back. He'd been sent to a lot of places, what with all those leads. But nowhere fancy. The favorites got the fancy ones—Honolulu, London, Brussels. The fanciest he got was Atlanta.

He'd had a lot of dreams, once, solving it. Still did, occasionally, though it was dead, dead, dead.

Could go months without thinking of it, but whenever the old guy used to come in the juices started up. Like he couldn't let the bastard beat him out. Didn't want to get beat.

And now, even by any of the shit the son might have.

• • •

Madeline sat with her hand on the cradled phone, face fiery. Then she lifted it and began dialing.

"McInstery Foundation."

"Mr. Ellis, please."

"One moment, I'll give you his office."

"Mr. Ellis's office."

She hesitated, felt her hand fighting to hang up. "May I speak to him, please?"

"Who's calling?"

"My name's Madeline Schwartz." Her voice seemed to be resonating in her head.

"Could I take a message for him? He's busy right now."

She started to hang up, then said desperately, "Is he in?"

"Yes, but I said he's busy."

"Could you tell him it's Madeline Magglio? He knows who I am."

From the silence, the secretary seemed to be trying to decide. "Hold on a moment."

But it turned into at least two minutes, and now that he knew she'd called it was too late to hang up. Yet she was tempted to, so tempted, he didn't know where she lived, she'd count to fifty—

"Madeline." The voice—it froze her for an instant. So amazing how it hadn't changed.

"How are you, Nick?"

"Fine. Hey, it's so good to hear from you. Where are you? Are you in Washington?"

"No, I'm—home. Nick—can I talk to you?"

There was a long pause. Then, a somber change in his voice, he said, "I'll have to call you back."

"When do you think?"

"Within the hour. Let me have your number."

Hanging up, she wondered confusedly should she call the school—she'd called in earlier to say she would be a little late, but this could be half the day. But she caught herself, it was so stupid, the last thing in this world to worry about.

The call came in a half hour. There was no hello, no preliminaries.

"Tell me," he said.

Oh, the publisher, the executive editor—she would imagine anyone like that in authority.

Hanging up, he stood with his hand to his mouth. He started to put in some coins again, to call one of the other papers, but was certain it would be the same. He called the public library to see if they could help. The operator said she would put him through to a computer service, but the line was busy, stayed busy, then abruptly disconnected. He was about to call back but, since he was here, he decided to try the *Sentinel-Observer* again.

"What's the executive editor's name?" he asked the operator.

"Mr. Colson."

"May I speak to him, please?" He kept fingering a handful of coins.

But Colson's secretary said he was busy. David, who hadn't really expected to reach him, told her he was doing research on a book and asked who could give him permission to use the library. After some thought she said the managing editor; but he turned out to be busy too, and whoever answered his phone switched the call to the assistant managing editor. After hearing David out, he asked did he work for any newspaper or wire service.

"No, I'm a magazine writer. I've done things for *Esquire*, the *Digest*, *Reader's Digest*— But like I said, this is for a book, I do mostly books."

"Look, you can go to the public library—" Then he stopped. "What kind of books?"

"Novels. But this'll be nonfiction."

"What"—he sounded skeptical—"are some of your novels?"

Oh, Christ. "I do mostly thrillers—paperbacks. I do a series on someone named Cade, a doctor—"

"Cade? You do *Cade*?"

•  •  •

He waited outside the elevators on the third floor, where the assistant managing editor had said he'd meet him. He could see into the city room, with its rows of desks, each with a word processor, and people moving about quickly but as though in an aquarium silence.

How different.

"We go through here," Pop had said.

It had been on the second floor of what looked like an ancient factory building, and they had to go straight through the typesetting room, with all its noise and men wearing little folded newspaper hats, to get to the newsroom. He'd been only about six then, and his father had pointed out that over there, where those men were sitting around a sort of horseshoe-shaped table, was what they called the copy desk; and he took him past other desks, through clatter and clutter and crunched-up paper on the floor, to his own scrungy desk in a corner.

"So this is your kid," the guy at the next desk said; and though he didn't lift his legs off his desk, he reached over to shake his hand. And a few other people came around, and two of them said, at different times, "He going to be in the newspaper business?" And each time his father answered the same thing: "No, he's got too many brains."

His father used to say that a lot when he was a little kid, how brainy he was . . .

The assistant managing editor was a short stocky man who tempered down his enthusiasm about Cade, said he liked to read to go to sleep, but he spent some time by the elevators asking David how he thought him up and did he use an agent to sell his first book. Then a young woman joined them, who the assistant managing editor said would take him to the library. There, a man behind the counter asked if he was looking for something that was published more than five years ago. If so, they'd give him clippings; otherwise, it would be in the computer.

"Can I have both?"

"Sure." The man sat down at a computer. "What would you like to see?"

David had already thought this out; he didn't want to come right out and say Tucker. "I'm interested in what you have on the city's services for runaways. I understand there's a shelter here called Homeward House."

"Okay. Homeward"—he was tapping it in—"House."

Things flickered onto the screen, including a cross-reference to Tucker, Roger.

"I'd appreciate it," David said, "if you can give me what you have on Tucker and on Homeward House."

The computer soon began printing out stories. Several on his death. An obituary—went to the University of Wisconsin, his wife's name, their children's names, his activities against nuclear testing, abortion. A history of Homeward House—Tucker had started it eight years ago—and a story about an award dinner for him. David had to ask for clips then, and he was given a batch in an envelope. He went through them slowly. The opening of Homeward House. The hotline. The stories, about two a year, went back to 1976, now 1975—

All at once he was holding a clipping in both hands, was quickly rereading it.

It told how Tucker, still the pastor then, had opened his church to house a large group of the homeless. He was quoted throughout the story; but toward the end was a different kind of quote, about him.

"He's an inspiration to all of us, he's really one of a kind," said Sandra Meghan, twenty-seven, one of his congregants and a volunteer.

David made some fast calculations. That would have been Sandy's approximate age.

# 10

Nick Ellis—only his wife and strangers called him Nicholas—strode down the terraced steps of his rambling Tudor home to where his chauffeur was standing by the open rear door of his car, a glossy-black Lincoln, barely acknowledging the man's attentive presence though it was the first he'd seen him that morning. He quickly thrust up the thick black lamb collar of his leather coat as he settled back, for the idiot hadn't warmed the car enough, then looked out silently as they headed down the long, tree-flanked drive to the narrow road that curved past miles of estates. Then he clicked on the little light behind his shoulder and glanced through a few sections of the *New York Times* and *Washington Post* as they drove out of Virginia and joined the morning traffic that converged on Washington.

The car pulled up in front of a large colonial, white-pillared building in Georgetown, where simple bronze lettering identified it as the McInstery Foundation. This time

Nick acknowledged the chauffeur with a slight nod as he got out—the man would now go back to tend the greenhouse and do odd jobs around the house—and walked quickly to the massive door. A compactly built man of forty-seven, with little built-in lifts that made him five eleven, he walked with a slight hunch to his shoulders, as though his head, large but not massive, was thrusting him forward. He squinted against the cold. Though thickly encased in his coat, he was hatless, his straight black hair, lined with gray, blowing.

Inside, the world was instantly hushed. There was even a hush in the way the receptionist said hello as she looked up from her curved white desk in the lobby. As he walked to his office, Miss Bruehlman, his secretary and office manager, stood up from her desk in the hall when she saw he was having a little trouble extricating his left arm from the sleeve; she helped, asking how his wife was, and hung it up in his office, behind what looked like a secret panel in the light-walnut paneling. Sunlight poured through the large bowed windows, next to which she'd carefully placed some potted plants.

"Mr. Mellaney came in this morning," she said.

"Yes. He was scheduled."

"Oh, I wasn't sure you knew. I'm sorry but I forgot to put it on your calendar."

"Well, I knew." He flickered a little smile at her, and her face, a little strained, eased up. Unmarried, in her mid-forties, she'd worked for him ever since he'd been here.

"I hope you don't mind," she said, "but I showed him around a little. Just a little. But there was no one else in. I told him you'd be in to see him soon."

"Fine."

She left him to the mail. A huge oil painting of John Henry McInstery stared over his back. It was his wife's father, the founder of McInstery Oil, today just a part of a conglomerate of enterprises throughout most of the world. Although the foundation had been in existence for about twenty-five years, Nick had changed its direction in the seven years he'd been married to Louise. Where it had primarily funded medical research, he had changed its focus to the promotion of world peace. In addition to awarding grants for work in the sciences and humanities that could be instrumental in fostering peace—ranging from studies of possible biochemical triggers of anger, to underwriting cultural projects, to research into such nitty-gritty things as the techniques of negotiation—the foundation also offered twenty-five fellowships for scholars-in-residence, international experts in a wide spectrum of fields who could work in the foundation on their various projects for from months to years.

After looking through the mail, he went to Mellaney's office. Mellaney, about forty-two, with a thin mustache and thick glasses, had worked at several of the *New York Times'* foreign bureaus. He had taken a couple years' sabbatical to write a book on the cultural roots of the Sino-Japanese war in the thirties that he felt had applications to the Mideast.

Nick always liked to be the first to greet the new scholars officially. He smiled. "Are you almost settled in?"

Mellaney grinned as he stood up and shook his hand. "Couldn't be more so. I want to thank you for shipping my things." The foundation had paid to move him here.

"That's the least we can do. Have you met anyone yet?"

"Just your secretary."

"Let's see who's in. As you'll see, we're pretty loosey-goosey here, everyone maintains pretty much their own hours. Except, of course, when we have a meeting scheduled. But I think you'll see why they like to be here. It's very quiet"—even the paintings, except for John Henry McInstery, seemed muted—"and we have a tremendous amount of resources. And I'm not just talking about our library and computer systems, though they're among the finest. I'm talking about the interaction among the people. Wonderful, wonderful people . . . Well, look, let me introduce you to who's here."

Next door was Grossman, a former assistant secretary of state and a specialist in Soviet affairs, who was forever on news programs whenever some explanation of Russian behavior was required; Vanbrussen, a behavioral scientist from Holland, wasn't in yet, but Gomez was, next door. Gomez, a Yale professor, was writing a series of popular articles on Latin American cultures and conflicts, which the foundation would also publish as a book. Here, two offices away, was Dellons, the celebrated movie critic, who was writing a book analyzing Hollywood macho men and movies, which the board of directors had thought inappropriate for the foundation, but which Nick had gotten through—"We want a different concept of macho. Tell me, who's more macho—the guy who climbs Mount Everest but needs a steady job that gives him a pension, vacation, and Blue Cross? Or the little self-employed guy who's never had anyone else pay for his vacations, let alone for the time he takes off to go to the bathroom?" And here, three offices away, was Carter, formerly of the British Foreign Office, distinguished-looking right to his graying mustache and elbow-leathered tweed jacket, who was writing a book on containing border disputes.

Nick, after a quick look at his watch, realized he had a meeting. Carter volunteered to do the rest of the tour, which would include the other scholars, the library, the conference room, and the foundation's publications offices—they published a journal as well as books and monographs. The meeting was an informal one in his office with his staff—eight people, most of them rather young and with recent M.A.s or Ph.D.s, who worked with the scholars on their projects and also handled the day-today running of the foundation. Some sat on the arms of the chairs, others against the window ledges.

"This, I hope, will be very short," he said. "I just want a rundown on where we stand on the conference."

The foundation was sponsoring an international conference, to be held in November, called The Science and Art of World Peace. It had been in planning for over a year, and was bringing in people from every discipline for five days of lectures, workshops, and informal gatherings. Nick looked around the room for their reports—PR, fine, all three networks would be carrying something, and a cable network perhaps the whole thing; housing—very good, Don, good work; some of the presenters still hadn't sent in their papers—well, try to stay on them, Lois, without seeming to push . . . You, Ray?

Nick's expression changed as the director of finance began his report—he'd turned down a speaker from Norway who had asked for airfare for his wife and two children as well as himself.

"Why didn't you come to me?" Nick demanded. His face had reddened. "Why would you do that on your own?"

"I . . . I thought that's what we always did."

"What we always did was come to me, damn it! Christ, a top nuclear physicist. *The* top. Are you crazy? We should lose him?"

He was still fuming as the group filed out. He looked at Miss Bruehlman, whose face mirrored his. "Goddam idiot! There are so many peace groups and marchathons and you-name-its who'd give anything to get him. Well, he's out. *Out.* This work's too important. I've got to depend on people!"

He heard the phone ring but wasn't in the mood to talk to anyone. Miss Bruehlman answered, then held it out to him. Covering the mouthpiece, she said it was Senator Bolding.

It took him just a moment to compose himself. He smiled as he said, "Bill." Then, "Good news. I heard yesterday but I couldn't reach you. Anyway, it's fine, it's a go."

"Oh, that's great."

Senator Bolding, a member of the Armed Services Committee, had written a dull, dull book analyzing the Spanish-American war, which every major publisher had turned down. And the senator wasn't eager for the foundation to publish it because he wanted to reach a general audience, looked on it as a best-seller. So, Nick had gotten the board of directors to agree to buy twenty thousand copies in advance, and one of the largest publishers in the country had agreed to put it out.

"Well, I'm very grateful," the senator said.

"There's no need to be. It's an important book. Damn important."

Afterward he sat staring at Miss Bruehlman out at her desk. Then, taking a deep breath, he went over and closed his door. He sat down and reached for his private phone; the calls didn't go through the receptionist.

He'd been trying Tucker's phone ever since the call from Madeline yesterday. So far no answer.

It was so many years since he'd seen Roger, and it was by sheer luck that he knew where he lived. There'd been a documentary on TV last year about clergymen activists, and a short segment was devoted to Roger.

The phone kept ringing.

But then, as he was about to hang up, a woman answered.

He said, leaning forward quickly, "May I speak to Reverend Tucker?"

There was a pause, then, "Oh, God."

Frowning: "Who's this?"

"Who are you?"

"My name's Ellis. I'm an old friend of Reverend Tucker's."

He thought he detected a gasp. "This isn't . . . Is this Nick? Is this Nick Ellis?"

"Yes. Who's this?"

"Nick, this is Anne. Anne West. We—we got married."

"Oh, God. Anne. Anne, it's so good to talk to you."

"Oh, Nick. Oh, Nick. Roger's dead."

And all at once he pulled in a long breath. He felt a surge of relief flood through him.

• • •

"Anne," he said, "where am I calling? Your house? Apartment?"

"An apartment."

"Look, I want to talk to you. Could you go to a pay phone and call me at this number?"

"I—I guess."

"Can you do it now? I'll wait for you."

He gave her the number, then waited. About ten minutes later the phone rang.

"Yes, Nick." She was crying softly.

He waited. "I'm so terribly sorry, Anne."

"I—I don't mean to cry like this."

"None of that. Come on."

"Just give me a minute."

He waited until she seemed to calm down. "Tell me. What happened to Roger?"

"I—I don't know." And she told him about Roger expecting a visitor, and her going out and then coming back to find he was dead. "Nick, I—I think he was murdered. I can't believe he'd kill himself."

"And you have no idea who was coming over?"

"No."

Not that it was connected in any way, he said, but had she ever heard of a Joseph Kyle?

"No." He wasn't surprised—the one time he'd read

about him was when he happened to be glancing through one of those scandal sheets. She said, "Who is he?"

"I don't want to go into too much on the phone. But I heard from Madeline. She said he'd been around to see her. Asked her things."

She didn't seem to understand right away. Then, "Oh, my God."

"But he's dead, he died. I understand just a few days ago. But then his son called her. David. She told me he asked her did she know Roger."

"Nick, I don't understand again." Her voice was frantic. "Who's the father, who's the son?"

"Look, I don't want to go into it too much, I'll explain it some other time. But this David Kyle asked her did she know Roger."

"Oh, Nick."

Just take it easy, he said. Madeline had said she'd only known Roger slightly, from when they were kids. "From what she told me, I don't think he knows where you live. But I just wanted you to know. If he gets in touch with you, I want you to call me. All right?"

"Yes." Her voice sounded faint.

"You'll probably never hear from him, but if you do let me know. Okay?"

"Yes."

"And remember this—there's nothing to worry about as long as you keep your head. Not one single thing. Okay?"

"Yes."

Again he waited; then this time he spoke in a lighter way. "So you and Roger got married. Do you have any children?"

She couldn't seem to answer right away. "Two. A girl and a boy. They're both married."

"Wonderful."

"And I'm a grandmother." Her voice had become much stronger. "My daughter has a little boy."

"That's wonderful . . . Hey, you don't know how much I've thought about you and Roger," he said.

**11**

Meghan—Sandy Meghan.

David stood by the revolving door in the *Sentinel-Observer* lobby, trying to get his head unmuddled, to try to think what to do. He had her name, a name his father might have killed in frenzy to try to get, but now what to do with it?

"Excuse me." A messenger carrying packages brushed against him. Cold air swept in with each turn of the door.

As of 1975 she'd been doing volunteer work at Tucker's church—but had she gone with him to Homeward House?

Try the church first? The shelter? And what could he say? Without arousing suspicion, somehow implicating Pop?

"Pardon me." And a glance over the shoulder from someone going by.

Outside, he swung on his raincoat in the sharp wind that had risen, but left it open as he walked to the luncheonette on the corner. He looked through the phone book, but there was no Sandra Meghan. Not even an S. Meghan.

He began flipping pages to the church, Holy Zion Lutheran. He was tempted to do what he did with Homeward, just call. But it was so easy for people to brush you off on the phone. He looked at the address, then at Homeward's. He jotted them down.

He sat down on the end stool of the counter. Needed more time to clear his head. But he also had this need to rush. "Coffee, please. Black."

He made himself sip it slowly.

In sixty-three Sandy comes to Boston, pregnant, a kid, and meets another kid, Tucker, whose family's afraid he's going to marry her. Then she takes off, supposedly to go to her parents, and sometime around then or later Tucker takes off, disappears for years.

What happened in the years between sixty-three and seventy-five?

He set down the cup, paid and put down a tip. On the sidewalk he looked around for a cab. One was going by with its off-duty sign on; another was occupied. Then he saw one on the far side of the street, and he let go the whistle he'd found as a kid he could do without fingers. The cabbie looked over behind the closed window and pulled to the curb.

He ran across the street to it and climbed in. "Twenty-two hundred Webb."

The church. It just as easily might have come out for Homeward House.

The one place he knew he couldn't go just yet was back to the hotel.

• • •

It stood on a corner, a large, stone church with a towering steeple. As the cab pulled away he stood looking up the long steps to the door. The last time he'd been in a church, except for a friend's wedding, was when Sara was christened. It had been in a Catholic church in lower Manhattan, the last of the cities they'd lived in before moving back to California. He'd been a little surprised Gina had wanted it, for she hadn't been in a church for years, either, though she'd never gone to anything but parochial schools.

He walked up the steps, tense, and opened the oak door to a vast, dimly lit emptiness. And a hush—except, as the door closed behind him, he could hear the distant sound of what seemed to be typing. He stood looking down the long, rose-carpeted aisle.

Davey, his mother used to say, come on. She used to drag him to church almost every Sunday, though she changed churches, and sometimes denominations, about once a year, because a minister would disappoint her or she'd hear marvelous things about another. And though David used to go reluctantly, he'd had no doubts about God looking down at you, and good people being there with Him.

But he could never get the boy to stay in heaven. The boy would always slip back to be outside the window in the dark, or up in the small attic, or somewhere around his pictures in the basement, or standing out there in the cemetery with the dead . . .

The typing was coming from the open door to a corridor on his left. A little way down the corridor were two lighted offices. In the first one a man in his mid-thirties was reading at his desk. He looked up and smiled. "Can I help you? I'm Reverend Hennings."

"I hope so. I'm trying to locate someone and maybe you can help me. I know she was a member of the congregation a number of years ago. Maybe she still is. Sandra Meghan?"

The minister thought. "No, I don't know the name. When was this?"

"It was at least until 1975."

"No, that was a little before my time. But let's see what we can do." He stood up and walked with David to the adjoining office. A woman in her fifties, with coiffed silvery hair, was typing away with a slight smile to herself. She turned, and the smile broadened. The minister said, "Mrs. Dove, maybe you can help this gentleman. He's looking for a woman named Sandra"—he looked at David—"Meghan? He says she was a member of the congregation until at least 1975. Do you remember her?"

"There was a program here for the homeless," David said. "I know she worked as a volunteer."

Mrs. Dove pursed her lips as she thought. Then looked at him. "A young woman? Say in her twenties?"

"Yes."

Mrs. Dove nodded.

"Yes, I remember her. Of course. She was quite active here. But I haven't seen her in a long, long time."

The minister excused himself, smiling. Mrs. Dove said, "I haven't seen her in eight–nine years, I think it is. She left about the time our previous pastor did—he died recently, poor man. A dreadful, dreadful thing," she said, shaking her head.

David waited, then said, "Would you have any idea where she went?"

"No, but she may have gone with him. He started— Are you familiar with the Homeward House?"

"Yes."

"Well, she may be involved there, I'd suggest you ask there."

"Actually I called there before I came here."

"Oh." She frowned. She glanced toward the door, then said, "One of the reasons I think she left, why some other people left when she did, is that there was some controversy here for a while. What happened, he was too active in outside things for a lot of people, a lot of people thought he was paying less and less attention here. I mean, he left voluntarily—he was a wonderful man—but as I say that's why some people left at the same time."

"Would you know any way I can find out where she lived?"

"Well, she was so active it should be on file somewhere, but offhand I wouldn't know where. I doubt if it's in current, but it could be in the storeroom." Then she looked at him with a question in her eyes. "I don't mean to be nosy but—you know—are you a relative?"

"No. She's an old friend of my wife's and mine—we're in California—and we haven't heard from her in a long time. I thought I'd try to look her up."

"Well, it may be in the old files—a million things are. I wouldn't be able to look now, but if you'd call me tomorrow, maybe then. But of course," she said, "I can't promise."

• • •

Homeward House was a rambling, gabled Victorian mansion, in a neighborhood of similar old mansions that seemed to be sagging and browning with age. The receptionist-secretary in the front sitting room remembered his call, and told him to wait and someone would be with him soon. He felt stiff with tension, but it still was less than when he'd walked into the church. He walked over to a large bulletin board, tacked with flyers and snapshots of missing youngsters. Tacked up, too, were messages— "Bobbie, if you see this, please come home, we won't bother you any more, we promise. Mother and Dad." "If anyone has seen Matthew Carlson, 15, red hair, please contact his sister, phone number below. She will not tell Mom or Dad unless he wants me to . . ."

"Sad, isn't it?" the receptionist said to his back.

He turned. "Yes," but could think only that at least somebody wanted them. Somebody, at least somebody.

"Sometimes a kid comes in here will recognize one of them," she said. "They're from all over the country, but once in a while they run across each other. Doesn't happen often, but even once . . ."

He nodded and picked up a brochure on a lamp table by the couch. Nondenominational, though founded by Tucker. A walk-in off the street for kids, though most were referred by agencies and police. Could stay as long as they wanted. No one forced to go home, but got counseling, including group. Most ended up going home . . .

Another brochure, a fold-over, was about the suicide hotline.

How, dear God, could a guy like this be in any way involved in the murder of a child? And the mother, the fucking mother, how could she work here?

A boy of about fourteen sauntered out of the house, and two girls came in, went in back. And a few voices back there, playful.

A woman came out and extended her hand. She was, she said, Miss Tyson, one of the counselors. "Ella says you're trying to find Sandy Meghan. All I know is she did some volunteer work when we got started. She did it for a couple months, I don't think more than that. Then I don't know what happened to her."

"Do you think it's possible to find out where she lived?"

"I really don't know, I—" She stopped. "Oh, here's someone might be able to tell you. Mrs. Tucker," she said, over David's shoulder.

He almost whirled. He stared at her as she walked in from outside—a short red-haired woman in a gray coat.

"Mrs. Tucker, this gentleman's trying to locate Sandy Meghan. I told him I don't know where she went to. Do you?"

"No."

"But didn't she live for a while in that rooming house where there was a fire?"

"She lived in a lot of rooming houses," she said, looking at David. "She was pretty much of a rolling stone. I'm afraid I can't help you."

"Well—I just thought maybe," he said. "Thanks anyway."

He started to leave.

"But if I happen to remember something or come across something," she said, "where can I reach you?"

**12**

That was it, he was getting the hell out of here.

He kept looking around for a cab as he walked. He was getting the first plane he could this evening. Just get the hell out of here.

But where was a cab?

He didn't even know what section of the city he was in; just that this street, and what looked like every damn street around here, didn't have a person on it, and hardly a car. Though it was only about four, it was darkening fast, the sky sagging with clouds.

Should have called for one from there, but he'd been so anxious to get out; hadn't just felt, but seen in a reflection in a glass, her stare following him.

"Excuse me," he called. A boy of about fifteen was starting to cross the intersection ahead. "How do I get downtown from here?"

There was a bus three blocks up, which took you to another bus. No, he didn't know the numbers. David walked quickly. It turned out to be a shopping street. And an empty Yellow soon came by.

David dropped onto the seat. The driver pushed down the flag but didn't lower his radio, which was just as well—no conversation.

David watched as the streets gradually filled with cars, headlights on. He felt a little calmer. Strange, how standing there with her there was absolutely no question he was face to face with the widow of the man his father killed. But gradually that was . . . stupid. His father was . . . Pop, and Pop couldn't kill anyone. He was just a good guy who for some reason needed this. Whose life wasn't enough. Whose work wasn't enough. Whose family . . .

Not enough. Obviously.

David stopped at the desk before going up. There was a message that Judy called. The first call he made from the room, though, was about flights. The only one he could get was close to midnight, which he took, though not sure he would keep it—it would get him in at a hell of an hour. He called Judy at home.

A little girl answered with a shriek of delight. "Yes. Hello! Good-bye! Hello!" And in the background were little-girl screams.

"Is your mother there? Is Mrs. Sears there?"

Judy apparently grabbed the phone. "Hello."

Oh, David, hold on, please. Madhouse.

It was, she explained from another room, Meg's birthday. Eighteen girls. "But tell me. I got your message, I couldn't wait to call you."

"Well—I decided to come here and I'm still here. But I'll be leaving either tonight or tomorrow, I don't know."

"What've you been doing?"

"The one thing I've accomplished is I've learned Sandy's name. Meghan."

"How in the world did you do that?"

He told her about going to the newspaper, and then

about going to the church, and then meeting Tucker's wife. "You know, all through this a part of me can't believe I'm here, that I'm—playing Cade."

"You're not playing anything, David."

"Well, whatever."

"What have you learned about Tucker?"

"Just that he was a good guy. This wild kid not only becomes a minister but apparently a king of men. And Sandy—she helped him. I'd give anything to learn what their relationship was—why he left Boston sometime after she did, why she shows up here years later."

She said, "He met her for the first time when she was pregnant." But there was a touch of a question to it.

"That's what I heard. But for all I know he could have met her before. Maybe he was the father."

She was silent, then she said, "What're you going to do?"

"Leave. I can't think of anything else."

"I mean, when will you decide?"

"I'll probably just toss a coin."

"I'd love to be able to say stay till tomorrow, I'll fly down."

"I wish."

"I wish it too. I—hold on." He heard the sudden sound of shrieking again; the party had opened into her room. He could hear her ushering them out, and a few voices calling for some kind of game or treat. When she came back on she said, "I'm sorry."

"No, you go ahead. I'll call you from L.A."

"David, I do wish I was there."

"I do too."

"Take care of yourself."

"You too. Tell Meg happy birthday for me. I'll talk to you."

Putting down the phone, he went over to the window and looked down at the headlights streaking the night. He felt lightened by the call, but soon it was as if an actual presence had gone and the room were emptier. He went over to his bag and hoisted it on the bed; he'd barely unpacked, had only a few things to put in. Instead he sat down on the bed.

That church, that shelter—them. She'd been in them. Knew people there, talked to them. Might still even be somewhere in this city.

And what kind of person? To be involved with charity, and yet . . .

Surely she'd either killed the boy herself or been a part of it. Or certainly had read of it over the years.

He was a little surprised to feel how fast his blood was going.

He thought of his father, in a room like this, perhaps even this one. Knowing he was so close. Frustrated. And years of frustration behind him. And in him all the hate for whoever had done this.

And suddenly he knew, with his whole body, how the Old Man could have cracked, could have, in a crazed instant, rushed and fought and wrestled . . .

●   ●   ●

Nick eased himself out of bed, careful not to wake his wife. He slipped into a maroon silk robe as he walked to his bathroom—hers was on the other side of the huge, Louis Quinze bedroom—and afterward dressed in the large alcove that served as his dressing room.

Downstairs, Nella came out of the kitchen when she heard him seat himself in the dining room. "Good morning, Mr. Ellis."

"Good morning, Nella."

She had put the *Times* and *Post* by his plate. He read the *Times* until she brought in his breakfast—always, unless he specified otherwise, orange juice, a three-minute egg, toast and coffee—and then occasionally glanced over at the paper as he ate. He looked up as Louise appeared in her ruffled, white dressing gown, then he lifted his face to kiss her on the lips. She was a bony, elegant-looking woman of fifty-six.

"I came down to thank you," she said, smiling into his face.

"Now, whatever does that mean?" He smiled back.

She rolled her eyes in the direction of the kitchen. "Like you don't know." She whispered: "I still hurt."

"You know I didn't mean to hurt you."

"I love it, I'll shoot you you ever stop." She kissed the tip of his nose and sat down next to him. Just coffee, dear, she said to Nella, then looked back at him, elbows on the table. "Let's play today. Don't go in, let's just play—do anything."

"Honey."

"I know, you've got the world to save."

"Not from the way you're saying it."

"Hon-ey." She immediately reached out and grasped his arm with her thin hand. "I mean it. That wasn't sarcastic. That *wasn't*—you're my genius," and she grasped his arm harder. She only released it when he smiled. "I didn't mean it that way, you know that."

Later, walking him to the door, she told him she was seeing Charlotte that afternoon. This was the eldest of her three children, and the last to warm up to him a little. The others had been all right once they'd heard he would certainly agree to a premarital contract.

They and their various husbands and wives could have all the stock and presidencies they wanted in McInstery Oil and its satellites; all he'd ever wanted, though he hadn't approached Louise about it until a few months after they were married, was to direct the foundation.

"Give her my love," he said.

"I certainly will." She stood next to him as he put on his coat. "Is Bill driving you?"

"No, I feel like driving."

He got there at eight-thirty, sure from the empty parking spaces that he was the first to arrive. But Miss Bruehlman was already there, straightening up her desk. The mail, he saw as he took off his coat, hadn't come yet.

It was going to be another busy day. He knew his schedule by heart, but he checked his calendar anyway. He was meeting with a delegation from Prague, had to go up to the Hill to do some lobbying at lunch, was meeting with some kind of committee from the American Psychological Association . . .

Miss Bruehlman brought in the mail. As he started going through it, he could hear the sounds of people coming in. And now the first of the phone calls.

He picked up the phone at Miss Bruehlman's buzz.

"A Mrs. Tucker."

He sat for a few moments like stone. Then he switched the call to his private line.

"Yes, Anne."

"Nick . . . I'm sorry . . . so early."

His voice stayed controlled. "What is it, Anne?"

"He—he was over. He's here, he's looking for her."

He took a deep breath. "When was this?"

"Yesterday. Late yesterday."

"Why didn't you call me then?"

"I—I don't know, I thought it was too late."

"Tell me exactly what he said to you and what you said to him."

"I don't know if I remember it exact, but he wanted to know where she used to live, I said I didn't know. But I said I'd call him if found out."

"Why didn't you just tell him you didn't know? Why did you tell him that?"

"I don't know, I couldn't think, Nick."

"Just calm down." Her voice would keep rising. He kept his own voice calm. "You say you know where he is?"

"He—told me where. Yes."

He sat back, his large face grimacing as he thought.

"All right, just calm down," he said. "Just stay calm."

# 13

David came down to the coffee shop before nine and, sitting at the counter with a cup of coffee, watched as people walked quickly to work through the ash-gray cold. On his second cup, he looked at his watch, though he knew it was still too early to call. He'd give Mrs. Dove until at least ten-thirty.

He called from his room at twenty after.

"Holy Zion Church. Mrs. Dove."

"This is David Kyle, Mrs. Dove. I was in yesterday? I'm trying to locate Sandra Meghan?"

"Oh, yes." Well, she'd found this one address for her, let's see, where'd she put it? Yes. "I was just thinking—I know she lived for a while in a place one of our congregants owned, a Mrs. Mayer. I don't remember if this is it or not, she hasn't been here in years either. But I thought I'd mention it."

"I really appreciate this."

"Well, good luck. You have a pencil?" Mrs. Dove asked.

• • •

The address was an old brownstone on Walnut Street, about a fifteen-minute ride from center city. If Mrs. Mayer did live here, she wasn't listed in the phone book.

Two young women carrying books in the curve of their arms and conversing rapidly came out as he walked up the steps—Penn, the cabbie had told him, was close by. There was a bank of six mailboxes in the vestibule. Though he hadn't given any thought to Sandy still living here, he instinctively looked for her name. And found Mrs. Mayer's.

He pulled in a breath and pressed her buzzer. A woman said over the crackly intercom, "Who is it?"

"Is this Mrs. Mayer?"

"No, who's this?"

"My name's Kyle, David Kyle. I'm trying to locate someone, and Mrs. Dove at the Holy Zion Church thought Mrs. Mayer might be able to help me."

"Who?"

"Mrs. Dove? The Holy Zion Church?" He closed his eyes for an instant. He couldn't shake the tension. There was a long silence, then the inner door—oak-framed, with smoky, etched glass—opened just enough for a tall black woman to eye him. Then she opened the door to a dusky hallway, a thick-banistered, curving stairway at the far end. Mrs. Mayer's apartment, the door open, was the first from the vestibule.

He stood just in the doorway; it opened directly to the living room. Mrs. Mayer, obese, swollen-ankled, sat staring at him from an afghan-covered chair.

"You're who?" Her eyes fixed him there.

"David Kyle."

"And who's this you're looking for?"

"I'm trying to find Sandra Meghan—Sandy Meghan. Mrs. Dove told me she used to live here."

Mrs. Mayer frowned; her eyes stayed on him.

He said, "I imagine it would have been at least seven, eight years ago."

"You don't have to tell me when," she said, still staring at him. "I remember every person, and I've been doing this thirty-six years. But I don't know where she is, how would I know where she is?"

"Well, I was hoping you would."

She raised her head slightly. "You a policeman? A relative?"

"No. A friend. But I haven't seen her in years. I happened to be in the city, and I thought while I'm here . . ."

She kept looking at him. "You knew her pretty well?"

"Fairly well, yes."

She nodded slightly, thoughtfully. "Tell me," and she motioned for him to come in. "Tell me. Can I ask you something? You're bringing it all back. Was she . . . a little strange when you knew her?"

He felt himself tightening even more. "What do you mean strange?"

"Well, like . . . very shy. Or, like, one minute very very shy, another time talking—you never knew."

He had to say something, for she was waiting. "That's pretty much the way she was."

"Excuse me. Emma," she said, a hand on her chest, "would you get me a glass of water, honey?"

Emma brought her the water and she gulped it down, still holding her chest. Then she took several breaths; she obviously had a problem breathing. Her hand came down, and she looked at him again.

"Funny, you're reminding me," she said. "She was like frightened of everything. I remember one time— Emma, you weren't here when she was, were you?"

"I don't remember the name," Emma said. She was standing in the archway to the adjoining room.

"No, you weren't here. I think maybe," she said to

David, "it was like the second day she was here. She was in here for something, I remember we were sitting here, and suddenly there's all these flashing lights outside—red, blue, you know police lights—and she almost jumped out of her chair. I thought what's this?—I wanted to get rid of her. But I soon found out she was frightened of everything. Had to really know you or wouldn't open her mouth . . . But she could be very kind, I guess you know."

He heard himself say yes, for she was waiting again; but he was thinking only of the scene, that jolt of fear . . .

"She used to knock on the door—she knew I was a widow, I'm alone—she used to ask did I need anything. And she was wonderful with needlepoint, did such beautiful things with her hands. But there was something strange about her. I used to think maybe she was in a hospital one time—you know, a mental hospital?"

"If she ever was, she kept it a secret."

"I used to wonder. And why would she let her sister raise her son?"

"She did tell you about that."

"Just that her sister was raising him. She used to go see him now and then. Where'd the sister live?—I think Chicago."

"I think so, yes."

"She used to go see him. Her Andrew." Her hand went to her chest again. Then, after a few breaths, "Can I ask you something? She never said and of course I never asked—was she married?"

Yes, no, then said, "Not when I knew her."

"I had the feeling not. I only knew her slightly from before, from the church. There was a minister there I loved. You wouldn't have known Reverend Tucker, would you?"

"No, but I heard what happened."

She shook her head slowly. "I'll never get over that. He must have changed terribly, something terrible must have happened. I haven't seen him in years—he left the church to do other things, so I left, though I was going to have to leave anyway—I got a little breathing problem, it's hard for me to get around. But he's the one asked did I have a room for her. She'd lost her room."

"When did she live here?"

"Well, you said it. About seven, eight years ago. And she was only here about a year."

"Can you think of anyone who might know where she went?"

"Well . . . Did Mrs. Dove mention Mrs. Tucker? She might know."

"I've spoken to her. But she doesn't know."

"Let's see, there were a few people around the church I used to see her with— She was shy, she was timid, but she was pretty involved in things there. No, I can't think of anyone offhand."

"Do you have any idea where she worked?"

"Yes, but it isn't there anymore. She was a waitress. The Picket Gate. Emma, the Picket Gate isn't there anymore, is it?"

"No, that's been gone two, three years."

"Let's see." She put her hand to her chest, then after clearing her throat, put it to her jowly face. "There were a few people at the church, Mrs. Dove maybe would know—"

She stopped, thought some more, then said yes. Raymond. "I don't remember his last name—everyone called him Raymond. He was pretty friendly with her. I don't like to talk about people, but you know why I remember. He was real—you know, real effeminate."

Mrs. Dove should know him; he might still be going to the church. "He was a waiter, as I remember. He used to use his van to bring old people to church, take crippled kids out, I remember. The church was always doing things like that."

"I appreciate this." And all the while he was trying to

think how to pose his next question. Then he just let it come out: "I was wondering. Did Sandy ever say anything about having an older child?"

Her eyes widened. "No. Did she?"

"She never said anything at all? No hint of it?"

"No." Then she frowned and said slowly, "You know, this is funny. I remember once, I don't remember what we were talking about—yes, we were talking about someone in the building had a baby—I said my godson's name was Jonathan, it was always my favorite name. And I asked what she'd call a boy she had one today. And she said all her life her favorite name was Toby . . . It didn't strike me until later, then why did she call her son Andrew?"

She was saying something else, but he barely heard. His skin seem to have lifted off his arms, chilled. For all at once the boy standing by the lonely grave at night, and pressed against his window, had a name.

**14**

Toby.

As he walked along the street the name kept taking on different sounds in his mind.

Toby. Tob-y. Tob-y Meghan.

It was the way kids called to kids—Tob-y. The way he remembered the kids calling to him from out in the alley instead of coming up and ringing the doorbell—Dav-ey. Come out and play, Dav-ey.

He kept walking.

Did any kids yell to Toby? Surely his parents, the mother, someone, said Toby do this, Toby do that. And finally when Toby didn't do something right or fast enough or was in the way or maybe didn't do anything at all, that fucking mother or husband or boyfriend—her or someone she knew did it, to be so afraid of police—had taken a pipe and smashed his head and then just tossed him away.

Toby.

It was weird that it even had to be that name, of all names.

Toby, like in Toby Tyler—almost the first book he remembered because it always made him cry; the little boy running from the circus, and his monkey Mr. Stubbs shot dead.

He'd only had to look at the page where Toby holds Mr. Stubbs, sobbing, "How I love you, Mr. Stubbs," and the tears would start.

"What's the matter, Davey?" his father asked. (It was always Davey until he was about ten, when his mother insisted on David.) And the feeling of being trapped, for he'd come out of his room unaware his eyes were still red. "Nothing."

How could he tell him, anyone, he'd just looked at a page and his eyes filled up? For Mr. Stubbs, dead, and Toby in his loneliness?

Like he could never tell him, later, how scared and yet how sad he was for the little boy. Not only murdered, but abandoned. Abandoned.

He walked in what he thought was the direction of center city. There were plenty of cabs, but he just wanted to walk. People were coming out of office buildings; it was noon. Some, hunched against the cold and talking in puffs of vapor, stood at lunch vans.

In the room, he just sat by the phone awhile.

It was strange how he'd never thought of this before. The boy and his father—it was always just something his father "did." But surely sometime, somewhere, he must have cried for him too . . .

He picked up the phone, fast. Punched the numbers fast.

"Holy Zion Church. Mrs. Dove."

"Mrs. Dove, this is David Kyle again." Please let her be able to help him.

"Oh, yes."

"I was over at that address. And you were right, it's Mrs. Mayer's place. She was quite helpful."

"So she's still there," Mrs. Dove said. "Oh my, I haven't seen her in years."

"Mrs. Dove, she mentioned someone she thought might be able to help me. But she only remembers his first name—Raymond. A waiter. Used to drive his van for church activities. I know I'm imposing on you, but do you know who she means?"

There was silence. Then she said slowly, "You know, I would like to help you, but I've been thinking. I don't think I have the right to give out names and addresses like this."

He grimaced. "Can I ask you this? I'm not asking who he is or where he is, but—are you saying you know?"

"I just can't give out his name and address."

"Then what about this? Could I trouble you to get in touch with him and say I'd like him to call me? Could we leave it up to him?"

Again silence. "I—guess. What's your phone number?"

He gave her the phone and room numbers. "Would you ask him this too? If I don't happen to be in, would he leave a message where I can call him, or that he'll call again?"

"I'll try to get in touch with him. And I'll tell him . . . Oh, how long will you be in town?"

He felt a little shock go through him—shock that this had blown out of his mind. That he had a flight at five.

He sat back with the phone.

"If he could call me as soon as possible I'd appreciate it. But I'll be here a few days," he said. Or, he knew now, as long as it would take.

• • •

Madeline was hanging her coat in the downstairs hallway closet when Cindy came partway down the stairs. No usual hello, no how was your day—just a coy little smile. "A man called."

Madeline looked at her sharply, but tried to sound calm. "Did he leave a name?"

"Noo."

"Cindy, stop that." But her legs had gone weak as she kept trying to adjust her coat on the hanger. It had to be, who else wouldn't leave a name?

Cindy followed her upstairs, but went to her room as Madeline closed the door to the bathroom. She'd been having this thing with her stomach, diarrhea, since this afternoon. She'd been eating like a horse, always did when her nerves went, so the diarrhea had to be in part from that. And the sheer terror again, after all these years.

Changing into a housecoat, she lay in bed awhile, but was too restless. And she'd also promised Herman osso bucco today—she hadn't made it in so long, though God knows she wasn't up to making it now. As she walked out in the hall, she could smell cigarette smoke from Cindy's room: she and Herman had tried to reason with her, threatened, shown her articles, but they'd given up on it. Most of her friends did, she said, and it was only once in a while, and it wasn't like it was pot.

Which they wouldn't bet on either.

In the kitchen, she opened the refrigerator and took out the veal shanks she'd bought yesterday, then looked for parsley, then for the carrots she was sure she had.

"Mom, you know Vince Bracillo?" Cindy was in the doorway.

Still looking for the carrots: "Yes, I know Vince Bracillo."

"He invited me and Kate and Nadine to a party at his house Saturday."

"All right." She was looking for the right pot now.

"Mom, would you mind if I marry an Italian?"

Madeline looked at her. It was one of *these* days too? When Cindy, who up until about a year ago couldn't get enough of telling her she loved her, was out to rip off her skin?

[ 104 ]

"Cindy," she said wearily, "right now I don't care who you marry."

"That's not true. Last week you said you only wanted me to marry a Jew. And I don't understand that. You're Italian, you were a Christian."

"And I became Jewish. I had a mikveh, you went to Hebrew school, had a bat mitzvah. Now, Cindy, marry whoever the hell you want, just leave me alone."

Cindy made a slight face, lingered for just a few more moments, then faded into the living room. Madeline dropped onto a kitchen chair. The flesh on her breasts seemed to be popping up with her heart. She started to get up to put the pot on the stove when the phone rang.

She wanted to race to it before Cindy swept it up. But she made herself walk slowly to it. She lifted it from the kitchen wall, stood with it.

"Hello?"

"Is this Mrs. Schwartz?" Nick. Cautious.

She squeezed her eyes shut. "Yes."

"Do you have a minute to talk?" Still very formal, in case someone else was on the line or maybe nearby.

"Just a minute, please."

She stepped into the dining room just enough to see Cindy watching TV in the living room.

"Yes," she said quietly.

"How are you?" His voice had softened.

"All right, I guess. I don't know. Sometimes all right."

"Look, I've been playing around with an idea," he said lightly. "I'm going up to Philly in the morning, I'm going to see Anne. I thought maybe you'd like to join us. It's what, an hour flight from Boston? We'd spend just a few hours—"

"Nick," and her voice became a forced whisper, "I can't, there's no way I can."

"It would be nice, Mad." Then his voice changed a little. "And it could be important."

"I—I can't, how can I? I'd need more time."

"Mad," he said quietly, "Anne called me." He waited. "He's there."

Oh, God! "Wh-where?"

"I don't want to discuss it on the phone. That's why I thought we should get together."

"I—I don't know how. Tomorrow, it's impossible, I've got so many—I *can't* tomorrow."

He said nothing for a while. She reached in back for a kitchen chair, sat down.

"I'll tell you what," he said. "Can you meet me at the Boston airport just for about an hour? Then I'll go see Anne. I'm willing to fly up there, then back to Philly, it's that important we talk."

"I—I don't see—I've got classes—"

"*Fuck* the classes, Mad, it's important."

She dug fingers into her hair. "What time will you be there?"

"I'd like it early. There's a plane, I looked it up, should get in a little before nine. And if I get a reservation I can get a plane to Philly—I can be on my way at ten-thirty."

"Where—where do I meet you?"

"At the plane. I'll give you the number. If there's any change I'll call right back."

Her throat had gone dry; the pumping of her heart had risen to her temples. "I'm—so scared."

And immediately his tone changed again. "Of what? Come on. Hey . . . come on. That's what I want to talk about. There's nothing to be afraid of."

• • •

David fell into such a deep sleep that when he woke he looked at the phone to see if the message light was on. It was the first time in years he'd slept during the afternoon. Had slept, in fact, into the night. He turned on the lamp, feeling a little disoriented. He saw through a squint that it was just after seven.

He sat on the side of the bed—all he'd done was take off the jacket, and the damn tie he hoped forever—and slipped his feet into his loafers, waited until his head cleared, then went in the bathroom. It was as if he hadn't peed for a week. Or slept for a week. He washed his face, digging the water against his eyelids, then hard around the back of his neck, and dried himself briskly.

Watch, he'd go down for dinner and then there'd be a message.

He went to the bar, which was mostly empty.

"Johnnie Walker Black and soda, please."

When the waiter brought it, David said, "Can I get anything from the dining room?"

The man brought him a menu, which he looked at as he took a sip of the drink. He decided on just a crab cocktail.

There were two men near the end of the bar, talking to each other, and a woman in her thirties at the other. A very light blonde, she sat with her legs crossed and an attaché case by her feet. He thought a distant thought, of screwing until the phone rang, but couldn't think of anything that would be a more dismal ending to the day than screwing a stranger. But she did make him think of Judy, of Diane of the game show and scripts. The bartender brought him the crab cocktail, then leaned back near the register.

The one person he'd never have to ask did you see my father was the bartender. Pop never drank, maybe because of his own rummy father, who had pulled out leaving his wife and four boys.

It was probably the only thing his mother and father agreed on.

He finished the drink after the crab cocktail, paid and went over to the lobby shop, where he bought the early edition of tomorrow's paper, *Esquire*, and a paperback reissue of Cheever's *Falconer*, which he'd always been meaning to read again. None of his—he looked matter-of-factly, though he already had that morning—were on the single turn-rack.

Upstairs, he turned on TV, looked for a game, any kind of game, but what turned out to be the Cleveland Orchestra was on. He kept it on, low, and sat with the paper under the Moorish-looking overhanging light. He glanced at the front page, then turned to the sports section, the only sensible part of a paper these days, and after reading it thoroughly, started with the front page again.

He tried not to think, or think too much. He turned pages slowly, glancing at everything, reading at least a few lines of most things. A local columnist now. He scanned the column—it reminded him a little of his father's, the names emphasized in blacker type.

At first his eyes went past the name—then his whole body seemed to leap toward it. Tucker.

In the is-it suicide, is-it homicide case of the Rev. Roger Tucker, we hear of a possible break. According to a mighty good source, a witness saw a man at Tucker's door on the evening of his death. The word we have is that he was gray-haired and was wearing a mackinaw.

David kept rereading it, as though something else would fly up. The one thing that didn't fit in was the mackinaw. There hadn't been any in his father's closets.

He went over to the phone. One of his nephews answered.

"Tommy, Uncle David. Is your mother there?"

Marie came on quickly. "Yes, David. How are you?"

Okay. Listen—

"Will someone turn down the TV?" she called. "David. How are you?"

"I'm okay. Look, I want to ask you something. Did Pop own a mackinaw?"

"A mackinaw?"

"You know, one of those short coats."

"I know what a mackinaw is. Why?"

"I was just curious about something."

"David. Tell me."

"It's really nothing." He felt stupid, this was so obvious.

"Well, he didn't own one. He . . ." Then her voice trailed off. She sounded frightened. "I just remembered. He borrowed Bob's. When he went to Philly. He got oil on his coat."

Oh, Christ!

"David, what is it?" Then, "Where are you?"

"Look— All right, look."

And he told her about being in Philly, about Tucker, the coat.

"Oh, God," she said.

"Marie, let's not jump to conclusions. He went to see the guy. We know that. But that doesn't mean anything happened."

"David, he was a mess when he came home."

"I know, but—maybe he'd heard about it, read about it. And he was upset. He thought he was onto something—"

"He was a mess, a mess."

"Well, we don't know."

"David, where are you?"

"The hotel? The Blaine."

"David, go home. Why'd you ever go there? You shouldn't have gone there. Go home."

"I am. Don't worry."

"Go home, David. Please. I'm worried about you."

"I will."

Her plea stayed with him long after he hung up. She was right, of course.

But if his father did it—if—*if*—the only way it would make any kind of sense, to the police, him, was if Tucker was involved.

**15**

Madeline walked quickly through the terminal, churning with the dread of seeing him and of someone she knew seeing her—she hadn't been able to think of anyone she could tell Herman, Cindy, she could possibly be meeting. She had timed getting here to the time of his arrival, not wanting to stand around, knowing planes were usually late anyway; but as she approached the gate she could see that the passengers were already streaming out. She searched the faces as they emerged, wondering would she recognize him immediately.

But it was so easy—the big head, slightly thrust forward, the same Indian-black hair, though touched with gray and no longer to his shoulders. He carried a rich-brown leather coat with a black fur collar.

He recognized her too—let go a big smile and came forward. She was afraid he would kiss her on the cheek, as if that would make the difference to anyone she knew, but he didn't, just took her hand.

"Madeline." And the same strong voice. He couldn't seem to stop smiling and just looking at her.

She wanted to get away from out here, but kept looking at him too.

"You look terrific," he said. "You really, really do."

"I thought I might not recognize you." She couldn't think of what else to say.

"Oh—still got hair, still got teeth. Hey, let's sit down somewhere and have a cup of coffee."

And she didn't want that—didn't know what she wanted. "Do you mind if we sit over there a while?" A section of empty seats; no flights were posted.

"Sure. Anywhere."

They sat on the row directly facing the windows. He put his coat on the seat next to him and sat angled toward her. She could feel her heart beating up through her throat; it was hard to breathe.

"Nick, tell me."

"First, I want you to calm down." He took her hand very briefly, just long enough to squeeze it; looked at her intently. "You look like you're about to walk the ceiling. And there's no reason for it. None."

"Why?"

"Because I know. And because I'm telling you."

"But he's there. Nick, I—I want to know. What did Anne tell you?"

"Just that he wanted to know did she know where she is, where she used to live."

"And Anne doesn't?"

"Not where she is. I don't know about where she lived—she apparently lived several places."

"And—him, is he still there? Do you know?"

He nodded. "As of this morning. I checked with his hotel."

"Nick, do you think he can find out? How can he find out?"

"I don't know, I don't know what friends she had. That's one of the things I want to talk to Anne about."

"Then why do you say there's nothing to worry about?"

"Mad," he said chidingly, "have any of us said anything all these years? Have we? . . . So. And Sand, what could she have said to anyone that wouldn't have come out by now? Long ago." He shook his head.

"But you're going there, you've got to be worried."

"Madeline, come on. I want to see Anne, I want to make sure she's all right. Just like I've come to see you. She sounds fine, but I want to make sure. And I want to—find out what I can find out. I haven't changed, Mad." And he smiled.

She felt some of her panic easing from her; but just some. "I wonder where she is."

He shrugged, lifted his palms.

She said, "Have you ever seen her, heard from her?"

"No."

She touched her forehead, tried to think of other things to ask, didn't want to remember them after he left. "Even if—if he did find her, why would she say anything? I mean, why to him? And why now?"

"That's right."

"I mean—why? It doesn't make sense."

He simply smiled. She could feel the popping of her heart slowing down. And wondered how he'd done it—it was more than words.

"So," he said, settling back, "tell me all about your family, what you do."

•   •   •

Detective Perry wondered at breakfast should he tell Mary. It wasn't unusual that he hadn't until now—he left most of his job at the place. But he felt strangely compelled to.

"You know who I heard from? Old Man Kyle's son."

[ 112 ]

Mary was pouring herself another cup of coffee near the sink. She said nothing as she came back with it.

"This'll give you a charge," he said. "He wanted to know did I want any of the stuff the old guy was still working on. I didn't say yes, I didn't say no, but I discouraged it. Who needs it?"

"I guess."

"Look, with all I got to do, right?"

"I'm sure you know."

He looked at her, frowning. He didn't want to say it, but he did. "You think I should have?"

"I really don't know. But, you know, what would it hurt?"

"What would it hurt? I'd have to look at the crap, I'd have to maybe go out. What would it hurt?"

"Then you're right, Ed."

"But I mean the way you say."

"Ed, I don't know what you want. I mean if you don't want me to say anything, don't ask."

He floundered for words, then said, "Aah!" He waved in disgust. Couldn't ever say anything to her; no wonder he never said anything.

Yet it stayed with him to headquarters; was with him at his desk.

Even if he wanted the shit, which he didn't, he didn't know where the son lived.

But of course he had the Old Man's number, didn't he?

• • •

Funny, David couldn't remember ever having had a conversation with his father. Never thought of it; had always assumed they did, and they must have, but he couldn't think of one.

Lying in bed, hands locked behind his head and the drapes closed against the morning light, he kept trying to remember, but all he could come up with were fragments

[ 113 ]

of things. Sentences, half sentences. Like when he was in the sixth grade and told him he was having trouble with shop—"Don't worry about it, you won't need it anyway." His mother, it was different, and then it would be more or less a monologue. And about sad things mostly, like about her arthritis or how pretty she was as a girl, as if that were a way different world, and how her parents really weren't for her marriage—his father's mother was coarse, and then there was the father running off.

He reached over for his wristwatch on the lamp table. It wasn't quite eight-thirty. He knew he wouldn't be able to hold out. If he didn't hear from Mrs. Dove by ten, he'd call her.

The phone rang while he was shaving. He walked quickly to it, naked, wiping his face on a towel. But it wasn't Mrs. Dove, it was Marie.

"David," and he immediately sensed fear in her voice, "I just got a call from a detective. A Detective Perry. Do you know a Detective Perry?"

"I've spoken to him. Pop knew him."

"He's trying to reach you. I gave him your number at the apartment, but I didn't tell him where you are—I—I didn't want him to know you're in Philly."

"Did he say what he wanted?"

"No, just that he wanted to talk to you. David, why would he want to talk to you?"

"I don't know. I called him when I was home, asked did he want any of Pop's papers. He said everything but stuff 'em."

"David, I'm afraid he knows something."

"Marie"—he sat down on the bed—"listen to me. Let's say they find out Pop was there. So? How could they say he did anything? How could they prove it?"

"I don't know, I don't know what they know. Are you going to call him?"

"I have to sooner or later."

"But don't call him from there. Call when you get back."

"I'll see."

"Don't see, do it. Call him when you get back."

"Marie, I'm going to do what I think's best." He hated this shit, always did. The last thing he'd ever needed was two mothers! But he quickly softened again. "Marie, I'm not going to do anything to hurt Pop. Now just stop worrying, okay?"

"All right. I shouldn't worry?"

"I'm telling you not to worry."

He sat for a while on the bed, then went back to the bathroom and quickly finished shaving. Marie was right—he wouldn't want Perry to know he was here, though it really wouldn't make any difference. David knew he would never tell him. And he was anxious to know what Perry wanted—how could he hold out until he got home?

David slipped on his jockeys, his slacks. But he didn't wait to put on his shirt. He called Boston information, then reached Homicide.

Perry? Hold on.

"Mr. Perry, David Kyle. I understand you called me."

"Yeah, I was just wondering. You said you had some stuff—I was wondering, you didn't bring it over."

"You kidding? You wanted it? You could have fooled me."

"Well, anyway," Perry said, ignoring it, "I was wondering could you drop it off, mail it off."

And let him know about—Tucker? David closed his eyes, hard, as he thought.

"I'm sorry," he said, "You really told me you didn't want it. So I dumped it."

"Oh? Okay. Just thought I'd ask."

David watched his hand set down the phone. He sat by the desk.

He was cut off now, alone. Almost a throbbing aloneness.

16

He didn't wait until ten to call Mrs. Dove, called at nine-thirty.

"He didn't call you?" she said. "I'm surprised."

"When did you talk to him?"

"Yesterday after I talked to you—around two, I guess. But I'm sure he'll call—if he said he would, he will. He's that kind of person."

"I can't ask any more of you than that, you're very kind."

He wondered, now, what to do about breakfast—go down? Have it sent up? After some thought he went to the closet and put on his shirt, digging it under his slacks and zipping up. Couldn't just stay in the room. But even though he was going down, he was aware his head was still a prisoner here.

• • •

"God, Nick," Anne said tremulously. "Oh, God." Tears filled her eyes. "I miss him so much."

She looked at him. "Nick, I—" She shook her head, then seemed to have to say it. "You know what I've been thinking, Nick? God forgive me, but sometimes—sometimes I see myself going over there and waiting outside and—I picture myself running over him."

He felt something lift away inside his chest; there was almost a glow in there. But his look was solemn. And he tried to convey with a nod and silence that it was perfectly natural.

He said, "Tell me, how did Sandy come to be here?"

"She just showed up, had read about Roger somewhere. We helped her out, did everything we could, and she seemed fine."

"Then why do you think she never told you where she was going?"

"I've no idea. She simply left. We didn't even know she did."

No, her parents were dead, and Anne didn't know of any relatives she still had in Detroit. And her sister in Chicago, she'd apparently moved.

He said, "Can you think of anyone she might have told where she was going?"

"She did know people at the church, and she was a volunteer at the shelter a few weeks."

"Would you try to find out?"

"Nick, I don't even know how to begin."

"You just think of people and you ask." He looked at her, knowing he couldn't treat her like Madeline. Madeline he had to keep calm; Anne he had to calm and yet get her to act. And she was the same Anne—thick. "Anne," he said, "I want to find her. I don't know if he'll ever find her, but I'm not taking the chance. And I want to find her first."

"But why would she suddenly tell?" The same thing he'd given Madeline.

"She probably wouldn't. But Anne, you I'm sure of.

Madeline I'm sure of. Because I see you and I've seen Madeline, and I know. But I haven't seen Sandy."

She nodded.

"So I want you to make a list of people she was at least fairly close to, try to find out the last place she lived . . ."

Although he hadn't expected to stay over—it was only a half hour by plane—he decided he'd better. And somehow it became important that he stay at the Blaine.

• • •

Though he'd been waiting for the phone to ring, would even find himself looking at it, when it came it was strangely startling. David reached for it quickly.

"Yes."

"Is this Mr. Kyle?" And instantly, from the voice, he knew—almost stereotypically effeminate.

"Yes."

"This is Raymond Hanson. I'm sorry I didn't get to you before, but I just couldn't. Mrs. Dove tells me you're interested in finding Sandy. I'm terribly sorry, I don't know where she is."

He felt himself sag.

"Did you," Raymond Hanson asked, "know her very well?"

"Pretty well, yes."

"Well, I would like to see you. Would you have a little time to see me?"

And all at once it was as though Raymond was the one who had to find her.

# 17

They met at four, near the bell captain's stand, Raymond Hanson apologizing for being late, which he wasn't. Very thin, of medium height, he took off his little Alpine hat, with its feather, revealing him to be completely bald; what wasn't bald, he'd shaved. Then he unwound his long scarf and unbuttoned a well-worn raglan coat. He looked about fifty.

David said, "Would you like to go in the bar?"

"No, out here's fine. And I have to be at the restaurant in about an hour."

They went over to the farthest chairs, where Hanson folded his coat and set it down and placed his scarf and hat on it. Except for a white shirt, he was dressed in black—shoes, pants, silky vest, and a bow tie.

Raymond Hanson looked at him carefully, then crossed his legs and placed his folded hands on his knee.

"Mrs. Dove," he said, "tells me you're an old friend of Sandy's."

"Yes." For some reason David hadn't felt too uneasy with him until now.

"Can I ask you something?" He waited.

"Sure. Anything."

"I know you won't tell me, but are you really from the police?"

Hanson too? "No. But I don't know how to prove it. I can show you my driver's license, credit cards, but that wouldn't prove it."

"Well, it doesn't make any difference, I was just wondering."

"No, I'm from L.A. And I haven't seen or heard from her in a long, long time."

"How long's it been?" He sounded more relaxed, genuinely interested.

David had thought about this, had come up with what felt right. "Eight, nine years."

"Oh. Then she was still here in Philly. I was hoping it was sometime after she left."

"No. That's why I'm asking around."

"And then you've got no idea if she got married. I thought she might have, she was talking about it."

"No, I don't. Was she seeing anyone in particular?"

"Not that I know of," Hanson said. "In fact I don't remember ever hearing her say she'd gone out on a date, was going on a date. But then she started talking about marriage—you know, marriage in general. Like did I think it was for her, she was scared of marriage, things like that."

"Why do you think she wouldn't have told you she was leaving? I spoke to her landlady—I'm not sure, but I think it was the last place she lived around here—and she said the same thing. She moved out without saying where she was going."

"Is that Mrs. Mayer?"

David nodded.

"Oh, *her*—she's a fat pig, she was always so nosy. I don't blame Sandy not telling her anything. But we, I thought we were good friends, I *know* we were good friends. That's why I thought maybe she was in trouble." He looked at David, seemed suddenly embarrassed. "That's really the only reason I came to see you."

"Did she ever act like she was in trouble? Mrs. Mayer said that she seemed frightened a lot of the time, had to get to know you before she could sort of let go."

"Oh, her. Well . . ." He paused. Then he nodded. "I never thought of it as frightened. More that she was nervous, moody." He stopped, then frowned slightly as he thought. "I remember one time I was in her apartment, she was in the bathroom, I was in the hall near her bedroom. Apparently she'd thought her door, the bedroom door, was closed, because when she came out and saw it open she looked at me like I'd killed someone. 'Were you in my bedroom? Were you in my bedroom?'—and I kept saying no. Then I got mad, I said why the hell would I go in your bedroom, and when she saw I was mad she was sorry, she almost began crying. She said she didn't know what got into her."

Looking at him, David asked, "Did she ever say why it got her so upset?"

"Later on she apologized again and said it was because the room was so messy. Like I say, she was sort of a nervous person, could be very moody. How was she when you knew her?"

"She was very shy," he said, repeating what Mrs. Mayer had said. "But when she got to know you she could be very warm and kind."

Oh, yes, Raymond Hanson said. Oh my, yes. Her work at the church. My. And this—this was something he would never be able to talk about if it hadn't been for her. "She helped me come out. I wasn't fooling anyone, but I kept trying. But there was this time, she was the first person I ever talked to seriously about suicide—and the whole thing came out. And she helped me—encouraged me to be myself, that it was okay to be myself, that—that fuck you if you don't like me the way I am."

David nodded. His mind was still on that bedroom—it had to be more than that—but he couldn't help feeling a strong sense of guilt that he was lying to this man, so open and trusting.

"You know," Hanson said, "I've always tried to do good to people. But there were people at that church, they didn't even want me to drive crippled children. *Children*. Like—like I was going to do something to them. But Sandy kept telling me the hell with them. And our minister and his wife—two beautiful little people—little, I mean, in size, not soul, not heart—they helped me, stood by me . . . So, she was a good person. But you know one thing I never understood?" he said, looking at him. "You know about Andrew, don't you? Her sister raising him?"

"Sure."

"That always puzzled me, puzzled a lot of people. She used to say he was better off there for the time being. In fact, when she talked about marriage, it was like the only reason to get married was Andrew would have a father. You don't know why, do you?"

"Her sister was raising him? Like she told you, she felt he was better off."

"She never—can I ask?—never had a breakdown or something?"

"No, not that I know of."

"When I'd see her nervous, moody—and like that time with the bedroom—you want to know the truth? That's the first thing I'd really think. But she was rarely that way, most times she was fine."

"If she ever had a breakdown," David said, "she kept it a secret."

Hanson said, "I was going to ask you did you know

[ 124 ]

where her sister lives, but I guess you don't, you'd be asking her."

"Just that she lived in Chicago at one time."

"I used to know where she lived—I called her right after Sandy left, but she either didn't know where she was or wasn't saying. Then I called her about a year later and the number was disconnected."

"Did Sandy," David asked, "ever tell you anything about her background?"

"Just that she came from Detroit and never got along with her parents. And that they'd died. Nothing much, really. Did you know her as a kid?"

"No. And she hardly talked about it—I thought maybe she did with you."

"No. Can I tell you something? It's like her life began with Andrew. Which is what makes it so strange—I know how much she loved him. You know how she almost lost him at birth, don't you?"

David, frozen, wasn't sure how to respond. He gave a little motion of his head, which he hoped could mean yes or no; would encourage him to continue.

Hanson said, "And to be so grateful to the doctor, to give the baby his first name. You know when she told me this? She asked me once if I could drive her up to the Poconos, she had things she wanted to give someone— clothes, food. And she told me about the delivery, how this was his nurse who'd helped. And she was sick now, pretty much alone. That's the kind of person Sandy was. So I drove her up."

"I'm curious, where was this?"

"A little place—I always remember it because I think of Paris—it's called Parrisboro."

"Would you happen to know her name?"

"Oh, I know her name, I've called her several times over the years. I thought maybe she'd heard from Sandy, they'd seemed so close. But she hadn't. So it's not going to do you any good to talk to her."

●   ●   ●

He called Parrisboro information for a listing for a Sandowski—no, he didn't know the first name.

"Do you have an address?"

"No, I don't." Hanson had said he probably still had the number, but he wouldn't be home until maybe one in the morning.

"There are two," the operator said. "W and Daniel."

"Could you give me both?"

Looking at the scribbled numbers, he pictured a little town in the mountains and night closing in and an old sick woman, if she was still alive, having a stranger say do you know a, I'm a, can I . . .

He dialed quickly. W.

It was still hard to do, but it had gotten easier.

And something extra was driving him—whatever the hell was in that bedroom.

"Hello," a woman said.

"Is this Mrs. Sandowski?"

"Yes."

"Mrs. Sandowski, are you a nurse? Were you a nurse?"

"Yes."

Somehow he hadn't expected this, that it would come so easily. "Mrs. Sandowski, my name's David Kyle. Kyle. I'm calling from Philadelphia?"

"Yes."

"A Mr. Raymond Hanson—Hanson—suggested I call you. He said he met you once. It would have been about eight or nine years ago. That you were a friend of Sandra Meghan's. Sandy Meghan?"

"Who?"

"Sandra Meghan. He said you helped deliver her baby, you helped save her baby. His name's Andrew? She even

named him after the doctor. And she came up about eight,
nine years ago to see you?"

"Yes, I know."

He was tempted to ask every question in his head—did
she remember the father being there, where was her medical record, did she remember her mentioning another
child, who was the doctor, who else might know—but he
said, "Mrs. Sandowski, I wonder if I could come up and
talk to you. It's very important. I wouldn't need any more
than maybe an hour of your time."

"You want to come up here?"

"Yes. Please."

"Can you tell me what?"

"It's about her. It could be very important."

Silence, then, "Who did you say you are?"

He raised his eyes to the ceiling. "David Kyle. And I'm
an old friend of hers. Really, it's important."

"And you're a friend of Mr. Hanson's?"

"Yes. You can call him."

There was another silence, a long one; but this time he
heard her speaking faintly to someone. She came back on.

"When," she said cautiously, "do you want to come?"

"Tomorrow?"

Hanging up, it was hard to believe he'd accomplished
it, wished he was on his way. He put on the lamps—the
room, almost without him being aware of it, had become
gray with dusk. Then he tapped out another number.

"Judy," he said. "David."

"My God, what a coincidence. I was going to call you in
about two minutes. Where are you?"

"Still in Philly. Sounds like a poem, but that's where I
am."

"I was just going to call you. How are you?"

"Okay. You? The children?"

"Everything's fine here," she said. "Tell me about you."

"Judy, I think I know the boy's name—I'm positive. Toby."

"Oh, David, how?"

"I've learned more about her, and that's one of the things—she loved that name. It just fits in."

"Oh, David."

"But there's a down side. I know Dad was—that he was there." He didn't want to be specific on the phone. "He was definitely there."

For a moment she didn't seem to understand. Then, "But that doesn't have to mean— It doesn't have to—"

"I know. But he was there."

"I've"—she sounded anguished—"got so many questions. What're you doing? Can you say?"

"Sure." He told her about Raymond Hanson. "Look, it could be what she said—the room was 'messy.' And she's crazy. That's the only thing that makes sense. But I keep thinking maybe she's kept a picture, a clipping, maybe a birth certificate."

"David," she said, after a pause, "are you going to be there tomorrow?"

"No." And he told her about Mrs. Sandowski. "Judy, if anyone told me two days ago—three days ago—that I'd be doing anything like this, I'd say he was absolutely one-thousand-percent crazy. I can't believe what I'm doing. You know what the odds are against her telling me anything? But I've got to do it."

"Then just do it. Don't question it."

"Hey."

"David, how far's this place tomorrow?"

"I hear about sixty miles, seventy."

"You've no idea how long you'll be there."

"No, but I can't see more than tomorrow, the next day. But I don't know."

"David—" Then she stopped. "David, you know why I was going to call? . . . God, I'm a little nervous. I thought if you were going to be there tomorrow, and you wanted it, I'd come down in the morning. It's the weekend, I can get my mother, I don't necessarily positively have to be in the place tomorrow— In other words, do you want a buddy?"

"Absolutely not. I want you."

"I'll call you right back about the plane."

He waited, his chair tilted back. Even the room seemed brighter.

It was a few moments before it struck him. Hard. He loved his daughter so much. Yet he'd forgotten tomorrow was Saturday. He'd forgotten to call.

• • •

Nick Ellis watched from the sofa as Anne made a call. But the person hadn't seen or heard from Sandy since she'd left. She looked at him, her face etched with desperation.

"I—I don't even know why I called her, she hardly knew her." Her hands rose slowly to her temples. "Nick, I can't think. I see faces but I can't think of names."

"You will," he said. "Just try to relax. It'll come to you. If not now, later. You'll see."

"I've gone blank. And—it's been so long since I've been at that church. Nick, what so many of them did to him— he was a Red, he wanted to feed people, he wasn't earning his pay, he wasn't looking after his flock—bullshit, all that bullshit! Nick, I *hate* them, I don't want to go to them."

He watched her sitting with her face down in her hands.

"It's—it's no good, I can't think."

It was hard sitting here like this. It was hard not to go over and take her by the hair, shake her, *hit* her . . .

"I—just—can't—think," she said, shaking her head with each word.

He kept looking at her. Then he stood up quietly and

**[ 129 ]**

went to the window. He stared out for a while, arms folded on his chest.

"So they called him a Red," he said, without turning. "Him."

"It—was terrible. Some people, not all. But it was terrible."

"You know, Anne?" His back was still to her. "You know one of the things I regret? When I saw Rog on TV I didn't try to reach him. I was afraid maybe he wouldn't want it. But I thought—the work he's doing, I'm doing, do it together. Him, me. It's a world gone absolutely crazy, Anne. And here he was doing the best he could, and I'm doing the best I can."

"He tried so hard, Nick. Oh, did he try."

He kept looking out. When he turned, she had changed position, was staring at her hands held tightly on her lap. He watched as the hands loosened and now as she sat with two fingers pressing her forehead, as if trying to push out a thought. She kept pressing.

After about a minute she picked up the phone, asked for information. Then she dialed.

He watched as she listened. Then she said to an answering machine, "Mrs. Dove, this is Anne Tucker. Would you call me as soon as you can?"

**18**

Judy came off the nine forty-five flight, carrying her coat and a small red overnight bag, and flashing him a smile and a wave. They hugged hard, then he kissed her quickly on the cheek, a little longer on the lips, then took her bag and they started walking in the direction of car rentals.

"I'm so glad you're here." And, his arm hooked around hers, he gave it a little squeeze.

"And free," she said, looking at the ceiling. "No kids."

At the car, a Buick, he threw his raincoat on the backseat. She stayed huddled in her coat and wool scarf as he pulled out.

"You remember the directions?" she said.

"No, I thought you were listening."

"You're kidding, I don't remember anything."

"Kidding. And you're in charge of the map."

"I'm great at maps, I just don't know how to close them."

Out of the airport, they looked for seventy-six; and there

it was, which he remembered was supposed to lead to the turnpike, then from there to some kind of road— Well, there'd be signs.

"Hey, even the sun's out," he said. "We haven't had sun since I got here."

"I thought it might snow. They said snow in Boston."

"Snow? On *us*? Say, what time did you get up?"

"Not early. Five."

He gave her a quick look. "You're kidding."

"No, seven. It only takes about an hour."

"Isn't there going to be a straight man on this trip?"

She laughed and unbuttoned her coat and put her scarf to one side. She shook her hair, as though it were long, and touched her straggly bangs. She was wearing a gray suit and a white blouse and dark-red pumps. There was a very faint trace of perfume.

"You had breakfast, didn't you?" he said. "I forgot to ask."

"Yep."

He glanced over. He absolutely loved this feeling of freedom. The boy, his father—everything was fading; even the woman they were driving to see was a million miles away.

It had become a ride out in the bright, cold sun.

"Hey," he said, and he reached out and put his arm around her and brought her close. He squeezed her and then let go.

"What was that for?"

"A wild, mad impulse."

She smiled and leaned her head back. "By the way, my mother said to say hello. So, hello."

"How is she?"

"Fine. I keep telling her to get married"—she'd been widowed for years—"but she says all the men are too old, they're over thirty."

"Your mother? A sense of humor? When did she develop that—when she was sure I was out of the way?"

"David, that's not funny." But she was smiling.

"Oh, did she hate me. I never understood it until I had a daughter. I'd have killed me."

"She didn't *hate* you. You just—worried her. I worried her enough, and you were the icing. But I was always good at school. David, why were you so bad at school?"

"Not *at* school—I got good marks. *In* school. And I wasn't bad. I never smoked on the grounds. I just didn't go when I didn't feel like."

"How many times were you suspended?"

"Don't say times. Once. One whole time. Warnings don't count."

"That was with Heffinger. You told him to shut up or something?"

"See? Depend on witnesses. Wrong."

"I wasn't a witness, I wasn't in that class."

"Well. He told *me* to shut up."

"And you continued."

"Just a whisper."

She laughed. "David, I used to envy you. I used to think where did he get the nerve?"

"Bad role model. Just a wise guy. But I had some fun."

"Look at that," she said, pointing to his window. They'd turned off seventy-six, were passing a small field where two beagles were peering through a split-rail fence. She looked back. "I love beagles. We had one for about seventeen years. And you know when he got mad at you he would go in the house?"

"Lovely."

"Just once in a while. I loved him. You had a cat, didn't you?"

"Oh, I had a cat but it died," he said with a sigh.

"You had two cats."

"Two cats is right. My mother loved cats."

"You know what I remember most about your mother?" she said. "She had a very nice smile. I liked her. I hardly remember your father. I only saw him once. Twice. Once

**[ 133 ]**

he was in the kitchen drinking coffee. We came to the house for something and he was in the kitchen drinking coffee. It was just hello . . . You know? I used to be afraid to meet him. He intimidated me."

"Really? Why?" He turned on his blinker and pulled out to pass a car.

"Oh, because he had a column. He was this famous newspaperman. And of course I knew what he was doing, I'd read about him. I used to think, how great it must be to have a famous father . . . You never spoke much about what he was doing, you know."

"Tell you the truth, for a long time I didn't think it was unusual. I thought everybody's father did something, so what mine did was write a column and look around about a dead boy."

"Really?"

"Maybe not exactly. Actually, I think for the first few years I was proud of it. But then I was, what—it was junior high—and someone kidded me about it. You remember a kid Jim Legger? I can see him right now. A little guy. Pimples. You remember him?"

"I didn't go to your junior high, remember?"

"God, we met late in life. Well, he started digging me. 'Your father bucking for sergeant? I didn't know he was a cop.' Crap like that. I kept telling him to shut up, he wouldn't, I got hold of him— I ain't especially proud of this, he was half my size—and I twisted his arm up his back. I kept saying are you going to shut the hell up? All I wanted was him to say yeah. But the little bastard, he wouldn't say anything. I could have pulled his arm off, he wouldn't say anything. And it was like he beat me. He did beat me, but he never did say anything after that."

"I think I'd have taken off his arm."

He laughed. "Naah, he'd have cried. Anyway, it obviously stuck with me. And after that, let's see, I remember reading a letter my father left around—some crank son of a bitch really gave him all sorts of hell, like who did he think he was. And I used to hear him sometimes on the phone—the cops weren't exactly thrilled what he was doing. So, if anything, sometimes it embarrassed me."

"Really? The story I remember reading, he was doing this wonderful thing. What a pity."

"Hold on, look at that goddam pothole." He slowed up and went around it. "The truth is, most of the time I never thought about it. It was like something that was just there, like part of the furniture or the roof. You know when I really started thinking about it."

"It's not hard to guess."

"And look what I'm doing. Pardon me if I repeat myself twelve times, but I still can't believe it."

"Well, you're not going to devote your life to it."

"I already have," he said.

· · ·

They stopped for lunch soon after they turned off the highway. It was a log tavern on a woods-flanked road; there were a few picnic tables on the grounds, settled for the winter on their sides. It was dark inside, especially coming in from the sun. There were tables along the bar, tables in another room. They sat in the bar. A good-sized trout was mounted near their table; a deer head stared from above the bar.

"I hear," he said, "their vichyssoise is delicious."

"Did you hear anything about their truffled lobster?"

"No, but we must try their veal tournados."

"And a wine?" She crossed her arms and smiled at him across the table. "Say a chardonnay?"

"No, no. It can be a little hostile. Their house wine."

She laughed and reached out and squeezed his hand. They settled on roast beef sandwiches, on Kaiser rolls, which turned out to be good, and each a mug of beer.

"Tell me," she said, "about where you live."

"The apartment? It's sort of early Gloria Swanson—stucco, palms, a pool. A balcony. Very nice. Sort of *me*."

She smiled. "How far are you from the ocean? I think you told me . . ."

"About two miles. Not quite beachfront."

"You still have a motorcycle? You did the last time you were here."

"No. Actually I hadn't used it for years. Just kept it around."

"I remember," she said, reflecting, "you always wanted a motorcycle."

He smiled. "Probably just to aggravate my mother. I could never aggravate my father. Did I ever tell you how it started?"

"Wanting to aggravate your mother?"

"The motorcycle. I read a story by Saroyan, always remembered the title, 'Where I Come From People Are Polite.' It's about this teenage kid who quits his job because he finds out that he's been hired to replace a woman who's been there for years. They owe him a few dollars, so he takes it and goes to a Harley-Davidson agency—he's always wanted a Harley-Davidson—and gives them the little check as a deposit and takes one out for a test ride. So he takes it and drives all the way from San Fran to Monterey. When he brings it back they can't believe he went all the way to Monterey, they thought he was just going around the block. And when they learned he can't afford to buy it, they won't give his money back. But he's too happy to care, he just loved that ride . . . So I guess"—he smiled—"it touched something in me."

"I would certainly think so," she said.

"Anyway," he said, after a moment. He looked at his watch. "I'd say we're about an hour away. You know we're actually a little early?"

"So we'll drive round and round a mountain."

[ 136 ]

"Do you feel we're on a mountain? California, we got mountains. So far it's a foothill."

Outside, a cold wind snapped open her unbuttoned coat as they walked quickly to the car. She clawed it together, arms clutching herself, for she couldn't get in on her side, she'd locked it.

"Hurr-ee."

She climbed in quickly and began adjusting the heat control even before he started the motor. Then, as he kept revving it, only cold air blew in for a while, and he brought her to him. She shivered against him; he kept rubbing her back, hard.

"Aren't—you—ever—cold?"

He could feel her shivering gradually subside. She lay against him quietly now. He lifted her face and put his cheek against hers, then turned up her face and kissed her lips. He squeezed her and then let go.

"You can," she said, looking at him, "turn off the heat now."

He laughed and released the brake. The road curved occasionally, and they climbed gently past little towns and long stretches of woods and farmland. There were patches of snow on the trees and fields, and frequent deer-crossing signs.

A sign said 20 mi. to Parrisboro.

They'd been riding quietly for a while, Judy with her head back. Occasionally he would look over, thinking she might be sleeping, but always she was staring ahead; and each time, sensing his look, she looked at him and smiled.

He said, "How're you doing?"

"I'm just enjoying it. Just taking it in."

He was aware, though, of a slight change in himself. He couldn't remember having really joked or laughed or just felt *good* like this since he'd come back; he'd left that part of him in L.A. But now he could feel a touch of tension.

The boy—he hadn't thought of the boy in a long while—was coming back.

They were passing through another town, just like most of the others, with a few stores in the center and steeples piercing the sky. Some more farmland now, then a crossroads with a gas station, and across from that a church with a graveyard; and soon after that, Parrisboro.

Her house was on the main road, near the edge of town. It was one of several narrow, gingerbread frame houses. Hers was painted green.

"Maybe you want to go in alone," Judy said.

"You've got to be kidding."

A man came to the door. He'd get his sister, he said, and he called behind him, "Wilma." A tall gray-haired woman in her sixties took his place. She looked at them without expression.

"Mrs. Sandowski? I'm David Kyle. This is Judy Sears."

She kept looking them over, then said come in. The living room was bright, warm. There were framed, crocheted hangings of flowers on the walls; the furniture was a sturdy maple with flowered upholstery. There was a little plaster statue of the crucifixion above the entrance to the hallway. The logs in the corner fireplace were blazing.

"Why don't you sit down?" she said. But her voice and face were severe. "But I must say I'm sorry I said yes."

The man, joined by a woman who might have been his wife, sat down quietly on the sofa. Mrs. Sandowski and Judy were the only ones who remained standing, Judy by the fireplace, her back to it, hands held out behind her.

"I'm really very, very sorry," Mrs. Sandowski said. She seemed to be getting angry at herself. "I don't know what you want, but I don't know you and I don't know anything about her, it's been years." She glanced over at Judy, who immediately said, "Do you mind if I stand here?"

"Of course not. Are you *cold*?"

"No, I just love a fireplace."

"Len, why don't you bring over that chair?" And he immediately pulled over a rocking chair. But Judy didn't sit down right away.

"And I've been admiring those flowers," she said. "Did you do them?"

Mrs. Sandowski looked around. She nodded.

"They are beautiful," Judy said.

"She could have gotten," the woman on the sofa said, "two hundred dollars just for that one. Without the frame."

"I can see why you wouldn't want to part with them."

"Can't do that work anymore," she said. "My hands . . ." She held out arthritis-knotted fingers. "I used to do good work. That one," she said, pointing, "was my first."

"Really?" Judy went over to it. "You'd think you'd been doing it all your life."

David kept looking at her, wanted to hug her. She came back to the fireplace.

"I just love this house," she said, sitting down. "And this *fireplace*."

"We have that going all winter," she said. "Last year I think we used six cords." She finally eased herself onto a chair, holding the arms and then letting go. She looked at Judy. "Did you," she asked, "know Sandy?"

"No, but I've heard a lot of things about her. I feel I do know her."

"Oh," Mrs. Sandowski said, gesturing, "you should of seen her when I first saw her. This thin, like a pencil—and dirty? Filthy dirty, hair all stringy. Looked like she didn't eat in a year. And this big stomach. And she was screaming, she was in terrible, terrible labor."

David wanted to ask a question—questions, but was hesitant, hoped Judy would keep it going.

"Where," Judy asked, "was this?"

"Over at Kendel Memorial—about ten miles from here. She came in an emergency."

"I was wondering why you didn't know her, it seems like such a small community."

"No, she wasn't from around here. A fellow used to live around here brought her in. He was driving a truck and he picked her up on the road, and then she went into labor and he brought her to Kendel. Bucky was so scared. Sometimes I'd see him, we'd talk about it, he'd say he still got scared when he thought about it."

David said, "How long ago was this?"

"I was telling my sister-in-law yesterday. I told her you were coming, and I tried to think what year. It was sixty-eight or sixty-nine. Maybe seventy, but I don't think so."

Which would be right. Two, three years after the boy was found.

He said, "Did she say where she was from?"

"Well, she started off by naming one place. Then when you'd ask her she might name another. And she was probably in all those places—you know, a hippie."

"And she almost lost the baby."

"A real miracle. It was her physical condition, it was God knows a million things, but Dr. Sorris got it out without even a c-section. And she was so grateful. Like you said, she named the baby after him. And she used to write to him from all over—he used to show me letters from her from . . . Houston, I remember, Phoenix, I think Maine. All over. She never did forget."

"Did she ever say if she was married?"

"She said yes, but we never saw a father. I don't think she was. In fact she never had any visitors. The only time anyone came— Well, what happened, we nurses went to the administration. We said you can't let that girl walk out of here with that little thing of a baby, it wouldn't live a week. So the hospital threatened to take it to court, and finally she gave the name of her sister, and her sister came and took the baby."

"When she came up here with Mr. Hanson, was that the first time you saw her after that?"

"No, she came up once before. I didn't recognize her—you know, clean, hair decent. She'd heard I lost my husband, I'd had a hip replacement, I was living alone then. So she brought me a lot of things. It was very nice, I was surprised. But then I never heard from her since."

"Is Dr. Sorris still around?"

"I don't know where he is. It's terrible what happened to him. His wife and his daughter and her husband were killed in an accident. All he had in this world. And there he was, what—sixty-one?—and he had nothing. So he just sold his practice and left."

"Didn't you ever hear from him?"

"No, that's the strangest thing. I was his chief nurse for years—hardly ever went in that OR without me. Last letter I got from him was right after he left. He wanted me to forward his mail until he got things straightened out with the post office. It was to some hotel in Philly."

David looked at her, startled. And from the sudden look on her face, she'd never questioned this.

"When," David asked, "was this?"

"You know," she said, and then she looked at her sister-in-law, "it was only a couple months after Sandy was last here?"

**19**

"No. No," Mrs. Sandowski said, shaking her head, trying to convince herself, "he wouldn't have gone to meet her—certainly wouldn't have gone off with her. No, she was—she was trash. She might have cleaned herself up over the years, but she was still trash. And she had to be half his age. No."

Her sister-in-law said, "Wilm, maybe that's why he never wrote you. Maybe he was embarrassed."

Mrs. Sandowski looked at her. Her face was suddenly fiery. "If he did that he should be, damn old fool."

"Mr. Hanson told me," David said, "that she was talking about marriage before she left Philly."

She turned to him. "She said she was getting married?"

"No, just wondered whether it was for her. Just talked about it. Said if she ever got married it was so Andrew would have a father."

Mrs. Sandowski was sitting with her hands clenched under her bosom, jaws tight. Then she began to nod, quickly. "I believe it. It all makes sense. Why else wouldn't he write? He knew I knew what she was—he knew I knew she wasn't worth this much of him." She held thumb and forefinger barely apart. "Not this much. He had such a brain on him, was so skilled. Oh, it all makes sense. Even her coming to see me—I thought how nice. But I swear, I'll swear to it, she was only getting her hook in him more. 'Look how nice I am.'"

"No need getting all upset, Wilma," her brother said. "Who cares?"

"Not even to write to me!" she flared. "Not to say! You know how many nights I got out of bed because he didn't want no nurse there but me? You know? 'Oh, Wilma, I don't know what I'd do without you.' And showing me envelopes from her—'She's in Denver now, Wilma.' Sure, whoring! I didn't realize how flattered he was. And he must have encouraged it, he had to encourage it." She had to catch her breath; then her fury, her jealousy surely, kept pouring out. "What is it with men? The brainier they are, the dumber. She was a total, complete tramp. But I can remember—I remember even as she held the baby she'd talk oh so sweetly, oh so sweetly, to the interns. She's this thin and we could barely get her cleaned up, and they're always coming in. And even Bucky—he brings this trash in, and then he's always coming up to the room, his tongue out."

David said, "Where did he pick her up?"

"I don't know," she said angrily. Then to her sister-in-law, "Would I love to find out if he married her. Even if he just ran off with her. Would I love it. There's some people around here still think he's a god . . ." She looked slowly at David, as though really hearing his question for the first time. "Bucky said she like stepped out of the woods . . ." She turned to her sister-in-law again. "Right near that lake? Osengo? She came out of the woods. She was a tricky little thing even then."

The way Bucky would tell it, she said, he was driving along and he saw this pretty thing on the road, trying to hitch a ride. So, being single and a *man*, he stops. But as soon as he opens the door, this girl backs off and Sandy comes hurrying out of the woods, pregnant as you can be, and climbs in. And she's waving and calling good-bye out the window, and this other girl disappears into the woods.

"I remember how he told it, he told it a hundred times. A big joke on him. Here he thought he had something, and then here he's with this pregnant thing who's waving out the window—'Good-bye, Mad. Bye, Mad.'"

For a few moments, as David kept looking at her, the name meant nothing. But then it sprang tall and wide.

*Madeline?*

Sandy? Roger Tucker? Madeline Schwartz?

• • •

"I'm trying to think—what else could it be?" Judy said as they drove. "I still only come up with Madge, but I don't think so. And Madonna. Mada."

"I don't know. But it's so goddam coincidental. The same neighborhood. On Dad's list."

And one goddam liar, if true.

They drove quietly for a while. It was as though something had drained out of both of them. He glanced at the clock on the dash. It was still early, just going on four. "Are you hungry?"

"No, not at all."

"Tired?"

"No." She smiled at him. But her eyes looked tired.

"Oh, I meant to tell you—you were great in there. I don't think she'd have said anything."

"She was very nice. Two strangers coming in. Poor thing, though."

He looked over at her. She was sitting back, looking out her window. He hadn't thought of that, how he'd come in and shaken up her life. And for what? What the hell now?

They kept driving quietly. Sometimes he thought she was sleeping, but each time he looked she looked back. Now and then she would point something out—what looked to be a ski slope in the distance; an adult bookstore just outside a hamlet. He concentrated on the road, a one-lane blacktop, curving, mostly down.

A long flat stretch of road now, and he took it up to sixty-five. It was all woods here, the trees close-packed. It went on for miles, on either side. Then suddenly he slowed up. A sign ahead said: LAKE OSENGO. He pulled over on the shoulder. She sat up.

"Somewhere around here," he said.

The lake was fairly large, but more like a swamp near the road, with gnarled tree trunks rising up dark and forbidding.

"Somewhere on either side of the lake," he said.

She said, looking around, "What could they have been doing here? There isn't a house in miles."

"Unless back there," he said, motioning vaguely toward the woods.

"Or maybe they got a ride here, then— No, I forgot," she said, shaking her head. "The other girl would have gone along."

"They had to be staying somewhere in there. And it probably was on the other side of the road, since the guy was heading to Parrisboro. Unless Sandy ran across to him." He U-turned and drove very slowly, looking at the woods. Nothing must have changed in all these years. He stopped at a narrow dirt lane. He looked at her, then turned into it. It was rutted and icy in places, then dead-ended. Many of the trees were skeletal and he could see through, but only to other trees.

He backed out, then drove back across the road and past the lake. There he U-turned again and stopped by another lane. He looked at her.

"Aren't you glad you came?"

"Yes."

"Look, I really don't expect to see anything. I just want to see."

They bumped along, once skidding slightly though he was going very slowly. Someone had dumped an auto engine back here a million years ago; it was rusted and partly covered with snow. Here and there were little clearings. The lane took a sharp twist to a field and then to the charred remains of a building, blackened timbers lying across the stone foundation. There were some rusted cans on the ground. He stopped.

Here?

He drove on, but the lane could go on forever, and it was starting to get dark, and it was nuts. He was able to U-turn at a clearing, paused once more at the burned-out building, then started to drive out. He stopped just before he came to the road. He felt a strange reluctance to leave.

"I wonder," she said, "if it really could have been that house."

"That house, a tent, sleeping bags, could have been miles from here. Could have had a car parked in the woods. All I know, Judy, that girl didn't come back in the woods to be by herself."

He didn't have to say it: maybe Tucker. But anyone. Or even more than one.

"You know," he said, "Sandy gave a million different places where she lived. And she wrote to Sorris from all over. And it could explain something. She could have had Toby anywhere—a barn, an empty house, a field, a commune. A car. Maybe never even went to a hospital. So there'd be no birth certificate, no record, maybe only a few people ever saw him . . ."

"But she did have Andrew in a hospital."

He looked at her, then nodded slowly. "And why," he said, "didn't that other girl go with her? And whoever else was back there, why didn't one of them go?"

He lifted his palms, then pulled out.

[ 146 ]

She leaned her head against his shoulder.

He parked in the garage beneath the hotel. In the room he set down her bag, then took a phone book from the desk. He didn't think he'd find him here, and he was right: no Dr. Sorris in Philly. He then pulled out the list of names from the folder on his desk. Halfway to the city he'd been wondering had his father marked down who had given him Madeline's name, would it be the same one who'd given him Tucker's. But there was nothing. So even if he wanted to try, how the hell could he learn more about—

He caught himself, looked over at Judy. She'd taken off her coat, was sitting on the arm of the chair, looking at him.

"Oh, Jesus," he said. He walked over to her slowly.

She let him raise her to her feet. He put his arms around her, and she pressed into them. His cheek was on her hair.

"I'm such a shit," he said.

"Oh, Romeo."

He lifted her face. "I am. A total, complete shit."

She looked at him. "No."

"Not total?"

She kept looking at him. He kissed her on the mouth, and though she returned the kiss her lips were barely soft. He just held her.

He said, "Should we get something to eat?"

"I'm really not hungry. I don't know why. Are you?"

"No. Not at all. But you've got to be tired."

"Not really. But it's sort of like I've had a very long cry. Tired, but not tired. It's been an emotional day, I guess."

"I'm sorry."

"No. No. I'm glad, but it was still emotional." She sat on the bed, and he sat next to her. "You know," she said, "I don't think I really ever thought about the boy. I mean, I thought about him, it was sad, I knew what your father

[ 147 ]

was doing. But David," and she looked at him and shook her head, "I never thought about him like this. He's got a name. His mother's got a name. She was in Mrs. Sandowski's house. She was in those woods. And that poor boy. That poor boy. He had a mother, a father, he was alive, he must have played games, he— I mean, it was twenty years ago, but all of a sudden he's alive. And David"—her eyes became intense—"I want to kill her. I'm against capital punishment, but I want to kill her."

He rubbed her hand, squeezed it.

"I guess I still find it hard to believe," she said, "that mothers and fathers beat up their children, kill their children. And even if she didn't actually do it, you're right, she had to know about it."

He put his arm around her. She let out a quivering breath. "I'm sorry."

"Don't. No. I'll tell you what." He lifted her legs onto the bed, then lay next to her. She toed off her shoes. They lay, she in his arm, looking across the room.

"I just want to say this and no more," she said. "I feel like I ought to call my kids."

"Why don't you?"

"No. I don't want to."

He could feel her body gradually relaxing. He could see in the mirror that her eyes were closed. But when he looked again they were open. She turned her face to him, and he kissed her. Her lips were a little softer, and they opened. He touched her tongue with his, kept turning round it, drew it in, let her draw his. He unbuttoned her jacket. She sat up and drew it off her arms. They looked at each other as they undressed. They lay on the cool sheet, the blanket flung away. He just held her, his lips under her ear; the perfume was still faint. He kissed under her ear, and she kept turning her head. He found her lips again, then his lips went to her throat, and then to each breast, long, wanting to draw them in. He kissed her little belly, breathing on it as he went lower. She opened her legs, then arched up to him with a gasp. She clutched his face, then drew him up. She circled him as he entered, then lifted up once, twice, let out a gasp, another, and then fell back.

She looked at him, her eyes wide; a look of almost shock.

"Don't move," he whispered.

"I—" She shook her head slowly, eyes still wide.

"Just stay like this."

"I—want to sleep."

"Then sleep."

"I don't want to sleep."

He put his cheek against hers.

"I'm so full of you," she said.

"Just let me hold you."

"So full of you."

She seemed to sleep. But then her body moved, just a little. He returned the move, just a little. She lifted again. He met her, then remained still as she kept lifting. She kept lifting harder, and her legs, which had fallen away, closed around him again. She kept lifting, and this time he met her at each peak, met her, met her, then harder, and he could feel her starting, and himself so close, then closer, and all at once even harder; and it was as though they rose up together, kept rising—and then fell away.

He held onto her. Her cheeks were wet.

He didn't know which of them was breathing harder. He held on, feeling his breathing easing.

He wanted to say he loved her. But why couldn't he say he loved her?

**20**

That morning, the phone in Nick's room rang at twenty after eight. Jolted awake, he reached over for it on the lamp table.

"Nick," Anne said, and there was terror in her voice, "she just called back—the secretary at the church. Nick, he was over to see her."

He sat up quickly. "When?"

"The past few days. I forgot to ask which. He said he wanted to know where Sandy was, he was an old friend."

"Does she know?"

"No. But she gave him her landlady—I forgot all about her—and she gave him a name, and he called Mrs. Dove back, and she said she couldn't give him Raymond's name because—"

"Look, you're not making sense. I'll be over."

He banged down the phone, took a fast shower—a compulsion; he couldn't wait to go over there—and shaved with the stuff he'd bought downstairs, and put on the clothes he'd been living in since he'd gotten here.

All Friday afternoon he'd been waiting for Anne to connect with someone; but it had to be today, when he had to go home for a few days.

He could feel his heart beating under his hair-matted chest—he was rarely conscious of its beating—and it worried him that he was losing his cool. He had made coolness a part of him; but this tension reminded him of those early days, after they'd split up and gone their own ways, he used to get scared about them, used to fantasize finding them and then . . . hiring someone. Hiring someone, or worse came to worst, doing it himself. But time had brought layers of comfort; and time had been comforting too, after he'd seen the story in that shit paper about the old man.

But now the son, the goddam son.

Waiting for the elevator, he thought of the sixth floor, how last evening when he'd come back from Anne's he'd had to struggle against getting off there and just walking by 691, and later, up in his room, against calling just to hear his voice. It would have been crazy; but it was frustrating to think he knew the guy's room, might even have just passed him in the lobby.

Going down, he watched the lights pop on. The sixth, but he was past it now. He flung on his heavy coat and, before stepping out, motioned for the doorman to get a cab.

"The Remington Apartments."

The driver lowered the flag. Nick leaned back, staring out his window. He felt so close to being exposed—not just about the kid, he rarely ever thought about the kid unless he had to, like now—but that everyone would find out he didn't have an IQ of 178, and that there'd been no college, not even that place in India which he'd learned no longer existed; that everything he knew came from things he'd picked up in books—so many books, scatterings of religions, philosophies. What he did have, that so many snots with their degrees looked down on, was not only the wisdom of books but the ability to think to the core of things and to act—like finally beating it, after high school, from a father who believed the world was coming to an end any second—Gog in the Bible was supposed to be Russia, Magog was who-the-shit remembered, maybe China, and gave most of his dough from the hardware store to that prick who was going to take them up some mountain where the saved were to wait. And from a mother who agreed with it all and never lifted a hand to save him from beatings, and who even screamed and beat on him when he finally let it all out and hammered that old fucking son of a bitch to the kitchen floor, wanting to kill him, only to kill him, but the bastard managed to crawl away, wheezing, rasping, "You're crazy, you're crazy."

Anne was waiting for him in the foyer of her apartment, the door open.

"Hey, ease up," he forced himself to say. "Ease it up . . . I smell coffee. I haven't had coffee."

"Let me heat this. It'll just take a second."

He went into the living room and sat on the sofa. She brought him the coffee. He said, after a long, forced sip, "So. What did she tell you?"

Anne remained standing. "Mrs. Dove said she gave him Sandy's landlady's name—I can't believe I forgot about her. And he went there, and she apparently didn't know anything, and she gave him another name. Raymond. Raymond Hanson. And him I really can't believe I forgot. I hadn't seen him for a long, long time, but he did come to Roger's funeral."

"Do you remember if he knew Sandy?"

"Yes. He did."

"And what about Kyle? Did he go to see him?"

What he did, she explained, was call Mrs. Dove for his phone number or address. But instead of giving it out, Mrs. Dove had called Raymond and left it up to him.

Nick said, "Do you know if he got in touch with him?"

"No."

"How well do you think this Hanson knew her?"

"Well, he was one of the people she was active with in church. He's a, you know, a homosexual, and some of the people gave him a rough time. But Sandy was one of those who stuck up for him, and so did Roger and I."

"I don't understand"—his tension was threatening to show—"why didn't you think of him yesterday?"

"I don't know. I told you I couldn't think. I still can't think too well."

"Well, I want you to call him now," he said.

She grimaced slightly. "I—I will later. Not now, I'm not up to it."

"I've got to go back today, Anne. I'm coming back, but I've got to go back for a couple days."

"I—I will later."

"Anne, please call him now."

But she didn't move. She stared down at her hands. Her fingers were picking at each other. "I don't think I can. I can't."

He said nothing. Let it come.

"After you left yesterday," she said, "everything backed up on me again."

"It's only natural," he said. Then made himself say, "We all have that."

"Sometimes," she said, still staring down, her voice a monotone, "sometimes I think let whatever happens happen. We—deserve what God does to us. You know something, Nick?" She looked at him. "You know why I'm convinced Roger killed himself? He wanted to make sure he went to hell. He used to say, maybe God would forgive the two of us for what we did to that—to that child. He used to say maybe He'd forgive us because we tried so hard to make it up. But I really think he wanted to go to hell."

Nick stared at her. He felt fire rising into his head.

"He was only a—child, Nick. There isn't one of us less guilty of his death than the others. You, me, Roger, Mad, Sand, Tony. Tony I used to envy because he's dead, but he's got to be in hell."

He rose slowly. He forced himself to rise, or else—he could feel it happening, it was starting to—he was going to grab something, that big heavy paperweight, or run into the kitchen for a knife.

He went to the window. He tried to think only of inhaling, exhaling, inhaling. But all at once he whirled and grabbed the paperweight, and he spun around to her, her hands flying up to her face—but then an infinitesimal bit of reason opening in him, he flung it against a wall. She let out a gasp and dropped on the sofa.

"I'm tired of it too, I'm sick of it!" But he managed to keep his voice down; his control was edging back. "I'm sick of everything." He glared at her. "Do you have any idea how hard I've been working to try to do good? It may be nuts, but I think what I'm doing may—just may help this goddam world from blowing itself up. But hell everything! Screw it! You want everything over? Do you? Do you?"

And suddenly he strode to the phone, punched a button—not the operator's. Not anyone.

"Give me the police. Please. Fast."

She stared at him in horror, then ran to him and tried to grab it from him. He pulled it away, but she grabbed again. And this time he let it fall. She quickly cradled it.

"Don't," she pleaded. "Don't."

"I'm sick of it, Anne. I'm so tired."

"Don't. Please."

She sat down by the phone, stared up at him. "Tell me," she said, "what to say to him."

"Whatever you want. I don't care."

"Nick, help me. Please."

"I don't know, let me think. That you heard he's supposed to call someone named Kyle. That Kyle also called
you, and you're afraid he's a nut, and maybe you're afraid
for Sandy if he ever does find her. And if he's already spoken to Kyle, try to find out what he told him."

She went to the phone. But it was a few moments before she dialed. Then, about half a minute later, she said
to Nick, "There's no answer. But I'll keep trying."

Nick looked at her, then went over for the paperweight
on the floor. He examined it. "It looks all right. I'm
sorry." He handed it to her, but she barely looked at it.
"I'm sorry I got mad," he said.

"No. It's my fault."

"Anne, I'm going to say this again. I'm going to handle
this. I swear to that. But if you weigh me down I can't, it's
not worth it."

"I promise, Nick. You say you're going away?" She
sounded a little alarmed.

"Just a couple of days. But we'll be in touch. And I'll be
back."

"I'll keep trying to reach him," she said.

"Anne," he said, "have you ever thought of calling
Madeline?"

"Not before Roger died. I—I really didn't want to see
anyone that would remind me of— But since he died, I
think of her a lot. An awful lot."

"Then why don't you call her?"

"I don't know if she'd want to hear from me."

"She feels the same about you. Call her. You need each
other. And I'll feel better. I'd love you two together
again."

She nodded. "I'll—think about it."

A tear slid down her cheek. He touched it with his finger. She looked at him.

"Hey, Ra," he said. "When's the last time anyone called
you Ra?"

"Oh, God. It's been so long."

"Tony thought he discovered America when he saw it in a crossword puzzle. 'I pronounce thee God of Sun.'"

"I was a real redhead then."

He smiled. "You still are."

"No."

"Ra." He was thinking of her suddenly with that brown, high-crowned, wide-brimmed hat she used to wear sometimes, like an Indian selling Manhattan. "I wonder if Sandy ever learned to cook?"

"Wasn't she terrible? You know, Roger became a very good cook."

"He was then." And a little skinny wimp. The gofer of the group.

"I mean gourmet."

They stood looking at each other. Then he said, "You going to be all right?"

"I promise."

"I'll call you. Later today. And I'll be back."

"Okay."

"Ra."

She smiled.

"Do you mind?" And he held out his arms and she came to him and he held her gently.

"What," he said, "did the Buddha say to Panthaka about greed?"

"Oh, Nick, I don't—" She looked at him.

"You forgot."

"'Greed is the real dust . . .'"

"Close. 'Greed is the real dirt, not dust . . .'" He said, "How about this? 'Unless we can agree to suffer . . .'"

"'. . . we cannot be free from suffering.'"

"Very good."

"Are you still . . . Eastern?"

"What did I used to say?"

"Oh . . . We're part of all things?"

He held her just a touch tighter. He could feel her thighs, her breasts against him. It was tempting to lower his hand. Not that he wanted to, but it might help. No, it would be a mistake now, and then to go. Later—just maybe. He'd see.

．　．　．

When the phone rang, Madeline thought it was still another teacher calling about the strike—some were happy it was off, others angry. But a woman whose voice she didn't recognize said, "Is this Madeline?"

"Yes."

"Madeline, this is Anne Tucker. Anne West?"

For an instant she felt a stab of fear. But then there was a rush of joy. "Oh, Anne. Oh, Anne, it's so good to hear from you."

"I was afraid to call, I thought you might not want—"

"No. No. I should have called you. I've been meaning to, but I thought you might not want it either. Anne, I'm so sorry about Rog. And I feel so rotten I didn't call. Why didn't I call you?"

"No, don't. It's so good to hear your voice."

"It's so good to hear yours. Tell me, Anne, how are you?"

The sudden silence brought another dart of fear. "I'm—okay. Madeline, Nick was here, I don't know if you knew."

"He said he was going to see you."

"He just left. But he's coming back in a couple days."

The fear became gathered around her throat. "Anne"—she looked out from the kitchen, though she knew no one was home—"tell me."

"He— You know who I mean by he."

Her eyes closed. "Yes."

"He's here. Asking people."

"Oh, Anne."

"Nick says—not to worry. And we are working—"

She leaned forward. "What do you mean by working?"

"I don't want to say too much on the phone. But—we're trying to find her first."

She kept staring out the kitchen door. "But, Anne, she wouldn't tell."

"I know. I guess. But we want to find her . . . But, Mad, I didn't call to worry you more. I really just wanted to say hello. I only wish you lived closer, I wish I could see you."

"I want to see you."

"Could you come, Mad? I'd come there, but I thought—maybe when Nick's here."

Her face reflected her torture. "Anne, I don't see how."

"I was just—saying. But I just wanted to talk to you. I feel better talking to you."

"Anne, let me see, let me think."

"I'd love to see you, Mad. I could—use you."

"And I want to see you. Let me get back to you, Anne. Let me see."

Later, she sat back in the chair, as drained as if she'd been running. She couldn't go there—and even if she could, she didn't want to. Wanted just to go back and forth to school, and cook, and watch TV, and go out on a Saturday night with Herm, and worry about nothing more than maybe Cindy's seeing a wrong boy; it seemed so trivial, anything about Cindy, a good kid really.

But she should be there.

How could you leave things to Anne? She was always a scatterbrain. Even her attempts to play the uke—a dumb, simple instrument—she spent months making nothing more than sounds, it used to drive Madeline nuts. And Anne used to think it a big deal to accidentally-on-purpose walk in front of the guys with her little tits out, and was really just dragged along because her lawyer daddy would send money to some PO number or Y until someone, probably some psychiatrist, told him not to. Madeline, on the other hand, had been Nick's right arm, he could depend on her to do anything; in fact was the one—though she couldn't believe it now—was the one who was the expert on boosting canned goods and sheets and tools, including once a big saw, while everyone else was getting the attention looking around the store.

She didn't want to go, didn't see how she could; but she should, she really must.

• • •

When she came up for the night, Herman was lying on his side in bed, the TV on. She didn't know whether he was asleep or awake. But when she slid into bed, he lifted his head slightly, without turning.

He remained intent on the show, though, even when she slid close and put her arm around him. She squeezed him, trying to bury herself and her fears in him, in this fatty of hers, this brilliant fat surgeon.

He lifted his head slightly, then turned and put his arm around her. All she wanted was this, the closeness, but then he kissed her on the mouth, then felt and squeezed her breasts, his hand going now to her vagina for a few seconds. Then, though she still didn't want this, she helped lift herself so he could remove the gown; tried to help him in, but she was dry. She kept trying, and now he was in, but it still wasn't really working until Nick, that black bandanna around his hair, began kissing her nipples, forever on one, forever on the other. She pushed him away, shoved him out of her mind, and kept holding onto Herman; but now Nick was in her, the tremendous size of him, and he lifted her legs over his shoulders, not caring that Sandy or Anne or Rog or any of them knew, heard—

She pushed him away again, came back to Herman, who was letting out little gasps now. And she gasped too, wanting Herman to hear. Then she held onto him tightly, in horror, for this was her world, she mustn't lose her world.

**21**

David and Judy woke up early and made love, then fell into a deep sleep again, arms flung across each other. It was almost noon when they stirred awake again, lazy, feeling good. He got up long enough to go to the bathroom, then opened the drapes to the sun and somehow to the feel of a Sunday. He brought the menu on the bureau back to bed, but she slipped out to go to the bathroom, and then they sat back against the pillows to decide who wanted what. He called room service.

After breakfast, she showered first—they were going to drive around the city; she'd never been here—while he lay half sitting, not wanting to think of it today, but thinking. Maybe the candy store guy, Sam Goldberg, had known Madeline, would remember her.

He got out of bed and looked through the folder; he'd written Goldberg's number in here somewhere. He turned the papers as the shower drummed. Here.

His wife answered. Yes, he was here, but he was in bed with a bad cold. "Can I help?"

He tried to think. "Could I trouble you to ask him something for me?"

"Sure."

"I'm David Kyle. I was over to see him about Sandra Meghan. David Kyle. Do you have that?"

"Yes," she said slowly, "I'm marking down."

"I was wondering if he remembers a Madeline Magglio from the old neighborhood. Magglio. I'm sure that was her last name. Her married name is Schwartz. Could you ask him that?"

"I'm still marking . . . Hold on." After a while she said, "He says he thinks. But he ain't sure right now. And he's watching his show. If you want to call back—maybe, I don't know."

"All right," though he hated to just hang up. "I'll call back. Thanks."

When he hung up, he saw that Judy was looking at him from the bathroom doorway, a towel around her.

She said, "Is something the matter?"

He told her. "And I'm not going to get anywhere with him on the phone anyway. I know it."

She looked at him. "If you want me to," she said, "I can go over there when I get back."

• • •

The ballroomlike living room hummed with conversation, while bartenders at two ends of the room served drinks and a chef in a towering white hat carved thin slices of Scottish salmon, balancing them gently on the knife, to rest on black bread. And butlers kept streaming in and out of the kitchen, carrying silver trays of escargot and stone crabs and miniature filet mignon sandwiches and blini with caviar and sour cream. It was only within the past few years that Nick had come to feel that this was his home, not just Louise's.

He drifted among the guests—chatting, smiling, serious. Most were Louise's family, with a scattering of friends: her granddaughter had come back from Brazil with a husband, and Louise wanted to introduce him properly. Occasionally someone would congratulate him on her marriage—usually an ass, but he liked it, it made him really family; but most wanted to talk about his work or the world: that they'd seen one of the foundation scholars on TV, or read an Op-ed piece by another, and what did he think of Russia's latest gesture? Now and then he would glance at his watch. He had made up his mind he would call Anne exactly at nine.

Last night, when he'd called, she still hadn't heard from Hanson. But he might have called too early.

At two minutes to, he went upstairs to his study and made the call.

"No," she said, "I haven't heard yet. And I left another message. I only hope he's not away."

He fought against saying call me anytime tonight you hear, but he didn't want to sound too anxious. "Well, he may be away just for the weekend. Look, call me tomorrow, I'll be in the office."

"Should I call him again tonight?"

"Whatever you want to do. But just relax. I don't like the way you sound again."

"No, I'm all right. Nick," she said, "I meant to tell you right away. I talked to Madeline yesterday. I called."

"Good." Christ, more than good; he needed them to help each other. "I'm delighted."

"She said she's going to try to come down. She said she'll try to when you're here. Do you know when you're coming back?"

"Let's see what happens. But I'll be there. Meanwhile, I want you to have a good night, you hear?"

He remained by the phone. Even with the door closed, the sounds of the party drifted in.

He could feel his anxiety growing again; was trying not to let it control him.

He'd worked so hard to be where he was now, had so much to do yet, was reaching so high—no less than the survival of the world. But that son of a bitch out there, looking for glory—

"Nicholas, you up here?" Louise called from the hall.

"I'm in here. I had to make a call."

"Sorry, honey, but some people are leaving."

"Be right down."

He kept staring at the door, breathing a little hard. She'd jolted him from some frightening thinking. Frightening but comforting. Of weapons and ways.

· · ·

David sat with her until they called rows twelve to twenty-five, and they stood up and kissed quickly. He carried her bag over to the line at the boarding gate.

She said, "Thanks for everything. Everything was great. And the dinner was scrumptious."

"You didn't eat enough."

She laughed. They'd gone to Bookbinders, near the river, and each had a two-pound lobster, with crab meat.

"Look," she said, "I'll try to see Goldberg tomorrow. I'll call you either way."

"Hey, I hate to see you go."

She smiled. "That I like. I'll call you tomorrow." Walking, she waved back at him.

He waited until she was gone, then went to the garage for the car. It felt lonely without her. He turned on the radio as he drove, but everything seemed like noise, and he turned it off. At the hotel he tried to buy tomorrow morning's paper, but all they had were a few leftover Sundays. He took one, thought for a moment about going into the bar for a beer; but that seemed the loneliest of all, and he went up to the room.

He threw the paper on the bed, sat down to look through it, then looked over at the phone. He'd intended waiting until tomorrow—he didn't know how Mrs. Sandowski felt about her Sundays—but was thinking why not?

Mrs. Sandowski, it turned out, was eager to talk to him.

"I was wondering," she said, "if you learned anything."

"No, but I've something I'd like to ask you."

Had Dr. Sorris ever mentioned anyplace where he wanted to retire to, or perhaps where he had particularly enjoyed vacationing?

"To tell you the truth," she said, "I thought of that when I didn't hear from him any more. I told myself I was going to find out. But then I thought if he doesn't want to write to me, why should I bother? You know? And I forgot about it."

Vacations, she said, he and his wife used to take vacations all over—Europe, Caribbean, they went to Japan, once took a cruise. But there were two places she remembered him saying where he wouldn't mind building a house some day. Little seashore places; he'd either been to both or seen pictures. One was in New Jersey—Ocean Bridge. The other was up in Maine, but she wasn't sure of the name. But she had the feeling it sounded something like Lanoka.

"I don't know," she said, "I guess you can call there and find out. I'd do it myself, but, you know, if he didn't want me to know . . ."

"Well, I'll probably try."

"If you do find out," she said quickly, "will you let me know?"

But there was nothing to let her know about. There was no listing for a Dr. Sorris in Ocean Bridge. And none in Landokwa, a coastal town.

He sat staring at the far wall, then went over and turned on TV. He flipped channels, but there was nothing he could bear watching. He picked up the paper, discarded certain sections immediately—food, society, business, comics—no, he'd save the comics—the classifieds, of course. He looked at sports, the front news sections, editorial page, Op-eds; tried TV again, and left it on to a situation comedy he'd never seen before and then was too lazy to turn it off. He went back to the paper, glancing up and down each page, sometimes reading. And there, grabbing him like a fist around the heart, it was again. Same columnist. Boldface. Rev. Roger Tucker.

. . . Well, our police source was right—an elderly man in a mackinaw did indeed leave the Rev. Roger Tucker's apartment the night of his death. But, it seems, it was about 20 minutes before the minister was seen falling to his death . . .

David felt something drop in him. He just sat looking at the story, a little weak. Then he grabbed up the phone to call Marie. But the line was busy.

He looked at the story again, as if somehow it might have changed. And then, through the hot flood of relief, it gradually sank in—that he'd actually thought his father capable of murder. And no, not just that. But that the pathetic old man in the wide-brimmed hat and long coat had really killed a man.

• • •

He called Judy a couple of hours later, to tell her.

"David, that's such a relief. I'm so happy."

They talked about how Tucker's suicide had to mean he was definitely involved; about that, and the weekend. But neither of them said anything about his being able to call it quits now. She seemed to know there was no way he could.

**22**

It was, David told the woman, important—couldn't she make an exception? But the woman at the American Medical Association headquarters, in Chicago, said she was sorry, he would have to send in the request in writing.

But, she added, they did publish a directory, the *American Medical Directory*, that listed physicians' addresses. Many libraries had it.

He called the main library, but the number was busy. He tried twice more, then was about to go there when he decided to see, first, what he might be able to learn on his own.

Maybe Sorris had gone to Ocean Bridge or Landokwa and left. A hospital there might know where he'd gone.

He got information for Landokwa and asked for the names of hospitals there.

"I'm sorry," the operator said, "I'm not in Landokwa and I don't know any names. You'll have to give me a name."

"Could you give me the police there?"

They gave him the name of the only hospital in the town. But the operator there said, "Sorris?" Then after a few moments, "No, we don't have anyone by that name."

"Who can I talk to who might know if he used to be on the staff?"

"I'll give you administration."

But a young woman who answered said she really didn't know where to look for that information, but if he'd call back in about an hour . . .

He stood up to leave for the library when Judy called.

"I just came from the Goldbergs. It has to be her. He said she was a hippie—ran away from home."

• • •

Anne Tucker kept opening and closing file drawers in her husband's study, frantically trying to find the auto payments book. They'd called a little earlier that afternoon— at first she'd thought it finally might be Raymond—to say they hadn't received a payment in two months. And it wasn't only this, she didn't know where to find anything, though Roger had told her several times—tax records, the few stocks he had, maybe even the phone bills. She sank down at his desk. She felt so helpless, stupid, frightened.

She didn't even want to go to the shelter anymore. She was sure everyone could see through her now, that she really didn't know anything about counseling, about anything; that without Roger's support she was a complete nothing.

If her children at least lived in the city. But then she was glad they didn't, with all this going on, with what might happen . . .

Her hand darted out to the phone at the first ring.

"Yes?"

"Hello, Mrs. Tucker, this is Raymond. How are you?"

And this, she'd been dreading trying to handle this, though Nick had coached her. "I'm all right, Raymond. And you?"

"I'm doing just fine. But I was worried something was wrong—I got three messages."

"No, nothing's wrong, I just wanted to ask you something." Her voice was threatening to break. "Has someone been asking you about Sandy Meghan?"

"Yes." He was puzzled.

"I was just—wondering. He was here, he asked me. And I know he asked Mrs. Dove. She's the one told me about you. I—I don't know, I just have a feeling about him. He worries me."

"Really?" He suddenly sounded concerned. "Why?"

"I just don't trust him. There's something about him. Did he tell you why he wants to find her?"

"He just said he was an old friend."

Be shocked, Nick had said, at whatever he says. "A friend? He didn't say a relative?"

"No. A relative? Is that what he told you?"

"Yes. I know he told Mrs. Dove he was a friend—that's what really started me worrying. Raymond, I—I'm worried about her. Do you know where she is?"

"No." His voice became distraught. "But God, I shouldn't have told him anything. I should have been suspicious, where were my brains?"

"What did you tell him?"

Her face went instantly agonized as he told her what he'd said about Andrew's birth, and about the nurse.

Nick—she had to call Nick!

•  •  •

Owen Grossman, former assistant secretary of state and foundation scholar for the past two years, stopped by Nick's office after lunch, ostensibly to chat about an upcoming meeting. But Nick knew he actually wanted to find out had he watched Grossman on last night's *World Report*.

Nick hadn't—deliberately, something he occasionally did to keep them from getting overinflated.

He was wondering, Grossman said, how the fall conference was shaping up.

"It's going very smoothly," Nick said. "It looks like it's going to be the biggest yet."

"Terrific." Then Grossman shook his head, to himself. "Had the damndest trouble with the earpiece last night. Did you ever have that trouble?"

Earpiece? When was this? Grossman, his face turning slightly pink, said, "Last night. On *World Report*. Kept coming off."

"Really?" And now the slight soother. "My daughter-in-law saw it. She never mentioned anything about that. She thought you were wonderful. She said you really put the Princeton guy in his place."

"Well, he's a predictable jackass. More and more nuke capability, better the chance of peace. The old story, never changes. Problem is they believe it."

"Sometimes," Nick said, "I wonder why people don't go rushing from their homes and run screaming through the streets—stop it, we've got kids, we want them and their kids to live out their lives—"

"You must be joking," Grossman said. In his fifties, he looked like the consummate diplomat—long white hair, rimless glasses, even the three-piece suit. "We have enough nuts doing that—chaining themselves, writing in blood on walls—"

"Owen," Nick chided with a smile, "I meant metaphorically. I mean how people can stand the pressure of the times."

"That's different. I wonder myself. Well," he said. "Work to do."

Nick watched him walk off. Occasionally he had to

remind himself to back off from his old thinking; to remember that the only way was the pragmatic way. Not too many years ago he wouldn't even stand on the same street corner with Grossman without dumping a bucket of shit on his head; but the man was bright, was known throughout the world, was just to the right enough of center to have the respect of much of the right, while others in the foundation were just far enough to the left of center. And, Nick always remembered with satisfaction, he'd grabbed him before the Carnegie could.

With Grossman gone, he found his thoughts starting to go back to Philly; but he controlled them and went out to the outer office to pick up mail that had come in while Miss Bruehlman was away from her desk. He was riffling through the envelopes when Anne called.

"He knows," she said, her voice trembling, "she had her—her second child in the Poconos. He knows—"

"Who's 'he'?" he cut in fiercely.

"This Raymond. And he says he told—him."

"Then tell me! Just tell me!"

"He knows that, he knows the hospital, the doctor, the nurse."

"Do you know the doctor's name? The nurse?"

"No."

"You never asked him?"

"I—never thought to. I was awful nervous."

Dumb, helpless cunt—as dumb and helpless as she ever was! "Did he say if Kyle's going up there?"

"I didn't ask, Nick."

"Anne," he said, keeping his voice low, "you've got to find out."

"Nick, I—don't think I can. I'm afraid I'll louse— I don't know how I did what I did."

"Anne, you've got to."

"When—when are you coming back, Nick?"

"I can't till after tomorrow. I'll be there Wednesday

morning first thing. But call. You hear me? And call me back."

Afterward he sat for a few moments with his eyes closed, as though from the sight of her—from the sight of everything. He was so torn. Tomorrow they were deciding on their new scholars—they were expanding the number of openings—and the foundation's advisors would be meeting with the board of directors; people were flying in. He had to be there.

Must be there.

He had such vital work to do, so much, so much to offer. But suddenly, after all these years, this—why this?

· · ·

Anne's first words to Madeline were a frightened, "Mad, he's mad at me."

Madeline's hand froze on the phone. "Why?" Then, after she heard, "Anne, where's this hospital?"

"Didn't you know?"

"Anne, how could I know? I just got her on the truck, I didn't know where she was going."

"It's up near where we were, the Poconos."

Her hand rose to her temple. "But she couldn't have said anything to them about us. They'd have come—"

"I don't know. But Nick wants to find out. He's coming here. Mad, can you come?"

Her palm went harder against her temple. "I don't know, I don't see how."

"Mad, try. You said you would. Please, Mad. We need each other. The three of us."

"I—I'll try."

She sat now in the silence of the house, her hands clenched tight on her thighs. She'd stayed home today, telling herself fuck it, fuck the whole school, the job, she was going to spend the day doing the house, giving it the cleaning her once-a-week girl never did.

But knew now, really all along, it was damn lie; just wanted to be near the phone.

But how could she go? What could she tell Herm, Cindy?

And she didn't want to go. Didn't want to be near him—that thing with his yin and yang, and the wisdom of the Buddha Shakyamuni, and even Christ whenever it served him—all that shit, with the rest of them huddled around, staring at him wide-eyed, or having it yelled at them when they didn't do something "right." And always with his talk of peace, peace, that violent man.

Didn't want to go. Mustn't.

But, God help her, they did need each other. And needed him most of all.

• • •

The librarian at the reference desk said yes, they did have the directory. Which of the geographic volumes did he want? Or did he want the index?

"The index, please."

The librarian brought him the latest one. He flipped through it quickly, then felt something sink in him. No Sorris.

David set the book down slowly, then went through the front pages to see who they said they listed. Every M.D., and osteopaths who belonged to the AMA.

Maybe he was an osteopath who didn't belong to it. Or maybe he was dead, he could be dead. Or maybe there was just a screw-up.

He looked at the librarian to ask if they had an earlier index or other directories. But three people were waiting to talk to her.

He waited a few minutes, then walked quickly to a public phone. Using a credit card, he put through a call to Ocean Bridge. There were, an officer told him, no hospitals on the island itself. But there were three within about fifteen miles.

"Masequan Hospital," an operator said.

"Do you happen to have a Dr. Sorris on the staff?"

"I'm afraid not."

"Can I speak to someone in your gynecology-obstetrics department?" Maybe he'd have better luck there than with administration.

"I'm sorry but we don't have one. This is a children's hospital."

Christ, at least that was half funny. He dialed the second number. No, no Dr. Sorris was on the staff. Sorry, the administrator's line was busy. Hold on, she'd give him obstetrics.

"Mrs. Matthews speaking."

"I hate to bother you, but I'm looking for a Dr. Sorris. An obstetrician. I was wondering if I could find out if he was ever on the staff. This could go back seven, eight years."

"I don't know. What's the name again?"

"Sorris." He spelled it.

"Hold on." She was away about five minutes. "Yes, he was, but I'm sorry to say he died. Several years ago."

He felt a fiery explosion in his chest. "Could you tell me how I can find out where he lived?"

"I imagine you'd have to talk to personnel. I really don't know."

She transferred the call, but a man in personnel wouldn't even look, said they couldn't give out this information on the phone; in fact, would have to have a good reason to do so, even in person.

Hanging up, he tried to think what to do—then quickly dialed information again.

Christ, why hadn't he thought of this before?

"Do you have a listing in Ocean Bridge for a Sandra Meghan?"

A pause, then, "No, there's no such listing."

"What about a Sandra Sorris?"

"How do you spell that?"

"S-o-r-r-i-s."

"Just a minute." Then, after a long pause, "I'm sorry, but that's an unlisted number."

# 23

Within twenty minutes, after a quick call to Judy, he'd checked out and was carrying his bag to the car. He flung in his coat and put the piece of paper with the directions he'd gotten from the auto club on the dash. The island was about ninety miles away.

His head reeling, he made his way to the Ben Franklin Bridge that spanned the Delaware River to New Jersey and maneuvered among the cars funneling onto it. On the Jersey side, after the toll, the road was still heavily trafficked, but gradually it began thinning out at major intersections and traffic circles, with cars peeling off in many directions. Now he had the road, a two-lane, almost to himself. On either side were woods, broken up by an occasional farm and, back deeper, a housing development. Then the woods took over almost completely.

He headed around another circle, cutting off at a sign that said Ocean Bridge. The speedometer was approaching seventy. Now it trembled close to seventy-five.

But he felt he could run faster.

Ahead, somewhere on that island, Sandy.

His head was clear now. Excitement was charging through it. And thoughts of his father kept breaking in.

What he wouldn't have given for this. What he had given.

It was hard not to think of the Old Man sitting next to him. And God how he wished it.

• • •

Night closed in a few miles from the island, and nothing eased it other than his headlights and a few scattered lights in the distance. He passed a darkened diner, then a small building that he took to be a real estate office, then what looked to be a clam shack, then a closed service station, a boat yard; and then there were lights ahead that turned out to be the long causeway that curved over blackness, a bay probably. And now as he approached the end, the dark mass of Ocean Bridge appeared, just a few lights dotting it.

Here. He was here, and she was here.

Off the causeway, he drove as far as he could, to a dead-end road. He had to choose left or right; ahead, undoubtedly, was the ocean. He tried left. The few buildings he passed were darkened. But here was a lighted service station. He pulled in, then went into the office where a teenager was staring out at him.

"Are there any motels or hotels near here?"

"I don't know which-all are open. There's one about a mile or two down." He gestured in the direction David was heading.

"How big's the island?"

"About eighteen miles."

Driving, he saw a grocery store that looked open, though barely so; they seemed to be saving on electricity. But the few other stores he passed were closed. And most of the homes—some looked like Cape Cods, others were built on pilings—were dark too. But ahead, on a high billboard illuminated by two gooseneck lights, was: SEA URCHIN MOTEL—Open Year Round. And an arrow pointed right.

The motel was at the end of the dimly lighted street. His headlights briefly swept across a dune as he turned in at the office. A line of units faced the street, another the ocean. There was a small light over the office, and a little sign said: RING. He rang, and a figure he could see through the thin drapes materialized from somewhere in back and opened the door.

"I'd like a room."

David followed him into the office; the man went behind the counter and peered through a big ledger, as if— though only two or three cars were on the lot—they were booked.

"How long will you be staying?"

"I'm not sure, maybe a couple nights."

"You want facing the beach or street?"

"Either one. The beach, I guess."

The man ran his credit card through his machine, then gave him a room number. "You want ice, it's in back, by the pool. But there's a soda machine in front. And you'll see coffee in the room."

David took the key; then, trying not to sound suspicious, he said, "Do you know anyone living around here named Sandra Sorris? Sandy Sorris? Her husband was a doctor?"

"No, can't say I do."

"I was just wondering if she still lived here," he said.

Carrying his bag, he walked along the wood walkway to the front, then past some fifteen units, only two of which were lit. A strong, salty wind blew along the beach; the ocean thundered about fifty yards away, as black as the starless sky, except for the churn and crash of foam.

The room felt damp, and was cool even for him. He fiddled around with the thermostat until he got the electric baseboard heat going. He set down his bag on a chair, used the bathroom, then went out. He could see a couple leaving at the far end; the blackness of their unit seemed so final he was sure they were checking out.

In the office he asked the man for a map of the island, which he produced only after going through several drawers, and then for directions to Manning Hospital, although it was too late to go there tonight. Before leaving he said, "Is there anyplace open for dinner you'd recommend?"

There was hardly anything this end of the island, the man said; most were on the other end. "But if you don't want to go too far you might try Pete and Mary's near the causeway."

There were more cars parked at Pete and Mary's than he'd seen on the island so far. But the bar was so long it seemed almost empty. He imagined it was two and three deep in the summer. One of the men wore a hard hat. There were plenty of tattoos, and most of the women wore sweatshirts. But the steak sandwich he ordered was exceptionally good, the mug of beer with just the right chill to it.

When the waitress brought him the check, he asked her about Sandy. But she didn't know of her either.

"You know whereabouts she lives?" she asked.

"No, that's the thing. She's an old friend, and I heard she moved here."

"You might try the Municipal Building tomorrow."

It wasn't until he was outside that he realized how quickly he'd eaten, how much he was racing. It was as if he'd been searching for her while sitting there, wanted to charge off in many directions at the same time. But what could he do tonight?

He hated to go back to the motel, thought about going

back in the bar or to another bar. But he wasn't in the mood for that either; was too itchy, couldn't wait until morning.

He headed back.

Somewhere on this island . . .

But even if he found her, what? After all of this, after all the years of his father, what then?

"Who's Toby?" That's all she had to say. "What child? What son?"

She might even call the police.

Suddenly, almost in alarm, he became aware of what he was doing. Squeezing the steering wheel, as if squeezing the truth from her throat.

• • •

He woke to darkness and the faint sound of voices and footsteps moving past his room. He turned on the lamp and looked at his watch, was disappointed to see it was only twenty to three. There was a distant sound of a car starting up. And he vaguely recalled the occasional coming and going of other cars that hadn't quite wakened him. A shack-up place for the mainland, no doubt.

He started to turn out the light, but knew he was too awake to try to sleep. He wished he could hop out of bed and start the morning. It was too warm for him in the room, and he turned down the thermostat almost to off. He opened the drapes just enough to look out. Beyond the dunes, the ocean had become quiet.

He didn't even have any books or magazines—he'd finished them in Philly and forgotten to pick up any others. All he had was an old *Reader's Digest* he found in the office, some of its pages ripped out. And even Judy—I wish, Judy had said, I was there; but had to whisper it and get off soon, for she was ensconced in her world again, with Donny insisting on calling into her room with a "headache."

He turned on TV, but only one of the two working channels was on—a summary of the day's news, which he guessed would be followed by a final melange of Niagara Falls and the Grand Canyon and the playing of "America the Beautiful." He left it on for the sound, tried to go through the *Digest* again, then put down the magazine.

He lay in the light, knowing it was going to be one of those nights.

He was picturing going to the Municipal Building, and them saying no, what's it for? And the hospital—why should they give out a dead man's address? Hit all the open places along these eighteen miles?

"I'm really close this time, David."

Had it been like this? *Knowing* something, but then going to see Tucker, and having it all end with the man's suicide? And going home frustrated and purposeless, to die?

It was so goddam sad, maddening.

No matter what had driven the Old Man to get involved, whether the need for his name in headlines, or he had nothing else going for him—no matter what, he'd cared about a little kid nobody else gave two shits for. *Nobody.*

David lay trying to calm himself, barely watching the screen as someone came on and made some kind of announcement; then it went blank. He left it on. It made a kind of humming sound.

He stared at the white screen, but his thoughts began to go to Judy. He thought of her in the Poconos and how beautifully she'd drawn the old nurse out, and her sadness about the boy, and being with her in the hotel—the marvelous burst of passion, and afterward just being together. And missing her when she left for Boston.

He missed her now.

It was calming thinking of her, even missing her.

He wanted her here in bed with him, and in a way she

was. But somehow—it was strange—he didn't really want it to be here, not in a shack-up place.

•   •   •

The TV was still on, brighter than day, when he woke at a little after eight. He made instant coffee and drank it standing by the picture window. The ocean was gray-green, teethy in the wind. Later, when he walked out, he saw that the cars he'd heard in the night were gone, leaving only his and what probably was the desk clerk's. He stopped in the office just long enough to find out where the Municipal Building was.

The island, this part of it anyway, looked almost completely closed. The houses—pastels and redwoods and weathered-wood grays—seemed as empty as their decks. Some, on high pilings, stood squarely at beachfront; others, toward the bay side, were on windswept, sandy streets. Some backed on street-width canals.

By the time he got to the Municipal Building, part of which was police headquarters, he decided against stopping here first. He'd need a damn good reason for them to give anything out, and he might only end up involved with the police.

He headed toward the causeway.

There were several people on the streets now; he passed an open grocery store and real estate office. He was thinking about stopping in, when he saw a drugstore. Surely a druggist would have know Dr. Sorris.

But the man behind the counter said he'd never heard of either of them; there were, he said, three other drugstores at the other end.

He turned onto the causeway. The sun had come out, and the water sparkled. Manning Hospital was three miles down the road he'd come on, a few blocks off on an intersecting road. He parked his car on the lot and sat looking at it—a two-story, beige-brick building.

Whoever he talked to might know her, might tell her about him, about this guy . . .

"So close . . ."

It was strange, how even his hands on the wheel suddenly reminded him of his father's.

He slid out and followed a nurse, in a thin sweater and hugging her arms to her, up the steps and into the lobby. He walked over to a huge circular reception desk at the center.

The administration office, he was told, was the first office down that hall there.

The door was open. A young woman at the first desk smiled and asked if she could help him.

"I hope you can. I'm trying to locate the family of a doctor who used to be on the staff. He died a few years ago. I lost their address and I was wondering if you still happen to have it."

What was his name? "Sorris—Andrew Sorris. He was an obstetrician."

"I'm not sure where to look," she said. "Let me talk to the assistant administrator." She stood up to go to a back office, when one of two other women sitting at the desks said, "Do you mean Sandy's husband?"

He felt a burst of fire in his face. "Yes."

"Oh. She does volunteer work here. Recreational therapy. Why don't you try the volunteers' office?"

It was four offices down the hall; but the glass door was dark. He wouldn't, he knew as he stood out in the hall, have gone there anyway. It would be the same as telling her he was here. He went out to the lobby and sat down, trying to think what to do.

In this hospital.

*Here.*

But even if he found her . . .

He was back to that. But find her first, see her, be sure. He wondered how he could find out where recreational therapy was—without asking, being obvious. There had to be a hospital directory somewhere. Looking over at the reception desk, he saw stacks of booklets and pamphlets; he went over and glanced through them. Health education things, mostly—regular blood-pressure checkups, mammograms . . . He scanned them, mostly because he felt that the security guard standing by the elevators might be watching him.

Then he saw a plastic-bound booklet a little farther away, hanging from the desk on a chain. It said simply MANNING HOSPITAL, and when he opened it the first thing he saw was a map—on one page, a map of a lower floor, and on another a map of this floor, and on another a map of the second floor. But though the maps were divided into rooms and sections, they had numbers instead of names.

When he turned the page, however, he found a list of offices and departments, with their numbers. Recreational therapy was Room LL215. LL?

Lower Level!

Just to see her . . . that's all he wanted. To be able to recognize her when she came out.

He returned to his chair with a couple of the leaflets. Occasionally he looked up, as if at some of the other people sitting there, but just to take in the guard. At one point the guard was talking to a doctor, his back turned. But when the doctor left, he surveyed the lobby again.

David looked back at a leaflet. Then, after a few moments, his eyes lifted slowly. And the guard was gone.

He stood up quickly, wondering if he should go to the elevator or the stairs. He decided on the stairs—might have to wait too long. As he walked down, he was suddenly afraid the downstairs door might be locked from the other side. But it was open. He walked slowly along the corridor. One hundred ninety-nine. Two hundred.

The door to 215, he could see, was open.

He walked past it slowly, glancing over. He saw several patients in robes at round tables. He stopped near the end of the hall, waited, wondering should he really peer in this time. His heart was almost pumping away his breath. He started walking back.

This time he saw a woman in street clothes leaning over one of the tables. But all he could make out was a green skirt and brown loafers.

•   •   •

He sat outside in the car, taking in every woman who came out. He'd been here over two hours now—and she could be in there all day.

And might not even be Sandy.

Every so often he would turn on the motor so he could put on the heater and radio.

And then suddenly he straightened. A woman wearing a three-quarter-length toggle coat, the hood back and light-brown hair blowing around her face, was coming quickly down the steps. He caught flashes of a green skirt, brown loafers.

He started the car. He didn't know where she was parked, but he could hear the sound of a motor. And now a car was pulling out somewhere behind him.

He had to go forward—another car blocked him in back—and he drove quickly to the exit. He pulled out to the street in time to see a blue compact make a turn into another street.

He turned into it, but the car was gone. He drove up and down streets, but nothing. Then he sped out to the road that led to the causeway. He wanted to stand on the pedal; was going close to eighty. But he saw only one other car ahead—a Jeep, coming away from the island.

# 24

He walked quickly to his room, barely closing the door in his hurry to get to the phone. He called information, then the hospital.

"Give me," he said, "the volunteers' department."

He was just hoping, expected endless ringing, but on the second ring: "Mrs. Holimen."

"Mrs. Holimen"—he leaned forward—"could you tell me if Mrs. Sorris is working today?"

"She was, but she left about a half hour ago."

Then it was—it had to have been her! "Do you know if she'll be in tomorrow?"

"Let's see." Then she said, "She's scheduled from ten to twelve. Can I give her a message?"

"No, I'll call tomorrow. I just want to talk to her about my mother."

"Well, she should be in."

He set down the phone, then drew a long breath. He let it out, then just sat there for a while.

He'd almost forgotten the hatred.

"They had to break his legs," Robby had said. And Robby, with him in the basement, pointed to the boy's knees. "That's the only way they could bend 'em. You die you stiffen up like a board. So they had to break 'em."

He hadn't wanted to believe they'd broken them. And though his father had never hidden the pictures from him, he couldn't ask him about this for a long time, for his father might guess he'd taken them out. So he'd waited until they were out on the desk and his father got off the phone.

"How'd they make him sit like that?"

"Like what?"

"Like that."

"They just did."

And that was that. He hadn't used the word "broken"—it was too terrible—and never brought it up again, just as he never let on how scared he sometimes was at night. So he never really knew, though he always thought of them as broken. And in a way, even though the boy had been dead and couldn't feel anything, those broken legs had been as horrible as the smash to the head and being left on the lot and being so alone at night with all the other dead.

And it was one of the things that fanned his hate, his revenge, whenever he used to catch them.

Sometimes it was just the father or mother, sometimes both, sometimes just an ugly man.

For he used to catch them lots of times, sometimes before he fell asleep, sometimes in the middle of the day when he'd just look up from a book with the thought—and sometimes when his father was down there hour after hour, or away.

•  •  •

It was, Madeline thought, one of the few evenings they were all in the living room together—Herman reading the newspaper at one end of the sofa, Cindy deep in a school book at the other end, she trying—God was she trying—to get through the little pile of homework on her lap.

As if sensing her thoughts, Herman looked up. He smiled. "That was a great dinner."

"I'm glad." She watched as he settled back again with the paper.

How had she been able to make it? And how was she able to sit here, looking so calm?

She wondered should she say it now.

Or, still, if it was crazy to go. Or crazy to stay, when just a day or two, or even just a *half* a day, of talking, comforting, strengthening . . .

"Look," and suddenly she was saying it, "I got a call today."

Herman looked up. He looked at her as he folded the newspaper in his usual way, lengthwise, creasing it sharply with one swift slide of his fingers.

"From an old friend. Lives in Philly. Philadelphia. Her husband died."

"Who is she?" He was folding the paper again.

"Her name's Anne Tucker."

"I don't remember you mentioning her."

"Oh—it was a long time ago. Her husband committed suicide a few weeks ago."

"Really? What a shame."

"She asked if I'd spend a day or two with her. I'd like to. I feel sorry for her. And I'd like to see her."

Cindy looked up at that. "Where you going, Mom?"

"I'm thinking of visiting an old friend for a couple days."

Cindy made a face, and Herman said, "Can you get off, or are you talking about the weekend?"

"I don't know. I'm sure I can."

Herman looked at her quizzically. Then, "Look, whatever's best, whatever you want."

"I'll see," she said.

But now it was settled, she was going.

• • •

Nick zipped up his garment bag and snap-closed his small suitcase. As he started to lift them, Louise said from the bed, "I wish you didn't have to go."

"I wish I didn't either."

"Come here," she said with a smile, holding out her hand. He came over and sat down on the bed. She took one of his hands. "Why"—it was with pretend-anger—"do you have to go there again?"

"I just do. I told you, I have to see the people at Penn."

"I *hate* Penn." And he hated, really loathed it, when she was this way—cooing, her lips pursed. She sat up and put her arms over his shoulders. He could see flecks of powder on her cheeks, the lines above her lip—everything she couldn't hide about her age up close. "What time," she said, "is your plane?"

"I've only got an hour. I'd better get going."

"I can be ready real fast. I want to go."

"You'd be bored to death."

"But I want"—the same coy voice, a little turn of the head—"you to bore me."

He had no patience for this shit right now. "Honey, I've got to go." He kissed her on the mouth. She held on to him.

"I wish," she whispered, "you could bore me right now."

"Honey." And loathed, as he so often did, his need for her, the money. "I've got to go."

She held him a little away from her, still smiling. "You look," she said, "so *mad.*"

• • •

Though she wasn't due in until ten, it was hard to keep from going to the hospital way too early, to see her drive in. But that would be pointless, the point was to follow her out of there. Still, he didn't hold out until much after ten.

Pulling onto the lot, he drove slowly along the rows of cars, looking. But it wasn't until the second time, going even slower, that he saw a blue compact, a Subaru.

He stopped quickly, just to keep looking at it, then drove on, thinking maybe he'd missed another one. But he hadn't. He drew into a space a row behind the Subaru, several cars away.

If she was finished by twelve, she should be out by a quarter after. Unless she hung around, maybe had lunch.

He had the urge to drive somewhere, come back; this was like staring at a phone, hoping it would ring.

But he kept staring at the entrance. Occasionally his hand would go to the ignition, turn it on for just a level of heat. The wind whipped around the car. People coming out bent into it as they came down the steps.

Still, he had to step out for a while, as much to breathe some fresh air as just to do something. And it was shortly after he got back in and was turning the heat back on that he looked up to see the toggle coat hurrying down the steps, the hood up. It ducked into the Subaru.

He had to fight not to take off right behind her, to wait until she had a little start. Then, staying about a block behind, he followed her to the causeway, then to the main road on the island, where she turned left. The light there turned red before he reached it, but he made the turn anyway. His was the only car behind her. She drove about four miles, then made a left, away from the beach. The street was lined with pastel ranchers with pebbled yards. She pulled into one down the street; he drew over to the side.

Moments later he realized how hard his hands were still fixed on the wheel. But it was almost as hard to loosen them. He made himself glance around, saw there were docks behind the houses, a canal. The good fucking life.

He kept the motor running as he stared at her house, wondered what to do.

In there, not only her but whatever she hadn't wanted Raymond Hanson to see.

He couldn't believe what he found himself thinking— looking for an unlocked window one night, trying to slip open a lock with a credit card, smashing a window.

And yet what else?

Suddenly his hands tightened on the wheel again, for she was backing out. She was heading down the street toward the bay. He reached the corner a few seconds after she made a turn. Now he could see her making another turn, back to the main street, the boulevard, that went the length of the island. She was heading toward the other end, past the causeway. He began to see a few more cars, more people out in the wind. There was a small super- market now, another drugstore, a theater, more shops, most of which were closed—jewelry, dresses, seashells, frozen custard.

She was pulling to the curb.

He stopped across the street, watched as she went into a darkened shop. Then the lights went on.

He sat staring; wasn't aware until now how heavily he was breathing. He slid out, not knowing what he was going to do, and crossed the street. He looked in the dark, almost-bare window of a shop several shops away, then in two other dark windows, not wanting to go there fast, he had to think. But he moved to that window now, ISLAND GLOBAL CRAFTS; there was a scattering of things in it— straw baskets, a mahogany cutting board, a wide- brimmed palm hat, a loom. He could see her back, mov- ing about. She seemed to be cutting open a carton; then he could see her reaching up to set something on a rack.

He felt dazed all at once.

Go in? Say Toby and hope she faints or screams? And then, so?

Suddenly the store went dark again, and as the blood churned through him the door opened. Her back was to him as she locked it.

"Pardon me, when do you open?"

She turned, startled. "Next week. But just for weekends."

"Is that loom Central American?"

"Guatemala, yes."

And now she was walking away, and he kept looking in the window with drumming heart, but looking after her at the same time. His brain felt glazed, he couldn't get clear what she looked like—but it was starting to come. A plain, open face, with wide eyes, and the very light brown hair. And though she had to be at least forty, thirty-nine at least, she looked, in those fast few moments, twenty-five, thirty.

And as she drove away he felt completely helpless. But even more than that:

Her?

*Her?*

## 25

It was snowing when he landed in Philadelphia, swirls of
it blowing along the streets to the curbs, but some of it
sticking. His big lamb collar up, he hunched into a cab
and asked for the Blaine. There, anxious to get to Anne's,
he told the driver to wait, giving him a twenty to hold
him.

He didn't believe for a second the bitch hadn't been
able to reach Hanson. Could tell in her voice—it got more
shaky with guilt each time they talked.

He registered quickly—the clerk recognized him from
before—and he followed the bellman up to his room. He
paused long enough to go to the bathroom, wet his hands
and face briefly, then started for the door. But there he
paused, wondered should he give in to it, then came back
and picked up the phone.

Just to hear his voice. It had become almost an obsession to hear it.

"Give me Mr. Kyle's room." He'd forgotten if his room
was 681 or '91.

There was a long pause. "We don't have anyone here by that name."

His body tightened. "I know you just did."

"One moment, please." When she came back: "Mr. Kyle checked out a couple days ago."

"Do you know if he left a forwarding address?"

"I wouldn't have that here. You'd have to come to the office."

There, he learned, Kyle had left nothing.

Given up? Gone home?

It was so tempting to think that.

But Nick had to think that he'd learned something, gone elsewhere—that the son of a bitch now had a couple days' jump.

Nick strode out, through sleet now, to the waiting cab.

• • •

Now tell me again, he said as they sat in her apartment, exactly what he said.

"You mean Raymond," she said.

Who the hell, he wanted to shout into her face, had they been talking about all these days? But he managed to say calmly, "Yes."

"What I told you. That—that this fellow wanted to know did he know where Sandy was. And he told him no. But they got talking and Raymond mentioned that Andrew was named after the doctor. And he knew Sandy kept in touch with the nurse, for she took him up there to see her."

"Nothing else," he said. When she shook her head, he said, "And you've been calling him at his place, not work."

She nodded. "Like I said, I don't know the number. Only that he works nights."

All right, let's go over this again, he said, this is what he wanted her to find out. He took out a small memo pad he always carried and clicked his pen. "Find out if he gave

Kyle the name of the hospital," he said, writing "hospital." "Where it is. Doctor's name. Nurse's name. And," he said, looking up, "if Kyle mentioned anything about going there."

He tore off the page and walked over to where she was sitting on the sofa. She looked up at him, frantically. She was obviously hesitant about saying something, but then it came out.

"Nick, I—I don't know if I can—I don't know how. Tell me how again. I mean, what'll he think my calling up and asking that? It's—it's so suspicious."

He sat on the sturdy cocktail table facing the sofa. He hadn't needed this as confirmation; and he had to stay controlled.

"Anne," he said quietly, "I told you he checked out. What I didn't say, what's concerning me, is maybe that's where he went. And for a damn good reason."

She winced slightly. "Nick, tell me again how to say."

"Just tell him this. Tell him you've spoken to someone—you don't have to say who. And from what you heard, you're more nervous than ever that he's out to harm her. Or I'll tell you what. If he wants a name, or you find you can't do it, I'm here, put me on. All right?"

She thought, then nodded slowly. She stood up. But when he asked was there another phone, she said in alarm, "You don't have to listen. That'll only make me more nervous."

"No, it won't. It's no exam. It's just that you might miss something—we all do. Hey," he said with a smile, "who's the one used to go out and come back with chickens?"

"Oh, Nick," but she had to smile. "I can't believe I did it. I used to hold them by the neck, they used to squawk."

"Squawk. Remember that time we pulled out with three flapping around in the car, and that car coming out after us?"

"Oh, Nick."

He smiled and put his hands on her cheeks.

"This," he said, "is easy."

But in the bedroom he pulled in a breath as he sat on the edge of the bed. He put the phone to his ear.

"Raymond Hanson."

"Raymond, this is Anne Tucker. Raymond, I—I was just talking to someone."

And she was doing it perfectly, Raymond's voice snapping with anger that he'd been so taken—no, he didn't know the name of the hospital, or the doctor's—just that his first name was Andrew—but he did know the name of the town, Parrisboro, and the nurse's name, Mrs. Sandowski.

"But she told me," he said, "she didn't know where Sandy was."

"Do you remember if he said he was going to see her anyway?"

"I don't, no."

"Raymond, would you help settle my mind for me? Would you be able to call her and find out if he called? I'm really afraid of the man."

He would. And oh yes, he'd call back.

Nick came out of the bedroom. Anne's face was as red as her hair. He smiled and put his hands on her shoulders. "See?"

She seemed to go limp. He put his arms around her. He held her for a while, and then let go.

• • •

"What," Judy asked, astonished, "does she look like?"

"Like—like any other person, I don't know what to say. Light-brown hair—almost blond. I really didn't get that good a look. A green coat. She volunteers at the hospital, she does something at this store—I don't know if she owns it. And she has this beautiful home."

"Do you know if she lives alone? Is married again?"

"I don't know, I only saw her alone. And I haven't seen any other car out there."

Did he have any idea what he was going to do? "Right now," he said, "just keep doing what I'm doing."

"David, what if you did talk to the police? Just talk, see what they think, might suggest."

"Judy, it doesn't work that way. If they suggest anything, it'll be get the hell out of here. Either they go in there or they don't. And if they do, and they don't find anything, that's it. And I know it shouldn't be."

She said nothing for a couple of moments. Then, "David?" He sensed tension in her voice. "David, if you're thinking what I'm afraid you're thinking, don't."

He didn't try to pretend he didn't know what she meant. It was as though, knowing him, she knew he'd gone back to that house several times this afternoon, looking at it, playing with ways to do it when the car was gone, trying to determine if the houses on either side or across the street were closed . . .

And he didn't want to lie to her. "I don't know," he said.

"David, don't. This isn't school. This isn't something where they just suspend you."

"No kidding." He couldn't help the sarcasm, but the annoyance he felt was more at himself for not having lied and just ended it.

"Then tell me you're not going to do it."

"Judy"—he was growing angry at her; he hated this kind of pushing—"I don't know what I'm going to do. It would be so damn easy for me to say I'm not, and maybe I should, but I happen to think too much of you. I don't know what I'm going to do. But you want me to say I won't ever consider it? I won't ever consider it."

"Oh, that's great, just great."

"I don't understand. You don't want me to lie, you don't want me to tell the truth."

"I want you to use your damn head, for God's sake."

"Well, my damn head tells me a lot of things."

A long pause, then she said, "You know something?" Her voice was rising. "You really want to know something? Do whatever the hell you want to do. But don't tell me about it, don't get me worried, don't get me thinking. I've got enough on my head."

"You're the one who brought it up."

"Go ahead, play lawyer with me, David, play lawyer— win the debate, win the case. But I'm just telling you. If you want to"—she was hesitating, then it came out—"if you want to fuck up your life, go ahead and fuck up your life. But don't get me caring for you, worrying about you, and fuck up mine."

"Well"—and this too just came out—"then *don't* start caring for me!"

"Good-bye, David."

"Good-bye."

His hand was quivering as he set down the phone. He didn't know who he was angrier at, her or himself. She meant well for him, but that was no comfort. She just didn't know what this was like, had no way of knowing.

• • •

He started to go to Pete and Mary's, but he didn't know why, he was too upset to eat. Instead, he made a quick turn and headed for her street. He'd just thought of something he wanted to see in the darkness, felt driven to see it immediately.

It had begun snowing, but he could see in the headlights that it was slowing up. And it was a wet snow—the wipers moved it away like rain.

He saw what he wanted to almost as soon as he turned her corner. Every house was dark but hers. He parked diagonally across the street and turned off the lights, then the motor. There was a light on at the side entrance, and just one light on in the house, in the back—a bedroom or the kitchen. Her car was in the driveway.

A light soon went on in the front room, then the one in back went off.

He could picture her, or someone there with her, going from room to room.

He wished he could see the rear of the house, get to the yard fronting the canal; see what windows were back there, if there was one on the back door. What he would also have to do is look at the houses across the canal, see which ones were closed up, who might be able to see what from where.

He wondered how often cops cruised through here. He hadn't seen a cop car yet.

And where he'd park. Not out here, the only car. It would have to be where there were other cars, or maybe, if he could, in back of the house.

He frowned as the light in the front room, probably a three-way, suddenly dimmed. Leaving? If she was, that had to mean no one else was in there. If there ever was a time—

He heard the car start up, saw a flare of red on the driveway. Then the car started backing out. He sank down in the seat, afraid it might head this way. But it was going the other way to make that turn down there.

He looked at the house. Then he turned on the motor and put on the lights and followed. He was pulled just to follow.

She'd already made the turn on the boulevard by the time he got there. He sped up a little, but another car came out of a side street and pulled in between them.

After about three miles, both cars drew to the curb near a two-story firehouse. Dozens of cars were on its lot and the streets. Two fire engines stood outside, to make room for the people. From his parking spot he watched her walk to the firehouse. After a brief wait he followed.

A woman stood just inside the doorway; she smiled at him. The place was crowded, though not filled, with people on folding chairs; a speaker stood at the lectern, his voice loud over the mike. David took a chair in back. She sat on the opposite side, two rows in front of him. He watched as she took off her coat. A woman sitting next to her was tall enough to have to bend to say something to her.

As you know, the speaker was saying, we're working very hard to get a light at Twenty-second Street.

Why, someone called out, is it taking so long?

Please, you'll have your turn, everyone will have a turn, the speaker said.

They were, he said, also still working on a light at Seventy-eighth Street. And now about the dunes. This was on schedule, they would have them restored by mid-spring. Meanwhile, those with beachfronts, it's your responsibility to get the fences back up.

The report took about an hour, then people stood up to comment or ask questions. And afterward, even though it had occasionally gotten heated, there was applause. Then everyone stood up, and most people helped fold the chairs and take them in a back room or stack them against the walls. A long table—actually several, pushed together—appeared, and then tablecloths, then two large percolators and paper cups and paper plates filled with cakes and cookies. The crowd moved around them.

He watched her, standing with the woman she'd sat next to. They went over to the table.

He got a cup of coffee and then stood back. He kept watching her. She was wearing a white, fisherman's type sweater and a wrap-around denim skirt. She seemed only to be listening; he never saw her speak.

He walked closer. She had a kind of Slavic face, high cheekbones. Her hair was in a short ponytail. He could see some lines on her face, especially at the eyes.

His chest, he became aware, ached with tension.

He was trying to think how to approach her when her eyes lifted to him, and he smiled. Thought he smiled. She looked back at the other woman without a change of expression.

He sipped his coffee, looked around, trying not to show his nerves. Then he saw the friend move away.

He stepped closer. "Pardon me."

She looked at him, as though caught at something.

"You've got some beautiful things in your store," he said.

She didn't seem to remember him.

"Do you carry any teakwood things?" It was the only thing he could think to say.

"Some. Yes."

"When did you say you were opening?"

"Next weekend."

"Oh. I'm not sure I'll be here. Any chance of seeing it before that?"

"I'm sorry." Then, without saying anything, she drifted over to the table, where she spoke to her friend. The woman looked over, then said something. She came back, just long enough to say, "That's the owner. She says if you'd like. Sometime after twelve-thirty tomorrow."

•  •  •

In his room, the surf tumbling close by, he looked at the phone as he pulled off his shirt. Then he went over to it, called the desk. He felt anxious as he said, "This is Kyle, did I get any calls?"

"No."

He sat back, wondering should he call Judy—wanted to share this with her, but mostly just to talk to her. But though he felt an emptiness of loss, he still had no idea what he was going to do.

## 26

He thought of them in the morning—the pictures. He went over to his suitcase on the floor and took out the manila envelope marked BOY and looked at them by the window. He set all of them down but one, the one showing just the face, straight on. As always, the eyelids caught his attention first—the right one closed, the left one just a sliver apart, as though the boy had been told to close them and was sneaking a look. David looked at the hair, the contour of the cheeks, the length and width of the nose, the curve of the lips.

He opened the door, and as the cold air blew in he looked at the picture again, in pure light, without the window between.

There was no question about it. It wasn't just his wanting something to be so: it was right there. It was, so eerily close, her face.

•  •  •

When Nick heard Anne's voice in the morning, he was sure Hanson had finally called. But it was about Madeline—she was coming in this afternoon.

"I should pick her up," she said, "but I told her to take a cab. I don't want to leave the phone."

"You were in all evening?" He'd left her at five.

"Yes. And I never used the phone."

"And," though he knew this was useless, "you can't think of anyone else."

"Nick, I've talked to everyone I can think of. I told you. And I've been trying to think half the night."

"And there's nothing Sand said. No town, no name, no hint—south, north, *nothing*?" It was so hard to believe, and she was such a stupid, stupid cunt, he couldn't stop trying and twisting.

"No. And I still can't think why she didn't."

"All right, I'll be over soon."

But he dreaded it, the waiting, looking at that face, trying to make conversation, keep her—and now soon Madeline—calm and steady.

He could barely keep himself calm and steady.

He picked up the phone again, this time to call his office. Miss Bruehlman read off the calls, and he marked down the important ones. More acceptances had come in for the fall conference, and Grossman had left for Moscow for the seminar on terrorism—he thought Nick should consider coming in a day or two—and his talk at Bowdoin was confirmed, and Vanbrussen would be on *Nightline* tonight, and, yes, she'd canceled all his appointments for today, should she for tomorrow? He thought so, yes. And of course she should call here with any messages . . .

He sat staring, his face flushed.

To be here? To be worrying about some little fucking shit out there—some crazy, the son of a crazy—who could wreck his life, destroy everything he'd done, could do, would do—goddam it, would do? To feel so helpless—

He swept up the phone almost the instant it rang.

"Nick," Anne said, "Raymond just now called. He just spoke to her. I marked it all down, but there's so much . . ."

He looked at the scribbled notes, then at her. "Did he say Sorris or Soris?"

"I only know what it sounded like," Anne said. She looked terrified that she'd done something wrong. "I didn't ask him to spell it."

"And the woman with Kyle, he didn't say who she is?"

"He didn't say and I—I didn't think to ask. I don't know if Mrs. Sandowski told him or not. All I know is he said she's very upset now."

Nick leaned back in his chair, trying to think out what Kyle knew now that he hadn't before. That there'd been someone named Mad, and where she'd gotten Sandy the ride. And that there was a chance Sandy had gone off with this doctor, maybe even married him.

He looked at the notes again, then made two calls to long-distance information. But there was no Andrew Sorris or Soris in Ocean Bridge, and none in a place that sounded something like Lanoka.

He immediately picked up the phone again, called his office. With all their resources, their library and computer tie-ins, Miss Bruehlman should be able to come up with an address.

• • •

David glanced over at the clock on the dash—he still had more than an hour to kill until twelve-thirty. He sat parked at the northern tip of the island, on a road that ended at the beach. Everything around here was closed— a luncheonette that sold bait and tackle, a custard stand, a souvenir shop, a little farther down a motel. Ahead the bay, gray and thorny, curved toward the ocean.

He headed back slowly, now and then turning into side streets toward the bay. It was lined with marinas here. He saw just one man; he was crouched in a parka on the bow of an old, peeling cabin cruiser.

Rectangles of pilings stood on vacant lots, waiting to be topped with houses. Some were being constructed, stood in plywood and bare beams; occasionally he could see men inside.

He passed her shop at twelve, drove on to the other end, where the island narrowed even more, almost to the width of the road itself. This, the whole island, was the kind of place he and Gina used to love. And how Sara loved the ocean. He thought of the movies they'd taken of her, she couldn't have been more than seven months, with Gina holding her hands and her feet thrashing the surf.

He couldn't think of Sara, here, without thinking of the boy.

He could understand cops the way he never had before. Beating the shit out of a guy you know has murdered, crippled. Knowing, really knowing, and snapping, because this is the only way you have.

He drove back, worried—as he'd been much of the morning—that she might not be there, that it might be the owner. But as he approached the block he saw her car. The only one.

The door was locked. He rapped gently on the glass. It was a little while before the door opened. She looked at him silently.

"I appreciate this," he said.

She closed the door behind him. Her face was expressionless as she said, "I won't be staying long. But you can look around meanwhile."

She went behind the counter. As he looked at the shelves—only partially set up—he would glance over. She was working on something—a leather belt, he saw now, punching holes through it, then cutting it.

He picked up an ivory piece, an abstract figure of a seal, just a little larger than his palm, and set it down. His eyes kept going over to her. As she sat crouched on a stool, he tried to look at her in profile. But she'd released the ponytail, and he couldn't see her face for the hair.

What happened that day, so long ago?

Had she alone killed him? Drunk? Tripped out? Or a pathological case, reaching out in fury for the nearest object to swing? Or was it a boyfriend, a husband, and she was shielding him?

He'd read of so many cases—a husband, a boyfriend, kills a child, and the mother, for Christ's sake, protects him.

Her child, her flesh and blood—yet *protects* him.

An animal wouldn't do it, would fight, try to kill.

"Where's this from?" He held up a small teak box.

She looked over at it for several moments, appeared to be thinking about it. "Australia."

"It's handmade, of course."

She nodded, then went back to her work.

"Very nice." He put it back, picked up a teak picture frame, then a gazelle. He looked at her again. "Do you do a lot of that?"

At first she didn't seemed to know what he meant. Then she looked at the belt, then at him again. She nodded quickly.

Like, he thought, an idiot's nod.

"Are any of your things here?"

"Not yet. I'll be bringing some in."

He began looking around again, was trying desperately to hang on in here, didn't know how, wasn't even sure what the purpose was. He asked about a number of things—some had no price on them—then finally, after two rounds of the shop, came back to the teak box.

"How much is this?"

She came around the counter, looked at it in her hand. "I don't know this one. Jeannine hasn't marked them all yet." She would try to reach her. But after dialing twice, and waiting, she hung up. "She isn't home."

"How could I find out?"

"I don't know today, I'm going to have to leave soon.

Could you call here later? Maybe Jeannine will be in, and I'll leave a note for her. Or can you call tomorrow?"

"I'll call or stop by."

In his car, he sat for a while, letting his body go limp, letting himself feel all the frustration and anger he'd had to fight to hold in. He kept looking at the shop.

He still had a tenuous link to her. But after tomorrow?

## 27

He hated to drive away. Back there in that head, bent over a strip of leather, was the whole horror; ahead, just this gray empty day and all of the night. He'd thought he had felt all there was of frustration, but this was a hundred pulse beats beyond. And there was absolutely no way out now, no way to just go over that causeway and drop the car off at the Philly airport and take a plane back to L.A. No way to just live with this.

He started to drive aimlessly, then thought of some stores he'd seen and made a U-turn. He went into two before he found what he wanted—some pads of legal-size paper. Maybe he could do some work on the Cade. He picked up a couple of newspapers, a daily from nearby and a local weekly, then went over to the paperbacks. They had two copies of his latest Cade. He picked up the top one, glanced at it before setting it back, then bought an Updike and a P.D. James.

At the motel, he ripped the plastic wrapping off the

pads, sat down with one—then just kept looking at it. He could hardly remember where he'd left off with Cade. Even more, couldn't get himself thinking about it. He pushed it aside, picked up one of the papers, began flipping through it. He paused to look at an ad headed YOUR MANNING HOSPITAL.

There were columns of boxed listings for various counseling groups. Drug abuse. Caring for elderly parents. Single parents. Then all at once one riveted his attention— NATURAL CHILDBIRTH. Under it was: Every Fri. eve., 6–8. And it was given by a nurse, and Sandra Sorris.

He kept staring at it.

It had to. Confirmed a field, an empty house, a barn, a commune.

He kept thinking of her with her hair down over her face, bent over a piece of leather.

He'd break into that house if he had to. But if only he could get inside that brain.

• • •

Why had she come?

It was like a drumbeat within Madeline as the plane rolled slowly to the terminal.

She forgot her reasons, knew only that she wanted to go back, just bury her head.

Her hands, icy, lifted her carry-on bag to her lap.

Maybe, she thought as she walked, it wasn't too late to call Anne from the airport, pretend she was still in Boston. Or maybe just go there for an hour, two.

But she dreaded even that—*loathed* Nick, didn't want to see Anne, who was from a different life—

But there she was, waiting. Madeline recognized her instantly—the same face, the same red hair; but Anne looked through her, then all around her, before her eyes came back. Then she walked forward quickly, waving.

"Oh, Mad." They hugged, hard, then looked at each

other. "Oh, Mad, it's so good to see you, I'm so glad you're here."

"I didn't expect you here."

"I know, I was waiting for a call. Let me look at you."

"Don't"—and then it just came out, as if it were important—"I've gotten so fat."

"No, you look wonderful. Do you have another bag?"

"I put it through. But I don't think I can stay long, I—"

"You'll stay as long as you want, I'm so happy to see you."

Anne started to bend for her bag, but Madeline took it. Then as they started to walk, Madeline felt a sudden turning in her head. She wanted to grab hold of something. "Anne, I've got to sit down."

She managed to get to a chair. Anne kneeled in front of her, took her hand.

"I—just feel a little faint. I'll be all right."

She felt her stroking her hand. "Maybe you ought to put your head down."

It was like hearing her from the past—always with practical advice, chicken soup for colds, Mercurochrome for every scratch . . . Madeline shook her head. "It's starting to go away."

Anne took the chair next to her, but still held onto her hand. Madeline pulled in several breaths. She felt cold all at once, clammy; but her head was clearing.

"Can I get you something?"

"No." Madeline looked at her. She wanted to say many things to her—Annie, why did we do it, why did we do it, who were we, why did we let him lead us around, *touch* us? But she said what was most urgent: "Tell me what's happened."

"It's—" Anne gestured helplessly. "I don't know, Nick's waiting for a call."

"About what? Tell me." For Anne suddenly looked in panic.

"He was up in the Poconos, he found out—"

"Who was up in the Poconos? Who?"

"*Him.* He was up in the Poconos. And he knows you got her a ride on the truck."

"Oh, God." Her hand flew to her mouth. "Oh, God, how?"

"He just knows, he found out."

"My *name*? He knows my name?"

"He knows Mad. That she called you Mad."

"But he doesn't know my full name."

"I don't think, I don't know."

Madeline's hand went into her hair. But even if he didn't, wouldn't he put it together, remember calling her?

"Where's Nick?"

"At the apartment."

Madeline picked up her bag. She still felt a little faint but was walking through it. And soon was walking so fast that Anne was almost running.

• • •

Nick was standing looking out the window when he heard the lock turn in the door. He turned, and Madeline walked in with her bags, followed by Anne. Madeline set them down and looked at him.

"Nick," she said simply.

She drew off her gloves and stuffed them in the pockets of her black down coat. Anne said, "Let me have your coat," and then helped lift it off her and hung it in the foyer closet. Madeline watched her take off her own coat and hang it up. Nick still stood by the window, looking at them. Her tension came across the room, to his. She didn't seem to want to come into the living room yet, reached into the closet for something in her coat, a tissue, and blew quietly into it and put it back. Then she looked at Anne, who said, "I'll put your bags in the bedroom."

"I'll take one." And Madeline followed her with it into

one of the two bedrooms, which, Nick heard Anne say, had been one of the children's. Then Nick heard Anne ask did she want to unpack now, and Madeline said just this one, she just wanted to take out a few things. Nick sat down on a wing chair.

They came out, Anne saying, "Would you like something to drink? Coffee? Tea?"

"No."

"Would you like something else? We have a bottle of something—it may be Scotch, I don't remember."

"No, nothing. I'm fine."

"Nick?" Anne asked.

"No."

Madeline sat down at one end of the sofa. She had on a pink cashmere sweater, which sagged with the bloat of her low breasts; he hadn't noticed, when he'd seen her last, that even her legs had become heavy. She wore a gold necklace and two rings, one a large diamond.

"Do you want," Anne, still standing, asked her, "to call home? There's another phone in the bedroom."

"No. I may call later."

She looked over at Nick; it was the first she looked at him at any length. He could see her throat move as she swallowed; her hands rubbed lightly at each other on her lap.

"Nick"—her hands were rubbing harder—"he doesn't know my full name, does he? I can't get it clear from Anne."

"I'm sure not. We'd have heard. Anyway, she rarely called you Madeline, did she?"

"I don't remember." She touched her cheek, frowning. "I don't know. And she went off with this doctor?"

"We're not sure either. But it sounds like he met her here. And she'd been talking about maybe getting married."

Her face becoming more distressed, she turned to Anne,

who was sitting turned toward her at the other end of the sofa. "I don't understand why she never told you anything. She was here, she worked with you and Roger. Did you have a fight?"

"No." Anne shook her head. "I've told Nick."

"You mean she was here for years, then gone. Just like that."

"Mad, you sound angry. Don't be mad at me."

"I'm not mad, I'm just *asking*."

"Even that. You make me sound dumb. You always did. And like I'm to blame I don't know where she is." She began looking around frantically, then back at her. "I didn't have a fight with her. But I'm going to tell you something, I—" But she didn't seem to know whether to go on. "I did have fights with Roger. Not fights—a few arguments. I mean, over her. And—I'm so ashamed. Like, he was paying too much attention to her—did she have a good enough apartment, a good job. I'm ashamed. But I didn't care that she left, I was glad she left. And I'm going to tell you something, Mad. I didn't care she left—and I thought of you."

Madeline looked at her, frowning.

"That's right," Anne said. "Like that time you didn't care."

"When I didn't care what?" She looked startled.

"When you put her on the truck? You weren't glad she was out of there?"

"That's not true!"

"It's true and you know it."

"That's not fair." Madeline lowered her head, put her hands to her forehead. Then her shoulders began to shake; tears started streaming down. Anne was crying too, quietly, pressed into her corner of the sofa.

Nick looked at them, wanted to just go over and grab each of them by the back of the head and smash their faces together. He said, quietly, very composed, "You're both acting pretty silly."

isn't," and hung up and said, "A wrong number." She started to walk away when it rang again. She picked it up, annoyed. But then she began nodding quickly at Nick, and said into the phone, "He's right here, hold on."

Taking it from her, Nick said, "Hello?"

"Mr. Ellis," Miss Bruehlman said, "the only Dr. Andrew Sorris we've been able to come up with is listed as deceased."

"When did he die?"

From the way she hesitated, he knew she hadn't gotten it. "I—I'm sorry, I'll check on that, I'll call you back."

"Do you have an address for him?"

Yes, they had two. One was in Parrisboro, Pennsylvania. The other, a later one, listed him as being affiliated with Manning Hospital, in Endewin, New Jersey. "I also," she said, "have quite a few messages for you."

He had to hold on until she read them off. The instant he hung up, he called Manning Hospital.

"Can you tell me," he asked the operator, "how I can find out where a doctor who used to be on your staff lived?"

"The only office I can think of is closed now. It's after five and they're gone."

"Let me ask you"—it was a sudden thought—"are you anywhere near Ocean Bridge?"

"Yes, we're about five miles away."

He hung up, looked at the women. Anne had hold of Madeline's arm as they stared at him.

"Nick, what is it?" Madeline said.

But he didn't want to interrupt his thoughts.

Maybe. Just maybe.

He picked up the phone again.

"Do you," he asked information, "have a listing in Ocean Bridge for a Sandra Meghan or a Sandra Sorris?"

# 28

The next afternoon, approaching the shop, David saw two cars parked outside. He parked half a block away, across the street, where he had an open view of the shop. He'd been afraid of this, didn't want to go in while someone else, probably the owner, was there.

He sat watching, the motor on, the heat low.

He wished he'd brought along one of the pads—he'd been scribbling away on Cade most of yesterday afternoon and this morning. And it felt just like that—scribbling; didn't even want to read it yet, just wanted to try to keep busy.

He wondered should he go somewhere for a sandwich and bring it back. All he'd had was early coffee.

Someone, he saw, was working in the window of a nearby sportswear shop, probably readying it for opening. He hadn't given any thought until today that they'd entered March. He was still trying to make up his mind whether to grab something quick, when he saw a woman come out of the crafts shop to one of the cars. It was the owner. But she wasn't wearing a coat or jacket, and he saw now that she'd run out just to get something from the car.

A half hour later she came out again. This time she had on a coat and a ski cap pulled over her ears. He waited until she drove off; waited a couple of minutes more, so it wouldn't seem suspicious.

Again, the door was locked. She came to it after a couple of gentle knocks.

She gave him no look of recognition; maybe just a slight nod, then stepped aside until he walked in. Then she went over to the counter and brought out the little box from underneath.

"It's eighteen seventy-five," she said. "And you'll see"— she turned it over, and showed a tiny golden sticker they'd since put on—"it has the artist's name on it."

"All of your things are handcrafted, aren't they?" A question he grasped at; was trying to think of other things.

"Yes."

"Well, I think this is very nice," he said, turning it in his hand. He handed it to her. "I'll take it." But now what? "Do you mind if I look around?"

She said nothing, began putting tissue in the box. He walked around, slowly. They'd added, he noticed, more things. He picked up a small brightly glazed figure of what was apparently a white leopard. "Where's this from?"

She seemed to have difficulty answering. "Here."

"You mean on the island?"

She nodded.

"It's very unusual." Which it was—somewhat crudely done, but that gave it a kind of power. And gave him something else to ask. "Is this person a professional?"

She seemed a little surprised that he asked. "No. I help

out at the hospital, in recreational therapy. One of the patients made it and I liked it, and I thought we could sell it for her."

"I really like it." He set it on the counter, then moved on, looking. Among the new items, he saw, were several leather belts, two handbags, and a jacket with long fringes.

He turned to her. "Are these yours?"

She nodded. Turning back, he had the curious feeling she might have brought them in because he'd asked about her work.

He took down one of the belts. "Is this the one you were working on yesterday?"

She nodded again.

"I thought so. This is the only one that's cowhide, isn't it?"

"Yes."

"Someone told me they generally require different tools to make."

"Yes, it's heavier than most leathers."

"The ones I saw didn't have buckles, they were like looped together. This is a beautiful buckle. You didn't make it, did you?"

"No. There's a man in Norfolk who makes them. We have a display of his buckles over there."

He looked at one of the bags, aware she was watching him. "This is some piece of work. Can I ask how you follow a pattern when you cut? Do you tape it on?"

"Usually. Or it might slip. But sometimes I follow by just looking at a pattern."

He looked at it more carefully. "You didn't add the fringe afterward, did you?"

"Actually I did." She came from around the counter. "Usually I don't. But the leather was too short to fringe, so I added it on." She turned it over. "I sewed it here, on this hem, so it doesn't go through."

"You wouldn't notice it."

"If you look carefully."

"I wish," he said, "I had someone to give these to. Beautiful work. Really. You don't make anything for men?"

"Yes, but I don't have anything right now."

"Do you make sandals?"

"I have, but I haven't lately."

"I bought a pair in Greece, I'd say nine, ten years ago. A little shop in the Plaka. Would you believe a poet sandalmaker? I bought the sandals because of his poetry. They're almost as good as when I bought them. I only hope his poetry lasts that long." He was hoping he'd see a trace of a smile, but nothing. He moved on, struggling to think how to keep this going. He looked at a small raffia basket, then a porcelain plate with little abstract figures on it. "I knew a woman who did this kind of work. I remember she said she only did underglaze painting. I believe the other is overglaze?"

"Yes."

"She said she did it because it was harder. I guess that's as good a reason as any."

"Do you do any crafts?"

It came as a surprise, out of silence—that she'd volunteered something, was not just answering a question.

"No. Not since I tried to make model airplanes that never flew."

"I—just wondered." She seemed to be sinking back into herself. "You seem to know about leather."

"Oh. I did an article on someone who did, and I picked up a little."

"I—was just wondering," she said.

She started to go back to the counter. He said, "Do you do most of your work here or at home?"

"Mostly at home."

"And home is here year-round?"

"Yes."

"This is the first time I've been here," he said. "And I was thinking, I'd like to spend a winter here. I can picture getting snowed in, and I don't think I'd mind it."

"No, we rarely get snowed in."

"There goes another fantasy. I'm going to ask you something I'm sure you hear a lot. Do you like it better in the winter or summer?"

"Winter. It's too crowded in the summer. You're not," she asked after a pause, "from Jersey or Pennsylvania."

"No."

"I was wondering. That's who most comes here. And New York."

"No, I'm not from New York either. California. Los Angeles."

She nodded. Then, after another pause, "You said you did an article on leatherwork?"

"Well, it wasn't only that," he said. "I did a profile on someone, and this was one of her hobbies."

She said, hesitantly, "What kind of things do you write?"

"A lot of articles. And books—novels."

Her face, almost expressionless through all of this, took on a slight look of interest. "What's your name?"

For an instant he could only think Kyle—but she might know Kyle. And the best he could come out with quickly was, "David Kale. But the novels aren't under that name. I use T. L. Weston."

She didn't ask why. "What kind of books do you write?"

"Thrillers. Suspense. They're paperbacks."

She nodded; everything seemed to require thought. "Are you just visiting?"

"I'm not visiting anyone, if that's what you mean. But I'll be staying here awhile. I heard about the island and I thought it'd be a good place to work."

"You're a writer," she said, "you might be interested in a book sale over in Endewin. It's a book fair at the Methodist church, but it's for the library. I think it's a dollar a book, something like that. This is the second night, I don't know what's left."

"Oh, I might go over."

She picked up the figure of the leopard. "Do you want this?"

"Yes, I do."

She looked at the bottom and read off the price.

"That's fine," he said.

He watched her wrap tissue around it, could feel her withdrawing again. She put it in a separate bag, with IS-LAND GLOBAL IMPORTS and a logo on it.

"Could you tell me," he said, "a nice place to eat here? I've only been to one."

"Which one's that?"

"Pete and Mary's? Near the causeway?"

"That's mostly a bar, isn't it?"

"Mostly. But what I had wasn't bad."

Well, she said, there were . . . And after some thought she named, with a little difficulty, four, two of which were on the mainland.

"Are any of them open for lunch?"

"There's one about two blocks from here."

He paid her for the purchases. She opened the register, then looked at him with dismay. "I don't have enough change. Jeannine just brought a little in. I'm short three seventy-five."

"So you'll owe it." He looked at her, wondering was there a best way of saying this. "Have you had lunch?"

She had been tearing off the receipt, but now looked up at him, a little startled.

"If you haven't," he said, "I was wondering if you'd like to go to that place around here."

"No." She shook her head quickly. "Thank you."

"Can I bring you something back?"

"No. Thanks."

He buttoned his raincoat, trying to buy time, to think.

He said, "You say it's close enough to walk?" He didn't want her to think she would have to go in his car.

"Yes."

"You would," he said, "be doing me a big favor."

She looked at him.

"You'll be back in an hour. I promise."

"I—really don't think so."

"An hour. At the most. And the most you'll have to lose is that it'll be a lousy lunch."

She kept looking at him.

"An hour," he said. "Tops."

Still kept looking. Then, wordlessly, she went in back. He could see, almost in disbelief, her putting on her coat.

For the first time since he'd walked in he was fully aware of all the tensions of his body.

"You know," he said, "I don't even know your name."

"Sandy Sorris."

He kept looking at her back there, pushing the toggles through the loops. And now, pushing the last one through, she was walking out to him.

• • •

It was a wind-beaten, clapboard little place, facing a cove. A surprisingly large number of cars were parked around it; it was so desolate here, otherwise. But they found a table by the long window. She gave a little wave to one of the two women behind the counter and took off her coat. But when he asked if he could hang up her coat, she shook her head. She folded it and placed it on the floor, between the table and window. He looked out at the bay; it was glittery in the sun. Choppy water slapped against the pilings of the empty docks.

When he looked back at her, she was studying the menu, which the waitress had left during the few seconds he'd been looking out. He kept looking at Sandy. Her hair was really much closer to blond than brown, with a touch of red to it. She was wearing it in a ponytail again. Her face looked small above her Icelandic wool turtleneck sweater; there were some freckles across her cheeks and forehead. He looked at the menu.

When he set it down, she was looking at him. Despite the few lines, her face was almost childlike. No lipstick. Her eyes were wide, a clear green.

He said, "Do you know what you want?"

"I'm going to have a chicken salad sandwich. And coffee."

"We've read each other's minds."

After the waitress took their order, Sandy looked out at the cove again. He thought of her as Sam Goldberg had described her—a little thing, no more than fifteen, big-bellied. He could see that. And he could see her by the side of the road years later, big-bellied again, dirty, scrawny, lifting herself into the cab of the truck.

And Toby's mother.

Never for a second wasn't she Toby's mother.

Toby with the legs they had to break.

"Do you," he said, while she was still looking out, "like boats?"

She nodded, without turning. "I sold ours. I kept it a couple years after my husband died. But I never used it, and so I couldn't see keeping it." She looked at him. "How long do you think you'll be here?"

"I thought for just a few days, but it's such a great place to write. And I think part of the story's going to be set on an island like this, so I'm trying to get the feel of it."

"Has anyone told you about the house on Sixty-third?"

"No. I really haven't spoken to many people."

"Well, it's supposed to have been used during Prohibition—there's supposed to be all sorts of tunnels in it . . . I'm trying to think what else. The bird sanctuary. The museum. Not very exciting, I'm afraid."

"Well, I'm not looking for an exciting place. It has a feeling I like."

The waitress brought their order. They ate quietly for a while. She said, "There's no place you have to go back to? I mean, you can stay here as long as you like?"

"Yes. I've an apartment in L.A., but it's just an apartment. I'm divorced, my daughter's with her mother."

"How old's she?"

"Six. They're in L.A. Do you," he said, "have any children?"

"I've a son. He's at Kenyon."

"I know it's in Ohio," he said, "but let me see if I remember where. Yes. Gambier."

She frowned. "How do you know that?"

"Well, they publish a famous journal. The *Kenyon Review*."

"Yes, I heard that. I never saw it."

No, she said, shaking her head, she didn't want any dessert. That had been just right; she'd better be going.

He helped her on with her coat, but didn't put his on until he was outside, when he had to catch it flapping around in the wind. She watched from deep in her hood. They had to walk against the wind.

"Aren't you cold?" she asked.

"Yes."

"Then why do you wear that little thing?"

"It's a conversation piece."

They kept walking, hunched forward. In the doorway, he watched as she unlocked the door. Then she said, "I'll get your things," and she brought the two bags from the counter.

"Thank you for lunch," she said.

"As I said, you did me a favor." He looked at her. For the past few minutes he'd been thinking only of ways to keep seeing her. "Can I push my luck? I'd like to go to the book sale. Would you like to go?"

She frowned slightly. "I have something at the hospital tonight."

"Any chance it'll be over in time?"

"Well . . ." Her frown deepened. "It should be over at eight."

"And the sale?"

"I think," she said, "they said nine." She looked at him, still trying to decide. Then, "Do you know where Manning Hospital is?"

Driving, he felt in a whirl of confusion. It was becoming even more unreal. Yet as he passed the road leading to the causeway, was heading toward the motel, he became aware of something else. And he didn't like it, was puzzled by it—and he shook off the feeling.

But he couldn't shake off that he'd felt, for a while, lighthearted back in that restaurant. As if he'd been out on a date.

29

Nick stood over Madeline as she spoke to someone in the Manning administration office. But the answer was the same he had gotten earlier—they couldn't give out the late Dr. Sorris's address on the phone. And would do so in person only if the request was in writing. He immediately turned to Anne.

"Try them again," he said.

"But I just tried them an hour ago."

"Anne, will you just do the hell what I say? Call them."

Ever since yesterday he'd had her calling several people she knew who owned summer homes or rented places at Ocean Bridge. But the few she'd spoken to had never heard of Sandy or her husband. But there were two she hadn't been able to reach.

And still couldn't now.

"You say," he said to Anne, "it's about twenty miles long."

"I—I think. Something like that. Maybe less. I was only there once."

"And it pretty much closes up in the winter."

"That's what I hear. But I don't know how many people live there." Her face looked agonized, as if she should know something more.

"Well, I'm going up there," he said. He'd been trying to put this off, from having to run around blindly. "You want to come?"

"What'll we do?" Anne said.

"You'll do?" He glared at her. "What I'm going to do. Go from place to place. This way we'll cover more."

"Can you go?" Anne asked Madeline.

"I—I really don't know. I have to be getting back." Like Anne, she seemed to be struggling for a way not to go. "When do you think," she asked Nick, "we'll be back?"

"I don't know, how do I know? We may go right up there and back, it may be that simple. We may have to stay overnight. But I'll tell you what," he said, staring from one to the other. "Do me a favor, both of you stay here. I don't need you."

"Nick, I didn't mean anything," Madeline said. "I just wanted to know."

"We just wanted to know," Anne said.

"Well, just tell me this. You going or aren't you going?"

"Yes," Madeline said, nodding. Anne was nodding too.

He sat down at the phone, wondering what was open at that goddam place if they had to stay. He tried to think how to find out, then dialed information to see if there was a chamber of commerce on the island. There was. A woman answered.

"I'm coming up from Philadelphia," he said, "and I was wondering if you could recommend a place to stay."

"Well, we're not allowed to recommend. But I'll tell you what we have. We usually mail it out, but there's just a few motels open."

Actually, she said, only three. And she gave him the names and phone numbers.

Even as he was dialing the first one, he knew what he wanted to find out.

"Sea Urchin," a man answered.

"I wonder if you could help me. I'm trying to locate a David Kyle. Could you tell me if he's registered there?"

There was a brief silence, then, "Yes, he's here, I'll ring."

His instant reaction was to hang up. But it would be too suspicious. He let it ring on, looking at the women. Then he set it down slowly.

He didn't have to say anything. They just kept staring at him.

He wasn't sure why, didn't want to put it in any concrete form in his mind, but he knew what he wanted.

"I think," he said, "it's best if I go alone."

"But—why?" Anne said. "You said we should all—"

She looked at him, then over at Madeline, who'd sagged onto a chair. Madeline was touching her temples, wincing slightly.

"What's wrong, Mad?"

"Nothing. Just—just a little headache."

"Could you go?"

Madeline looked at her briefly, then at him. Her face had gone plaster-white, but her stare was fixed.

"Do what he says," she said, slowly, still staring at him. "Let him go alone."

To do, her stare said, whatever he wants, whatever has to be done.

•　•　•

Nick went into the hotel while Anne waited out in the car. He gathered up his things and checked out, though he might be back. Anne had the motor running as he climbed in.

"It's only about ten minutes away," she said. A rent-a-car place—the one at the hotel wouldn't have a car for a couple of hours. But she had trouble pulling out of the large parking spot; the car kept lurching until she got it going.

"I—I'm sorry," she said. And he knew, it was no big mystery, her nerves; he was worried about her nerves. Not so much about Madeline's anymore; not with that look.

She said nothing as they drove, but he could occasionally hear her draw a breath. She pulled onto the large lot of cars, said, "I'll wait till you come out."

He went in and used a credit card and they brought the car around to the front. He motioned for Anne to wait, then drove over to where she was parked. She pulled down her window.

"When will you be back?" It seemed hard for her to get the words out.

Instead of answering, he slid out and got into her car. She looked at him; she seemed about to cry.

"Tell me," he said, "what you're so worried about."

"I'm—not." But it was almost like a question.

"I want you to tell me."

She shook her head. Then she said, "I'm just scared again. More."

He took her hand, drew it a little, and she slid over. He put his arm through hers. "Hey," he said, "I'm in control here."

She looked up at him. "I—don't know what I'd do."

Then she leaned her head against his shoulder. He looked down at her.

"Nick," she said.

He could be wrong, but he didn't think so—why she'd told Mad to take care of her headache, she'd be back in a few minutes.

"Tell me," he said.

She looked up at him. There was a slight wince to her eyes as she kept looking. Then she shook her head and buried it against his chest. He could feel her heartbeat through their coats. And the last thing he needed was this. He looked down at her hair.

She sat up soon. "I—I'm sorry."

"About what?" And her being embarrassed was worse, could be more dangerous.

"Come here." He put his arms around her and brought her close. He could feel her hands on his arms, drawing him to her. She pressed her face against his chest. "I'm not scared like this," she said. Slowly she lifted her face, and he had to kiss her. Her tongue darted in instantly. She was feeling around for his back, under his coat. She placed her cheek against his. "Nick, I—I wish I could tell you."

He said nothing.

"How many times," she said, "I'd remember, thought of you." She lowered her head to his chest again. "Nick—are you happy?"

He looked down at her head, trying to think what was best. "No." And more than that, how to get on his way.

"Oh, Nick." She squeezed him tightly. Then, "Can I tell you something, Nick? I—hated her. Sandy. I was so jealous . . . I—I'm sorry," she said, drawing away.

But he brought her back; mustn't leave her like this, embarrassed, the embarrassment turning to anger. He put his arms around her, under her coat. She raised her face, and he kissed her. Her tongue was wild inside his mouth. He touched her sweater-covered little breasts, squeezed them gently, the nipples, then reached under her skirt, to the crotch of her pantyhose. He pressed his forefinger against it; she began pushing, slowly at first, then faster. He could feel it dampening.

"Oh, Nick."

He looked at her as she pressed her red hair against his shoulder, her hips thrusting toward his finger. It was like watching something from afar.

[ 230 ]

"Oh, Nick." And her voice was rising. He kept watching. "Oh, Nick. Oh, Nick."

And now her whole body lifted against his hand, kept jerking and trying to lift higher, then went higher still and dropped away. She lay silently in his arms. Looking at her head, he felt nothing for her, cold; if anything, a touch of loathing within the overriding rush of anxiety to get going.

"I don't know why," she said, shaking her head against him, "I don't feel embarrassed. I feel good."

He hugged her hard, his eyes going to the clock.

•  •  •

Driving off the causeway, the first thing Nick did was stop at a service station for directions to the Sea Urchin. As the attendant started to walk off, Nick said, "Do you happen to know a Mrs. Sorris? Sandra Sorris? Her husband was a doctor?"

"Sorry, I don't."

Five cars were parked on the Sea Urchin's lot. The clerk asked if he'd like a beachfront, the price was the same as the others, off-season.

"No, give me a room facing the street." He wanted to be able to see the cars out there.

In the room he found he could see three of them easily. The other two he could see only by pressing up against the window and angling his head. He went to the phone and called the desk.

"I've forgotten Mr. Kyle's room, could you give it to me?"

"Yes, it's number fifteen."

He walked out, saw that it had to be on the row facing the beach. He walked along the walkway, passed it; the drapes were closed. He stopped at the end, pretended to be looking at something out there, then walked back, again slowly. Then he went around to look at the cars.

[ 231 ]

If Kyle had a room on the street, chances were the car would be in front of his unit. This way he had no way of telling. He went back to the room.

Wherever he sat, he could still see only those three goddam cars. And even if he saw Kyle get in one, he wouldn't know him. Except he was probably fairly young, at most in his forties.

It was getting dark.

About forty minutes later he heard a motor roar. He couldn't see who was in it, but he flung on his coat and went out to his car. He followed it for a block, then saw there were two men in front. He slowed up.

In that moment, two other cars went by, undoubtedly from the motel, speeding off in separate directions.

He sat frozen. His head seemed to be swelling with frustration and fear. And a blinding kind of rage.

# 30

She was waiting just inside the entrance as he pulled up in front of the hospital. As soon as she saw the car stop, she finished buttoning her coat and came out, the hood dangling. She walked around to his side; he lowered the window.

"I'll get my car," she said, her hair blowing, "and you follow me."

"Would you like to go with me and I'll bring you back?"

She looked at him, then walked slowly around to the other side and got in. She immediately lifted the hood and put her hands in her pockets.

"I'm sorry," he said, "I'll put the heat higher."

She sat with her hands in her pockets as the warmer air responded quickly.

"Okay?"

"Fine."

"You'll have to tell me how to get there," he said.

Just, she said, make a right when you get out, then another right at the first light, and it was only a few blocks from there.

They drove quietly for a while. Then he said, "Did you have one of your classes tonight?"

"It's a Lamaze class. I help out once a week."

"Really?" he said, glancing over. "You're not a nurse or a midwife, are you?"

"No. I got interested through my husband. He was an obstetrician."

"Is that how you had your child?"

She didn't answer right away. And he was instantly sorry he asked—it would accomplish nothing, only to make her more guarded.

"I would have," she said quietly, "but it became an emergency."

"I see," he said.

When he glanced over next, she was looking out her window. She kept looking out. He said, though he knew, "Is this where I turn?"

"Yes."

He could see the church now, the entrance brightly lighted. Cars lined the curbs.

"I'll leave you in front," he said, "and I'll find a spot."

"No, that's all right."

He parked a block and a half away. They had to walk into the wind, she holding the hood to her head. As they reached the curb he instinctively wanted to take her arm, but didn't. She began walking quicker, half turned to the wind.

Inside, an arrow directed them to the basement, where a woman at a desk just inside the auditorium smiled warmly and gave each of them a large brown paper bag. The room was filled with long, book-lined tables, and books were piled in cartons on the floor. Most were three for a dollar. The place was crowded, some people carrying a bag of books in each arm or in a shopping cart.

He watched her wander off. He glanced curiously at the titles, but his eyes always went back to her. He saw her, once, talking to a couple, but she soon drifted away, was walking slowly along the tables, occasionally picking up a book, setting it down. He tried to concentrate on the books, but couldn't; it was as though he might look up and find her gone.

"Is this yours?" Her voice, in back of him, surprised him, for he had lost her briefly. She was holding an old, dog-eared paperback.

"No, I use T. L. Weston."

"Oh. I saw the initials. And it's suspense."

She put it back on a table that held only paperbacks. They walked along it, looking. But no. Now, wordlessly, they began drifting along together, to other tables. She picked up a Judith Krantz, and looked at it and asked if he'd read it.

"No."

She looked at it again, then put it in her bag. She selected two other sagas, and he picked up an anthology of Maugham stories and a biography of Sinclair Lewis. The auditorium had almost emptied out.

He offered to go for the car, but she shook her head, though she let him take the bag. He turned on the motor quickly, but couldn't turn on the heater yet; it would only blow cold. She was huddled deep in her coat, seemed to be shivering.

He said, "I could use a cup of coffee. How about you?"

She nodded quickly. "There's a place a couple blocks around the corner."

It was a diner, almost filled. They took the last empty booth, in the far corner. She took off her coat, let him take it from her and hang it up.

"Would you like something to eat?" he asked.

"No. Just coffee."

Her eyes seemed to go everywhere but to him. He

looked at her. She was wearing a gray wool sweater, the collar of her white blouse tucked over it. Her face was solemn.

He found himself fighting off a sense of deceit. Of disbelief. That somehow he was terribly wrong. That she not only couldn't have killed her little boy, she couldn't have known about it.

It was hard, even, to remember everything that led him here, that made him sure. Except he was sure.

He said, "Do you ever go away in the winter?"

She looked at him and shook her head. "No, I've loved it here. But I am moving."

"Really? Where?"

"I don't know yet. But I think maybe Santa Fe."

"It's beautiful there."

"That's what I remember. But I haven't been there in many years."

"Have you sold your house?"

"No. I just gave it to a real estate agent."

"And you'll sell it without knowing where you're going?"

"I think so. I just think it's time for a change."

He smiled. "I love that."

She seemed puzzled.

"I mean," he said, "moving when you want to move. Which is why I've made up my mind not to own anything again. Certainly not a house. Not even a car."

She nodded. "I can understand that."

The waitress brought their coffee. Sandy sipped it black, as did he. He said, "Where did you live before you moved here?"

"Philadelphia."

"Is that where you're from originally?"

She shook her head. "No. Detroit."

"Do you have family there?"

"No. No one close, anyway. And you? Are you originally from California?"

"No." And wondered tensely should he say it. Then he said it: "No, near Boston."

He took a sip of coffee.

"I think it's a beautiful city," he said. "Have you ever been there?"

She took a sip of coffee too. But, before that, she shook her head.

• • •

He pulled next to her car in the lot. She lifted the hood to her head.

"Thank you very much," she said. "I enjoyed it."

"No, thank you. Are you kidding?" He sat angled toward her. "Are you going to the shop tomorrow?"

"I don't know, I don't think so. We're pretty much set up."

"Then can I ask you? Are you free in the afternoon to take a ride? I'd love to see the area."

"You've seen the whole island, I'm sure."

"Not really. And there are those towns across the bay."

"I really don't know what I'll be doing," she said, frowning.

"Can I call you?"

She looked at him. "Well—I don't know if I'll be at the shop. I'll give you my number at home."

Afterward, he sat watching her start her car. Then he followed, staring at the car in his beams; staring, rather, at the dark shape of her head.

The lie, the lie.

And such an innocent face.

And to be able to live with such a horror, to be able to eat, sleep, walk, work!

He hated to cut off onto the street to the motel, to let her drive on ahead; somehow, had to get into that goddam house.

There were at least eight cars parked at the motel. He locked up and walked around to the front. Each occupied unit had a light on at the door, yellow; there were three here, widely spaced. The surf crashed, silvery. He unlocked the door, closed it, threw his raincoat on a chair. He had to go to the bathroom; with all that was on his head, in his heart, he still had to go.

Who, he thought, sitting on the edge of the bed, would believe this? That here he was with the lady his father would have given both legs to catch up with, had given away years of his life to try to catch up with. That here he was talking to her, smiling, looking at books together. And didn't know what to do now, except try to get into that house and just hope.

The phone rang, and he grabbed it at the first ring. But it was the clerk—sorry, he called the wrong room. David put it back on the hook, feeling thumps of disappointment that it wasn't Judy. He kept looking at it, then at his watch. It was ten of eleven.

He'd been tempted to call her several times. Now, somehow, though it was late, the disappointment made it impossible to hold off.

She answered.

"Judy, me," he said. "And before you say anything, I'm sorry."

"No, don't," she said. "Don't. Believe it or not, I've been wanting to call you all night. But Meg has a cold, she hasn't been letting me alone."

"Let me call you back. Or you call here."

"No, no, I want to talk," she said quickly.

"Then let me say something. I am sorry."

"I don't hear it. And I'm the one who should be sorry. I talked to you like you were a kid."

"No. You talked to me like someone who's been with me all the way. And you have. And if it weren't for you up in the Poconos, I'd still be, I don't know where, but I wouldn't be here."

"Come on. Hey, I'm so happy you called."

[ 238 ]

"How are you?"

"I don't know how to play girl games," she said, "so I'll say it. I was miserable. Till now."

"God, I've missed you."

"I love it when you pray."

He smiled. He started to say something, but didn't. Wanted just silence, and she seemed to want to prolong it.

"I was just holding you," he said.

"If you don't let go I won't let go." Then she said, "Don't let go but tell me. Tell me everything."

"Are you ready?" And he told her about being in Sandy's shop and buying the couple of pieces; about lunch and just coming back from the book sale and maybe seeing her tomorrow.

"No, I wasn't ready," she said. Then, "You say she knows you as Kayle?"

"Yes." But, he explained, for some reason he'd let her know his real pen name.

"David," she said, "can I ask you something? How do you feel about her not knowing who you are?"

Judy was so damn perceptive.

"It's a weird feeling. But I can handle it."

"If I know you at all, it's got to be hard on you."

He thought she might say something again about talking to the police. Instead she said, "Look. Whatever you've been doing has obviously been right. And whatever you're going to do I'm sure'll be right. Whatever," she repeated.

Afterward, thinking back on it, he was sure she'd really read into him. How a part of him—only a part, but it was there—wanted to head off over that causeway and let Sandy alone.

# 31

Shortly after eight the next morning Nick walked out of his room to find there were only three cars out there in addition to his own. Cars had been coming and going much of the night, but now the whores and whoremasters were gone. His hands deep in the pockets of his thick leather coat, the fur collar up, he walked slowly past each car. One had New York plates, another Rhode Island, the third Maryland.

Which of those? All he knew was that the first he'd heard of Kyle was when he was in Boston, next Philadelphia, then up in the mountains in Pennsylvania before coming here.

As though sauntering, he walked past them again, front and back. Then something hooked his stare. A sticker on the bumper of the Maryland car, a Buick. A rental car.

Of course. It didn't have to be from the state where you rented. His own had an Ohio tag.

In the room, he found that he could see the car only if

he sat at an awkward angle by the window. He tried to think what to do, then lifted a mirror from the wall and set it, angled, on the dresser. Now he could see it from the chair at the dresser or even sitting back on the bed.

He sat fully dressed against the headboard, dark suit, white shirt without a tie, and his overcoat in quick grabbing distance.

About ten minutes later he quickly lifted his legs from the bed, could hear creaking sounds—someone coming along the wooden walkway. Then there were voices, a man and a child, and he could see them, now, walking to the Rhode Island car.

The adrenaline was going too fast for him to sit back right away. He waited awhile, sitting on the arm of the chair. He looked at his watch—almost nine. He started to go back to the bed, but then heard creaking sounds again. He turned to face the window. A man—he couldn't see his face, just a flapping, tan raincoat—was walking by. And now, in the mirror, he was bending over to unlock the Buick.

Nick swept up his coat, opened the door just enough to see the car back out and then go forward. He pulled on his coat as he strode out. The Buick was just turning into the boulevard. He started up quickly, but tried to pull out too fast, and it stalled. Then threatened to flood. It was a couple of minutes before he could get it going.

He drove about a mile along the boulevard before he spotted it. It was parked with several other cars at a small, storefront place that advertised breakfast and lunch. He took a table near the corner, where he could see everyone without turning. There were about seven people at tables, and two at the counter. One of the two, a very tall, lean guy with brown hair, had a tan raincoat folded on the stool next to him.

Nick stared at him; could hear, faintly, his own breathing.

Him. Had to be. Not only the car, but the age—early thirties.

He was drinking coffee, between chews of coffee cake.

The crazy.

The wolf.

Nick glanced up quickly at a waitress who materialized suddenly.

"Just coffee," he said.

He kept his eyes on him.

*That*, after *him*?

He studied his face, almost wanting to see the pores of someone who could do this to him, could drive him to the edge. A nothing. One of those *Gentlemen's Quarterly* nothings, who had nothing to offer the world but how to wear a sports jacket casually.

The waitress set down his coffee. He kept staring at him, even as he took slow sips. Then suddenly he put the cup down. The bastard was paying the waitress, now was getting to his feet. Nick watched him go by, then took a dollar from his wallet, set it on the table, and stood up. He waited inside until he saw the Buick pull away. Then he strode out to his car.

He wondered, following, if Kyle had already found Sandy, was going there. But David turned into the street to the motel.

And now, as Nick pulled up, he saw him disappear around the front.

Nick sat there, staring at that corner. He wanted to run after him, pound on that door, leap at his throat. Or at night, somewhere, with a rock, just smash, smash—

He sat back, slowly. Again he was aware of his breathing. But it was heavier, this time.

First, find Sandy. He needed Kyle, to find Sandy. And if she wouldn't tell, that's all that mattered.

• • •

At five that morning Madeline stopped trying to sleep— she'd gotten an hour at most. She got her robe, thankful she'd brought her heavy one, but she was still freezing. What did that idiot put the thermostat on? She felt her way through the dark to the bathroom, then waited until the flushing ended before opening the door again, then groped her way to the kitchen. She managed to find a wall switch that lit only a small neon light that illuminated just the sink and stove: she didn't want the light to disturb Anne, who had her door open.

She searched the barely lighted cabinets for coffee, found only instant, then looked around for something to boil water in. Anne appeared in a robe in the archway to the kitchen.

"I'm sorry," Madeline said, "I didn't mean to wake you."

"You didn't wake me. Were you able to sleep at all?"

"Maybe an hour."

"I've been up since three. I was afraid to move I might wake you." She rubbed her eyes, her disheveled hair, then lighted the overhanging lamp at the table. She filled a kettle with water. "I thought maybe he would call last night."

"He just got there."

"Not at night. He'd have gotten there before night."

"Then he had nothing to say."

"I thought maybe." She stood by the stove until the water came to a boil, then brought over two cups, cream and sugar. "Do you want Sweet 'n Low?"

"No, I don't want Sweet 'n Low," she said quietly.

"Do you want toast? You want eggs or something like that?"

"No." It was hard not to scream it. "Nothing."

Anne sat with her at the table, her back to the white window curtain. Madeline looked at her as she sipped her coffee. It was starting again, or maybe never had left—the disgust. It had been so obvious Anne hadn't wanted her to go with them for the car—You don't have to, Mad, stay home, take care of your headache. In that sweet little voice she always could put on. And oh her great concern when she'd come back—How are you, do you feel better, it's dreadful out—and all the while that white, white face had come back the color of blood.

Still? After all these years, and your husband a few weeks dead, to still run after his—his droppings? That's all they were—droppings, his great big favors!

"Do you think," Anne said, "he'll call today?"

"I don't know." Madeline couldn't even bear looking at her.

"I mean, do you *think* he might?"

"Yes, I think he might. No, I don't know."

"Mad," she said, hurt on her face, "you're mad at me again."

Madeline looked at her, then shook her head quickly. "No, at him. What asses we were."

Anne stared at her. "He didn't make us do anything, Mad. We didn't do anything we didn't want to do."

"That's a damn lie."

"No. It's the truth."

"He had this—this power over us, we were kids—"

"Mad, is that what you blame everything on? Is it? Mad, I may not be the smartest person in this world, but there's one thing I've never done is fool myself. I told you I was jealous of Sandy? Wanted her out of the city? Mad, with all the love we used to preach, I always hated her. And you did too."

"Anne, that's a lie."

Anne looked at her incredulously. "How do you do it? Tell me. How are you able to forget? Mad, you know how many times you told me? And you didn't even have to tell me, it showed. Mad, tell me—tell me, how do you forget?"

Madeline turned away. She felt tears starting, closed her eyes against them.

"You know," Anne said, "I've been wondering. And I swear this explains it. I've been thinking—how could you have moved back to Boston? *Boston?* How?"

Madeline wanted to kill her. She wanted to kill her because she'd moved back because her father had died—had dropped dead in his barbershop—and her mother, half-dead herself, and with swollen legs, had to be cared for until they could find a nursing home. And then when the people or whatever it was she'd run away from were gone, there was Herman, the person, the way of life, she'd really been running to.

"I really want to know," Anne said. "Was it punishment? Did you want to get caught? Or was it something else you forgot? Did you think about it at all? Much?"

Don't!

And yet—

So rarely. In the past ten years, almost never.

She was sobbing now, convulsively. And then she began nodding quickly.

"Oh, Anne. I did—I hated her! Hated her she had his baby. I was always saying things to him . . . like why didn't she keep him quiet, didn't she know he was busy, why was she always leaving things around. Things like that . . ."

She kept sobbing, her head down. Then, almost imperceptibly, she became aware that Anne had taken her hand. She was holding it, stroking it.

"I'm sorry," Anne said gently. "I'm sorry. But I just couldn't handle it alone."

• • •

David started calling her at noon, alternating between her home and the shop. It wasn't until almost four that he reached her, at home.

"Hi. David," he said. "How are you?"

She didn't answer right away—it was as if his voice had startled her, that she'd forgotten she'd given him her number. "All right." Then, after another pause, "You?"

"Good. Hey, I thoroughly enjoyed yesterday."

"I did too." Everything seemed to follow a pause.

"I've been trying to reach you. I hope it's not too late for that ride."

"I'm sorry, I had to go out," she said. "But I think so. I just got in."

He looked at himself in the mirror, holding the phone. He kept looking as he said, "Then how about dinner? Can I talk you into dinner?"

"I don't know," she said hesitantly.

"It could be a late dinner—I like late dinners. It could be an early dinner—I like early dinners."

"I really—" She stopped. "I don't know." He could almost see her thinking; was trying to will it, turn it, direct it. "Well . . . I guess. Can it be around seven?"

Afterward, hand still on the cradled phone, his eyes went to the mirror again. His face reflected the tensions of the call. He stood up and went to the window. The day, sunny since morning, was taking on the slight turn of evening. A couple, thick in parkas, was walking near the surf. A seagull stood facing the ocean; another was flying against the wind, kept soaring higher.

He wondered, staring out, what seeing her again, or fifty times, would do.

All he knew was that he wanted to see her.

• • •

The wind had died with the daylight, but it had gotten colder. The motor struggled to turn over, then finally caught. He kept it running for a couple of minutes before pulling out.

The boulevard was empty of cars, though later, about a mile from her street, he saw headlights in the rearview mirror. They were distant; in the brief glance he gave them, looked like two tiny crystals.

He pulled into her drive and left the motor running, for the heater.

He had to wait almost a minute before she came to the

door. Then she said, "I'm sorry, I'll be right with you," and left the door open for him to step in while she opened a closet and flung on her coat. He found himself staring at a framed photo on the piano. A teenager, handsome, face slightly lifted, in cap and gown.

Her eyes followed his.

"That's my son," she said.

His skin had gone prickly. It felt so eerie, looking at Toby, if only he had lived.

# 32

That face stayed with him as he drove. He had the urge to race to the motel and get the pictures and put them in front of her face; could even see himself forcing her to look at them as she tried to turn away. Yet here they were like any two people out on a dinner date, she with her hood thrown back and her hair spilling over, and her small, gloved hands holding her shoulder bag on her lap. And making small talk about which restaurant to go to.

"They're all good," she said. "But if you like seafood or Italian, I guess maybe Saterly's."

"Sounds fine. You?"

"Fine."

She gave him directions, but his mind began surging off again, and soon he was sure he'd made a wrong turn somewhere. When he turned to her to ask, she didn't seem to have noticed, was looking out her window.

He said, "This isn't the right way, is it?"

She looked around quickly. "This will be all right. I'll tell you where to turn."

The restaurant was in what was originally a huge, frame beachhouse that stood on pilings. Completely white, it was illuminated by spotlights on the ground. It was a little more crowded than he'd thought it would be—obviously people from the mainland came here.

The hostess, holding menus to her, led them to a table that looked out on a large deck, and beyond it to the surf.

"This," he said, "is very nice."

She nodded and looked at the ocean. A few faint stars distinguished it from the sky. She was wearing the Icelandic turtleneck sweater she'd worn before. Her hair, out of the ponytail, curved over her forehead, brushed her shoulders.

"I imagine," he said, "they serve on the deck in nice weather."

"Yes." She looked at him. "They have big umbrellas. It's a beautiful view. You can't see right now, but you can see the bay as well as the ocean. Actually," she corrected herself, "you can. Do you see those little lights over there?"

He thought he did, then was sure. He nodded. Those were buoys, she said. She kept looking out there, until the waiter came by and asked about drinks.

"No, I don't think so," she said to David.

"Sure? A little wine? Perrier?"

"No." She shook her head.

He ordered Johnnie Walker Black and soda. When he turned back to her she was reading the menu. He looked at her, at the slight part in her hair, and thought of her fright at the sudden flash of police lights in her landlady's apartment, and of Raymond Hanson and her panic that he might have been in her bedroom, and of her uneasiness with strangers everyone spoke of. She looked up just before his drink came.

He said, "Have you decided what you want?"

She nodded. "I'll have the veal marsala and linguine."

And of the boy, the boy. "No appetizer?"

"No, that'll be fine."

"Let's see." He sipped his drink, then opened the menu. He wasn't really hungry, hadn't been since he'd come to Ocean Bridge—but blackened redfish was the most appealing. And a salad. "How about at least a salad?" he said.

"All right."

"Antipasto? I see there's a Greek salad. Caesar salad . . ."

"No, just a tossed salad. And the house dressing."

Her eyes immediately began to drift around the room.

"So," he said, "how was your day?"

Oh, she'd been at the hospital, then had gone with Jeannine to help her select some things for her house. "It was nice." Then, "How was yours?" which surprised him—she'd seemed, after pointing out the buoy lights, to be growing locked in herself again.

"I did some work. Looked at the ocean a lot. And made some calls. To you," he added.

"I'm sorry."

"I'm afraid," he said, "you don't look very sorry."

He thought he detected a brief touch of a smile—it would be the first he'd seen. Then she looked up at the waiter, who'd suddenly materialized. David asked if he could have his redfish extra hot, and the waiter nodded, writing. The busboy came with rolls, and the waiter soon followed with their salads.

They ate silently, then he set his aside, unfinished, to hold it off until the entree. He took a final sip of his drink.

He looked at her, then out to the ocean. "I wonder if it ever comes up to here. I guess it would in a good storm."

"I imagine. It's been through a few hurricanes."

"What do you do in a hurricane?" he said, looking at her. "Leave? Stay?"

"Just stay. Well, once I had to leave, they made us."

Their entrees came. He eased off a piece of fish with his fork, looked at her as he chewed.

"This is very good," he said. "How's yours?"

"Good."

"Have you ever had blackened redfish?"

"No, but I've been meaning to."

"Give me your fork," he said.

"No, I'm doing fine."

"I'm one of those," he said, "who insist on sharing. Especially with those who don't want to."

And this time there was a smile, a real one. He took her fork and cut off a piece.

"Oh, I forgot," he said, "I asked for extra hot."

She took the fork, chewed thoughtfully, then swallowed. Hard. Her eyes widened a little.

"It is," she said, "hot. But very good."

Afterward, they settled back. She touched her napkin to her lips, which was like a signal to the waiter. Coffee? Dessert? Just, they agreed, two coffees.

"So," David said, "tell me."

"Tell you what?" It was strange—now, she almost instinctively offered a trace of a smile.

"Anything. All right, Detroit. Tell me about Detroit."

"Gosh, I haven't been back there in years."

"Then about your mother, father."

"Let's see." She folded her arms on the table, looked at the ceiling. She looked back at him. "My father was a high school teacher—a gym teacher. But he was a little ashamed of it, he felt the other teachers didn't look on him as a real teacher. And he always wanted to be the football coach, but they made him the soccer coach. It might not sound like much, but it was the grief of his life."

"Why shouldn't it sound like much?" he said.

She shrugged. "It was very, very important to him. I remember he used to come home and say there were like five people at the soccer game and there were ten thousand at the football game. My mother used to say why don't you quit. They used to have big fights over it."

"Did your mother work?"

"She started working in a department store when I was, what, I think when I started high school."

"Was it the same school where your father was?" He fingered the handle of his empty cup, his eyes on her.

"No. Thank God. For his sake. I wasn't much of a student. I hated school, I don't know why. I did very badly. And of course I've been sorry ever since that I never went to college. My husband," she said, after a pause, "wanted me to. But I don't know. He was a very special person," she said, as though to herself. "A very kind person. And a wonderful physician."

"That's such a beautiful word the way you say it."

"Physician? That's what he was. Well," she said. "Anyway."

He looked at her. And for the first time her eyes really lingered on his. Then she lifted the napkin from her lap and put it on the table. Her eyes began to drift again.

He was amazed—he wanted to put his hand on hers.

The waiter came with the check. David asked him to wait, and he scanned it quickly, and chose his American Express card at random from the other cards. They went over to the coat room, and he helped her on with her coat, and walked with his on his arm. He put it on at the door.

The wind had risen a little, and she half turned her back to it as they headed across the pebbly lot to the car. He unlocked her door, while she stood with her hands deep in her pockets, then he went around to his side. He turned on the motor quickly.

"I should have had you stay inside until I warmed it up," he said.

She shook her head, under her hood, her hands still in her pockets. Her shoulders were hunched.

He wanted to reach over and draw her to him. He was sure she would come easily; might even, with the slightest touch on her cheek, lift her face.

The boy's *mother*!

He couldn't believe he was thinking this of the boy's mother!

He set the automatic gearshift, released the brake. The heat was starting to come in.

He said, "Could we take that ride tomorrow?" Yet what was the point? The *point*?

"I'm afraid not tomorrow," she said. "I'm going away."

He looked at her quickly. He felt a searing throughout his chest. "Where are you going?"

"I'm going to New York with Jeannine. We're going to a crafts show."

"How long will you be away?"

"I think three days. I'm not sure."

He drove, never more aware of the loneliness of the streets under the tall curved lamps, of the closed shops, the summer houses; drove past the street to his motel, that fucking, lonely motel, with the empty gray beach and dark ocean; was driving away from those pictures, was driving to a good-bye, I'll see you.

And then return to the loneliness, to the pictures.

To the boy with the peering eye and little smile and the broken legs.

Her street, and he was turning into it. Her drive, and he was slowly turning into it. She put her hand on the handle of the door, but he came around and opened it.

"Thank you so much for dinner," she said. "I really enjoyed the evening."

"I'm glad. So did I." He was aware of each deep breath.

He watched as she went through her shoulder bag for her key.

And even if he waited the three days? Four?

She was turning the key in the lock.

The word was suddenly rising in him, building. He kept staring at her back, bent toward the lock; told himself not to, don't, it—

"Toby."

It just came out. Like a bell on this cold clear night. She stood motionless, then straightened slowly, her back still to him.

Then she whipped around. She stared at him, her face in shock.

"Who—are you?" Then louder, "Who are you?"

She kept staring, eyes wide, mouth open. Then she whirled back, flung open the door, closed it. He could hear something drop against the door, perhaps her, sagging onto it. Then he heard the bolt-lock snap shut.

## 33

He stared at the house, stunned.

Like this? This is the way it ended? After all these years of the boy? All these *years*?

Whatever she'd saved of the boy—pictures, a diary, letters, whatever—she had to be ripping up now.

And he? Just get back in the car? Just drive to the motel and somehow try to get through the night, and then leave and try living out the rest of his life with what he knew?

But though he walked to the car, it was only to stand there and stare at the house.

Why did he do it? He could have waited until tomorrow night, when she was gone, and broken into the house. Could have torn it apart. Or have finally just gone to the police and say fuck it, here's what I know, you'll need a lot more, do what you want.

Could still do that, though there'd probably be nothing now.

He sat down in the car, but only to keep staring there.

Didn't know why—it had been so spontaneous. Just that so much of him wanted to protect her.

• • •

Nick watched as the car's lights went on and it backed out of the drive. When its taillights disappeared around the corner, he drove from across the boulevard to her block, stopped in front of her house.

He had lost them soon after they'd left the house, and he'd decided to come back and wait. He hadn't been able to see her face—but was sure: his instincts were always right. And Kyle wouldn't have just hung around the motel all day if he hadn't already found her, the son of a bitch would have still been scratching around.

He slid out of the car and looked at her home.

He looked calm but was churning. It didn't make any sense her telling Kyle anything, she had everything to lose. But if she was the cunt she was then, she was dumb, could be twisted.

He walked up the drive. A car, undoubtedly hers, was parked farther back. He rang the bell, then after a brief wait rang again. Still nothing. But she had to be in there. Unless she'd left with him again.

Walking back to the street, he looked at the whole front of the house. A few lights were on behind the thin, closed drapes. But then he thought he saw a glow toward the back of the drive, as though a light had just gone on there.

He walked back to the door and rang again.

Where was the fucking cunt?

He started to walk to the rear, to try maybe to see a shadow through one of the drapes. Nothing. He looked back at the canal—she had a dock, every house had a dock. She'd really come up in life. This place had to cost a quarter of a million on up.

"And what's yin?" he couldn't help thinking. But it was the way he thought of her mostly, when he thought of her at all—the high school kid he got talking to in a Detroit pizza parlor. And then it got around to the battered paperback he was holding, and he started trying to tell her about yin and yang, the simplest crap. But though she had a head like a sieve, she tried to pretend, and a couple of days later took off with him. The thing he liked about her was she never made a fuss, even when she got pregnant; you could turn her this way, that. And though her family tracked her down and managed to get her for a while with threats of taking away the kid, he knew she'd come back, though sometimes he used to wish she hadn't.

He walked back to the front door. This time he knocked on the window as well as rang the bell; knocked again. Then, frowning, he stared toward the back. The light back there, the one with the glow, had gone off again. He placed his forefinger against the bell, pressed with the full strength of his arm.

He didn't know if she lived alone, and didn't care—whether it was with a husband, a sister, chief of police, the pope—

The door flew open. And she stood there, face distorted with rage.

Then, as they stared at each other, it became stamped with shock.

"Oh, my God," she said.

"Sandy."

"Oh, God." Her hands rose to her temples.

"Can I come in, Sandy?"

"Oh, God." She kept staring at him as he came in. Then she began shaking her head, hands still against her temples. "What's happening? What's happening?"

He looked at her—he'd half expected her to still have jagged-edged, close-cut hair. He sensed that if he tried to touch her she would recoil, maybe scream.

"What's happening?" She was staring at him dazedly. Her hands began to drift down, but her eyes remained wide. "Why are you here? Who is he? You must know him!"

"I've been trying to get to you first. He's—someone trying to find out. But he's not the police. He's just trying to find out."

Her eyes still on him, she sank down on the sofa. She kept staring at him.

"He knows."

He felt a massive thump in his chest. "How do you know?"

"He mentioned his name." Her voice was a monotone. Her eyes stayed fixed on him.

"Whose name?"

"His. *His*."

"Sandy, whose name?" He wanted to shake her.

"*His*. Toby's." Tears began to form. "Toby's."

"How did he mention it?" Calm it! He had to look calm, sound calm.

"He—just said it. Toby."

"Just like that?"

"I—was going in the house, and he said his name."

Oh, Jesus. "What did you do? What did you say?"

"Nothing."

"Sandy, tell me. You're hiding something."

"I—I was shocked. I said, 'Who are you?' I must have screamed it—'Who are you?' And I ran in."

Oh, Jesus. But had to act calm. "Did you say anything more than that?"

"No."

"Sandy, tell me."

"I am telling you."

Still, the cocksucker knew! Oh, did he know!

"All right, let's just calm it," he said. He sat down next to her on the sofa. "Everything's going to be all right."

She looked at him. Then, with a slow shake of her head, "I—don't know if—I want it to be all right."

"Sandy," he said.

"I don't know."

"Come on." Stay calm. He took her hand; it was stiff in his. "You've gotten a terrible jolt. Come on." He began stroking her hand. "Come on."

Her hand gradually softened. He could see that her chest wasn't heaving as much. But calming her was just step one. And he mustn't rush it.

"Guess where I just came from," he said. "Anne's. Anne Tucker. How come you never told her where you were going? That you were getting married?"

"I—I always knew she didn't like me. And I wanted to be out of her life."

"No," he said.

"It's true. She always thought I was after Roger. And it was never true. So I just thought I'd let them alone."

He looked at her for a few moments before saying, "Do you know that Roger died?"

Her eyes burst wide. "Oh, no. When? How?"

He told her about the suicide, about the old man's visit. She bent her head, crying softly. He kept stroking her hand, looking at her. He waited until she was just sitting there, drawing in quiet breaths.

"You know who's with her?" he said. "Mad. Madeline. She's going to be with her for a few days."

She didn't seem to care.

"She married a doctor," he said. "And she turned Jewish. She's a school teacher, has a daughter. She's put on quite a bit of weight—I didn't recognize her right away." When she still showed no reaction, he said, "Listen, I've an idea. Why don't you call them?"

She shook her head. "I don't want to," she said quietly.

She took her hand from his and wiped her eyes with her fingers. Now, he felt, was the time.

"Sandy, I want to ask you something. If the police ever come to talk to you, do you know what you'll say?"

She looked at him, startled.

"Just remember this," he said. "He can't prove anything—he would have done it by now. So he really knows nothing, and they know nothing. You reacted to the name? You didn't react to the name. It was his imagination. He knows nothing, you hear me?"

She kept looking at him. And the look growing in her eyes was frightening.

"As long," he said, "as you deny it."

She looked down at her hands now; they were clenched in her lap. She kept staring at them, seemed to be tightening them.

"Sandy?"

She didn't look up.

*Sandy!* "Sandy?"

Hands still twisted, she lifted her eyes slightly.

"They know nothing," he said.

"But I do."

"Sandy."

"I—know."

"Sandy, what do you know? It was an accident."

She shook her head slowly. "It wasn't an accident. You did it. You."

"Sandy, they were all there!"

"They were part of it, but I know you did it. I know you!" She looked at him fiercely. "Oh, do I know you! You've never once asked me. About him." And she looked quickly at the picture on the piano, then back at him. "You haven't even asked his name. You've never even known if it was a boy or a girl."

He looked at the picture. Where the hell had his head been? He said, "I've had so many things on my head."

"Not even his name," she said.

"Sandy, don't do this to me." Don't do this, you fucking cunt! Don't!

"Don't do this to you? To *you*?"

# 34

Striding to his car, David almost broke into a run. He backed it out quickly, and almost without stopping shot forward.

He sped along the boulevard. It was going on two. The overhanging streetlights barely held back the night.

A car, he saw, was parked in front of her house. Frowning, he drew up behind it. And saw, with a full burst of alarm, that the door was wide open.

He got out quickly, his thoughts ricocheting to suicide—that she'd tried, or had since succeeded; that she'd first called around, frantically. He started up the drive, then froze. A cry somewhere to his right—he thought a cat—and now the sound of running—she was running from behind a house up the street.

"Sandy!" He raced after her. She stopped, turned, then flung out her hands, gesturing wildly.

"David! Watch!"

He whirled and saw a blur of something and curved his

arms above his head. Pain exploded through his left hand, shot up his arm. He dropped to one knee, somehow rose, grabbed at something with his right hand, the wrist that held the weapon, strained up with it, saw the blur of a man's face, kept trying to push the arm up, kept pushing against him. He staggered forward with him, then fell with him. He punched at the face with his right hand, rose, staggered for a few steps, almost dropping, then straightened, ran. She was still there, hands to her mouth. And now was running with him as he grabbed her arm.

Had to get off the street—the streetlights! Tugging her, his left hand dangling, aflame, they ran to the rear of a house, ran across the pebbled yards that fronted the canal, then sank behind some bushes at the side of a house. His left hand was trembling; he tried to swallow down the pain, keep it deep in there.

She was gasping against his shoulder, on the bad side. He reached across to her with his right hand, held her head to him. Don't cry out, for God's sake don't.

The crunching of pebbles somewhere. The sky was studded with huge clusters of clouds, and now and then the moon broke through.

He rose to one knee, trying to tell where the crunching was heading. Here! He yanked her up, and they ran to the front, then along the street, then to the rear of a house again. They sank down. She fell against him, on the hand. He gasped, almost cried out, and might, it was coming—but he lifted her from it and raised his face to the sky, teeth clenched and holding the hand to him. It was easing just a little. And just a little had to be enough.

The crunching again.

It was following the sound of their own crunching.

"Come on!" A quick whisper and he was rising with her again, and they were running, this time to the boulevard. But it was too bright, and he tugged her, running, across the boulevard, past a scattering of dark houses to the beach. They ran onto it, along the dunes, each step leaden now in sucking sand. Then they slid down the dunes and lay there. The sand was damp, cold, crusted. The waves, roaring as they crumbled, slid along in foam.

"I—I'm sorry." She was gasping.

"Don't. Shh. Don't."

"I—I'm sorry." She was trembling violently. Her face was like ice in his palm as he held her to him. The air was glacial. She had on just her turtleneck and a skirt.

"Here, help me," he said. He unbuttoned his coat. "Can't get it off, I hurt my hand."

"No."

"Help me." He was trying to twist out of it. But this fucking hand. Smashed. "Help me." He twisted toward her. She pulled and drew it down his arms. He bit against his lip, head bent. But, there. He sat breathing through his mouth, holding his hand. She swept the coat over her.

"I'm so sorry. I'm sorry."

"Don't."

"Oh, God, there he is."

They could see his dark figure coming down the dune from the street. He tugged her up and they slogged along the side of the dunes, slipping down, slogging on. They sagged down again, in a little gap between dunes.

They sat hunched over, trying to get their breath back. She was shaking. He kept holding her to him, stroking her shoulder, staring always to his left, body coiled, ready to spring up.

"I—I'm sorry. He—made me call. I—I'm sorry."

"Don't. No more. Don't."

"Shouldn't have— Should let him kill me—"

"Come on, no more." And wished he could cut off this fucking hand. Make some kind of sling. "Who"—he kept sucking in breaths—"who is he?"

"Nick— He—he—he killed Toby. His own—killed his own—ours—killed my little boy. Said"—she kept gasp-

[ 265 ]

ing—"said—it was an accident. And they all—people who were there—said—an accident."

He kept stroking her shoulder, her back, his eyes always to the left; held her in as hard as he could.

"Said—said an accident."

"No more now. Later." Was afraid her voice, though so soft, would carry.

"I—I'm so cold."

She had a long spasm of shivering. He kept rubbing her; pressed his cheek against her head; wished he could close over her with the other hand, the throbbing hand, the fucking throbbing hand.

"We—we were going to break into some stores. Needed food, clothes . . ."

"Later. No more." He put his hands to her face, as much to warm her as to quiet her.

"And he was planning it." She had to keep stopping to breathe. "Said—said keep Toby away—was bothering him. Was only playing. I—tried. I knew how angry could get. His temper. So I tried. But I had—had to go out. And when I came back—"

She was crying now, quietly; he could feel the tears on his hand.

"They said he—he fell on something. Said died on the way to the hospital. And they—they said—they were afraid no one would believe, so they left—left him."

Another long spasm—her body convulsed within his arm.

Had to do something. She'd freeze to death here.

"Made myself believe. He was like—God to me. To all of us. Didn't want to leave. Wanted—with him, stay with him. Stayed. Left only because—because I was afraid for the new baby, became pregnant. And God almost took— took him away, but my husband saved . . . Didn't ever want Andrew to know . . ."

He pressed her head harder to his cheek, but just for an

instant, then peered out a little farther from the slight opening in the dunes. Could see nothing in the blackness. They had to keep walking, moving, maybe just smash into a house, take a chance with the clatter of glass, try to find a knife, something.

"He was such a beautiful boy."

He looked at her.

"Such a beautiful little boy."

"I know." He touched her hair. "I know. Come." He tried to tug her up, but she sagged back. She shook her head.

"No."

"Come on."

She kept shaking her head. "Doesn't matter."

He tugged hard, and she rose slowly. He put his arm through hers, began walking with her, ran a little, walked. The moon came out for just a few seconds, not long enough for him to look back. She was sagging on his arm.

"Come on. There." A house that stood darkly behind the next dune. She fell to her knees, partway up; he pulled her up, then fell himself, got up. And just then the moon came out.

He glanced back along the silvered beach and saw him, about fifty yards away.

She'd looked too, and froze, and kept looking back as he dragged her along. But he had her trying to run now, against the sliding sand; she was digging in with him, struggling up. But then, near the crest, she stopped, turned.

He was almost at the foot of the dune.

David grabbed for her arm, but she tore free, and now was running and sliding down to him. Racing after her, he saw her flailing at him, saw a blur of him swinging, heard hideous thumps, saw her drop. David leaped at him, fell over with him, kept punching with his right hand, then grabbed the arm with the hammer, tried to reach it, to get to it—had it, he had the handle, had to wrench it free, was trying, they were rolling over. And now he had it, really had it, and as they were rolling over again he swung once, twice. Again.

He lay facedown in the sand, then gradually pushed himself up, crawled to her. And though the moon had gone in, even in the blackness he could see the running mass of blood on her face. And how still, how terribly still she lay.

## 35

He reached out and touched her shoulder, hoping some-how it would move beneath his hand. His hand slid down to her hand, to icy, sandy fingers; lingered there for a few seconds. Then he stood up quickly, hearing a moan from the dark mass to his left. It lifted its knees, an arm. They flopped down and lifted again.

He wanted to go to that hammer, hit him again, again.

He ran up the dune and off the beach, pressing his left arm to him, each step a jolt of agony, past all the dark houses to the boulevard. And now he was running along the boulevard, looking for just a pinpoint of light. Some of these houses had to be occupied, just had no lights on; but he didn't know which, had to keep going.

He was aware soon that he'd come to her street; could see light from the house. He could only walk now, each breath a blade, but kept trying to break into a run.

The open door, and he walked into the silence, past the picture, and sank down at the phone, in the midst of her presence. He sat bent over for a while, gasping, then held the phone between his shoulder and jaw and dialed the operator.

But he couldn't remember the street. It was either Seventy-third or Seventy-fourth, or maybe Eighty-third.

He'd wait, he said, out on the boulevard. And there, within minutes, he saw the distant dazzle of lights of a lone police car. He stepped into the street, began to wave.

At the beach, in the glare of the headlights, he walked with the officer to the dune. The beam of the officer's flashlight shot ahead, then to the left, the right, then farther out, in a slow, slow arc—and settled on her. David scrambled down there with him.

An open, fixed eye stared out from the blood. He turned away. He felt something turning in his skull, fought not to pass out, to go to one knee. Then through the tumble and roar of the surf, he heard the moaning again.

Other police cars were pulling up, other officers walking and sliding down the dune. He watched them hovering over the figures, heard the whooping sound of an ambulance, coming fast.

Then he felt, through a daze, a hand on his arm.

"What happened?"

He looked at the officer. He started to say something, couldn't, then felt his eyes fill up. He held his arm tighter to his chest; a full awareness of the pain was back.

He pawed at his eyes.

It wasn't just this pain. There were so many pains.

•   •   •

They took him to the hospital first. A metacarpal bone was fractured, but it didn't require surgery, and they put on a cast from his elbow to his fingers. The police took a statement there, then he was told he could go back to the motel but to wait for word from them. An officer drove him back, and sat out in the car as he went to the room.

His hand was starting to throb again. They'd deadened

it, but he could feel the growing sharpness of the pulsing. They'd given him pills, but he wanted to hold off.

He stood by the window, looking out at the dawn. He felt really cold, for the first time in so long. And the beach and surf were even cold to look at.

It was hard to remember the last time in his life he'd cried, but he could feel it building again. He went over to the bed and sat back against the headboard. He ran his arm across his eyes.

Soon, starting to sink into exhaustion, sleep, he heard footsteps outside, then a soft knocking. It was a detective who'd questioned him at the hospital.

"I talked to Boston," he said. And the way he said it meant they'd learned that the crazy story about a boy was true. Then he said, "Look, you say you got some pictures."

David took them from the envelope, and the detective turned on a lamp and sat on a chair. He kept looking at them, and then at a snapshot.

Afterward he handed several snapshots to him.

"We found these in her place."

And there she was—no more than seventeen, scruffy, rumpled, crop-haired, pretty and sort of smiling, with three other people and with trees in the background.

And this one of her with two other people, one of them—who?—Anne Tucker?

It was Anne Tucker.

He set it down and picked up another. And this time he felt a blast of flame in his chest.

Different place—a field somewhere—and some of the same group. And she was holding a little boy, who was sitting upright in her arms, eyes crinkled as he smiled, and full teeth showing.

Oh, Jesus.

Oh, God.

"Can I take some of your pictures along?" the officer asked.

He kept staring at the snapshot. He nodded.

"Take all of them," he said.

# 36

Detective Perry rubbed his eyes before getting out of the car. He hadn't slept more than five hours in the past three days, had flown down to Philly, then driven over to Ocean Bridge; and though Anne Tucker had opened up right away, the Schwartz broad still hadn't said anything until after she agreed to come back here to Boston. So he'd had to sit in with her too.

He walked up the steps to the Kyle home. The sister, whom he'd called to find out if her brother would be in, nodded a brief hello and asked him to come in. "He'll be down in a minute."

He sat on the firmest chair he could see—his back, after all these months, had begun bothering him again—and unbuttoned his coat and finally took off his hat. A bunch of newspapers were over on the sofa and the adjoining lamp table.

They probably had every fucking one of 'em.

You'd think the papers had nothing else to print.

Page after page. And the headlines.

SON FOLLOWS FATHER'S STEPS TO UNKNOWN BOY
UNKNOWN NO MORE
PEACE FOUNDATION HEAD ACCUSED CHILD-KILLER

And one, a tabloid, with just one word on the front page, almost from top to bottom: TOBY!

David was walking down from the second floor. And even the fucking cast on the arm, the perfect injury, the big hero home from the war.

"How's it going?" Perry said.

"Okay."

His sister, who'd been waiting for him to come down, left them alone.

Nick Ellis, Perry said, was still listed as critical, but the odds were he'd make it. But with his face half smashed and his larynx and a few other things in his throat crushed, he wasn't about to do any talking soon. But Madeline Schwartz had finally opened up, confirming everything Anne Tucker had already told them, and adding a little more.

No changes in the main story—it was a shit-eating little group, with this guy as head who thought he could change the world, that traveled around, holing up at different places, stealing and begging and occasionally doing odd jobs to support themselves. Kids kept joining and leaving, but the group at the time of the murder was Nick, Sandy, Madeline, the Tuckers, and a guy Tony, who'd OD'd sometime afterward. And Nick was still the one who'd done it—the kid had been "bothering" him while he was planning some break-ins—and everyone was there but the mother.

"The few things Schwartz told us," Perry said, "doesn't add up to much, but we'll need it all. She and this Roger Tucker first got involved when they met Sandy in their neighborhood and she filled their heads about this guy.

Let's see what else. Yeah. She and Anne delivered the baby—Anne told us she'd done it alone. I don't know why either of them want credit, they admit they were jealous of her and the kid. She was his lady. In fact, she would have had the second kid there, but Schwartz said she warned her to go, that it could happen again. Like," Perry added, "you'd need someone to tell you that. That was some fucking mother."

Some fucking mother, he repeated, looking at David.

He was just now getting to what he'd really come here for.

"Do you mind," he said, "if I ask you just a few questions? I know you've been asked just about everything. But there's still a few things I'm not quite clear about."

David looked at him, said nothing.

"What did you do that night," Perry asked, "after you said 'Toby' and she slammed the door on you?"

"You're right," David said, "I have been asked everything. I kept driving around, then I went back to the motel."

"But I'm still not clear on why you didn't go to the police."

"I was afraid it would be just her word against mine."

"Then"—he had the son of a bitch now—"what would you have done if she didn't call you?"

"I don't know."

"You mean you might have let her just go on?"

"I didn't say that. I said I didn't know."

Perry waited before saying, "How often did you see her before that night?"

David stared at him. "Perry, why don't you come right out and tell me what's on your mind?"

"I'll tell you what's on my mind. I called to ask for your father's notes and you said you threw 'em out. Why?"

"I didn't say I threw them out of my head, did I? Look," he said, his face tightening, "I don't know what you're driving at, and I don't care. But you're starting to bother me. And something else. In all the interviews I've given, the one thing I haven't said—because I wasn't asked—is that I called you and asked if you wanted them. And you said everything but put 'em in my ear."

"That's a damn lie."

"Well, next time I will say it. And you can say it's a lie, okay?"

Perry felt his face swelling with blood, wanted to punch him out, but he said, "Look, I came over just to fill you in. I didn't have to do that."

"I understand."

"I think you did a great job. And I just had to do mine, that's all."

I understand, he said again.

What a bunch of bullshit, Perry thought, walking to his car.

Kyle was getting all the honors—*Time* and *Newsweek* had to be next—and on top of it had probably been fucking the broad. And, shit, between here and court—wrapping it all up—doing your fuckest to see they got time—this was when, though nobody knew it, the real police work began.

•   •   •

David opened the door to the basement and turned on the light. He walked down slowly. He hadn't been down here since he'd come back yesterday, hadn't wanted to until now.

He stood at the bottom of the stairs and looked over at the desk. The swivel chair was turned around, as though his father had just stood up from it and left.

He walked over and stood looking at some of the things still on the desk, the little stand-up calendar, pencils and ballpoint pens in a ceramic jar, a small plastic magnetic container of paper clips . . . Then he looked at the photos on the walls—his father with Marciano, Berle, old local celebrities and politicians and athletes. His gaze finally went to the picture of his father at the grave. The long coat, the wide-brimmed hat, eyes staring down.

He kept looking at it.

His name was Toby, Pop.

And you were right. Wasn't the son of spies the CIA knew about but couldn't reveal, or a guinea pig in a scientist's experiments, or the president's hidden illegitimate child.

He was . . . just a kid.

He looked at the framed old news story next to it, the first of the stories about him. He wondered what his father would say if he could see the papers. Especially the ones with their pictures next to each other.

Would have gotten a kick out of that, and, Christ, reading what the commissioner said—"One of the most dedicated people I've ever met." No more pain in the ass, Pop. And all the people who'd sprung up to say they'd always known that some day . . .

He sat down on the chair, arms folded on the desk. He'd sat here many times when he was a kid, but never like this. Trying to listen for long-gone sounds up there—his own sounds coming home from school, Marie yelling to lower the TV, his mother running the water in the sink. And all the sounds from outside.

All the sounds his father heard.

He opened the middle drawer, though he knew there was nothing in it anymore. Only a few fragments of erasers.

He just looked at it, then slid it closed.

What would he have done if she hadn't called? He hadn't lied, didn't really know. Couldn't see himself calling the police. And couldn't see himself dropping it. All he knew was that he still ached.

For the boy. And for her.

He put his hand on the top of the desk, rubbed it lightly, then tapped at it before standing up, a kind of good-bye.

# 37

Judy picked him up at the house to take him to the airport. On the way they would make a stop.

"I bought these," she said. She pointed to the backseat, and he looked over and saw a bouquet of roses. He squeezed her hand on the wheel. Later she said, "Have you thought any more about a book?"

"No." His agent had already gotten a number of offers to do one on the case, as well as offers for movie rights. Maybe some day, though he doubted it. But parts—feelings, maybe insights, God knows—surely would be a part of other books he would do. He said, "I hope no one's there."

"I doubt if there'll be."

The mayor and half the politicians and cops in the city had already been there, with all the press, the network coverage. He'd backed out of that, preferred it this way.

The cemetery lay quiet in the sun. They stopped at a small building near the entrance and went in and got directions. They passed a mound of golden earth, waiting, then found the right lane and walked down it slowly.

There.

Judy held out the roses and he took just one and put it on the grave, amid all the other flowers that had been left behind. He covered part of the long stem with dirt, just to let it lie awhile longer. She set down the others. They stood there. His hand found hers, his fingers going between her fingers. He squeezed lightly. She squeezed back, and placed her head against his shoulder.

The headstone was covered with a small white cloth. There was printing across it, one day to be chiseled on a new stone.

TOBY MEGHAN

March 9, 1963–April 19, 1966

DEAR LORD HOLD TO THEE THIS BEAUTIFUL BOY